Novels by Mary Carter

A FORTUNE IN DIMES

THE MINUTES OF THE NIGHT

THE MINUTES
OF THE NIGHT

THE MINUTES
OF THE NIGHT

a novel by

Mary Carter

An Atlantic Monthly Press Book

LITTLE, BROWN AND COMPANY · BOSTON · TORONTO

The author wishes to thank the following for permission to use copy-
righted material: Robbins Music Corporation for permission to re-
print the lines from "Deep Purple," music by Peter DeRose, lyrics by
Mitchell Parish, © copyright 1934 (renewed), 1939 Robbins Music
Corporation, New York, New York. Used by permission copyright
proprietor. Joy Music, Inc., for lines from "(How Much Is) That
Doggie in the Window," © copyright 1952, 1953 by Joy Music,
Inc., New York, New York.

PS
3553
A7825
M5

ATLANTIC–LITTLE, BROWN BOOKS
ARE PUBLISHED BY
LITTLE, BROWN AND COMPANY
IN ASSOCIATION WITH
THE ATLANTIC MONTHLY PRESS

Published simultaneously in Canada
by Little, Brown & Company (Canada) Limited

PRINTED IN THE UNITED STATES OF AMERICA

to

PEARL VICTORIA CARTER

All characters in this book are fictional and intended to represent only those people who inhabit the writer's imagination.

THE MINUTES
OF THE NIGHT

The time of this novel is the future; but it might equally well be the present or the past, whenever fear gains the ascendancy over reason — the time of the Yeti.

I

THROUGH his doze John Lucas heard the sharp crack of
the furnace, an invisible bowling ball rolled down the
hall, and he was wrenched to full arousal on a bucking bed.
Far below him the San Andreas Fault gnashed its boulders.
Hearing the roar of its clanging caverns, feeling himself teeter
on the ledge of the continent, he thought: *I may die.* He
vaulted in a leap over minor regrets, opportunities missed,
pleasures forgone, and came face to face with revelation: at
the end of life, he had never risked it. Never to have wrestled
a gorilla, dangled from a crag, leaped from an airplane! Never
to have played out, with rope and muscle, the solitary moment
when all he was was his alone; never to have held his life
whole between his two hands. He waited, in a flood of the
most stunning grief, for the final crunch which would swallow
him bed and all. It did not come.

The roaring subsided. The timbers of the house creaked
gently and settled into stillness. In her own bed his wife
sighed, stirred, resumed her light breathing. She had not
awakened. She had not called out. Even in her sleep she had
gauged the danger and found it surmountable. While his
heart rattled, Sally slept.

*   *   *

Ploink.

Somewhere a tap dripped. A wind had come up. Clematis leaves clawed stiffly at the window. John Lucas lay and stared into the darkness.

When he was eleven years old a dream had permeated his days: to charter an airplane, fly over Susan Rindelhelm's house, and parachute into her back yard. He had plotted the space of lawn between her back porch and the alley where he had to land in order to avoid the telephone wires. What — if this single act of dedication had been fulfilled — might he have become? A man who has dangled his mortality between his own two hands, even if only once, will never be the same man as one who has not.

He sifted through lost possibilities. He had been in danger. As a soldier he had faced death, and with the requisite grace. But it had not been an act of free will. War — *life* — was an interdependent community project. You hacked your way through it alongside supporting cadres, with camera and gun. John Lucas groaned aloud. Crags and gorillas existed. Had he deliberately avoided them? (The Rindelhelm Project had been balked by lack of cash. The charter fee for a half-hour of the biplane and pilot's services, portal to portal, was astronomical. If the county airport had been nearer to town he might have managed it. Bitter chance horns in early in life.)

Several times, when pushed, he had fought personal, physical battles, but there had never been any question of mortal danger, either to Lucas or to his opponent. He was a huge man, impermeable to mere fists; and like many such men, peaceable. His gift of strength was wasted on his nature. He groaned again. At forty-two years of age such dreams of glory could only be quixotic. What relevance to the world he embraced — the world of decency, intelligence, responsibility, citizenship — had this atavistic spasm, this chest-beating? It was ludicrous.

And yet the revelation had come. It had struck at the moment of his imagined death, and therefore he knew it to be authentic, even if the immediacy of his death was not. Evidently he was not to die tonight. But sometime it would come; he would have to face the moment — and the revelation — again. What would he do then?

At four o'clock in the morning, that iron hour, truth trembled around him like ionized particles, waiting for the electrifying current to sweep them into the frozen pattern of his life's polarity. His nerve-endings stretched to one long vibrant filament; with them he probed the dark for the switch. *What would he do then?*

Ploink.

A drip formed, swelled, trembled exquisitely, *ploink*. John Lucas's old-fashioned neurons discharged an exact amount of corresponding energy. He could hear the next drop forming, growing heavy. Never had he been so excruciatingly tuned.

Ploink.

That goddam tap! He burst from his bed, lurched to the bathroom and, panting, choked the enemy into submission. The faucet snapped. With astonishment he felt the broken metal in his palm. Was this the way his power was to be put to use — mutilating his own household? He had used only a pitiful fraction of his available adrenalin. His body did not know it was outmoded. He took a tranquilizer to plow under the excess crop.

But restlessness had seized him. The hidden plumbing rumbled like a subterranean monster. The floor felt unsolid beneath his feet, as if it had not settled back firmly onto its foundation after the quake. He toured the house, checking locks and testing windows. Even in the dark all was familiar under his hands. He himself had designed and helped to build this house. Now for the first time its familiarity irritated him. Knowledgeable as he was of its far reaches, scaled as it was to his towering size, he nevertheless felt boxed, in contours so intimate the walls seemed to brush his shoulders as he prowled, the ceiling beams to ruffle his hair.

He listened at bedroom doors to the breathing of his children. Asleep, Cissie perfumed the air with her sweet breath; Mark's room stank of sneakers. Asleep, how trusting, how secure under this roof, were his children! They had not been awakened by the quake. Their lives stretched far ahead and full of promise. Chris's door was closed; behind it he slept in adolescent mystery, sweating with dreams, private and unapproachable. John Lucas felt a prick of envy. He remembered those dreams. When he was seventeen they had rocked his nights; he had carried them with him into the days. Nourishing them through the waking process which he could sustain sometimes for a full hour, fatigue a sensual ache in every muscle and a sense of levitation rising from his mattress, he would lie drifting motionlessly, navigating Time with his delicious cargo, until at last he would be brought up against his mother's voice strung like a hawser over the stream, and she would haul him in word by word and tie him up firmly to the dock. He would then arise with all the injured rawboned dignity of his youth and stomp to the bathroom. As he stood pouring out the night's warm fluid he would feel inexhaustible promise rise in his body, and he would dress and stalk downstairs in a rage of ego, knowing something great was going to happen to him this day. Each morning was mysterious then.

John Lucas shuffled back to his room and sat on the edge of

his bed and listened to his wife breathing gently. She too was secure. It was her nature.

Oh, Sally Lucas was of sturdy stock indeed. She stacked up splendidly Life Force–wise. The ground could crack open at her feet and she would survey the fissure with the same scientific interest with which she tapped the barometer each morning. She was fond of natural phenomena such as weather, rashes, the formation of crystals. On the kitchen counter was a large soup bowl whose bottom was furred with what looked like a bluish-white mold; it was a "garden" of salt crystals, a mixture of ammonia and bluing saturated with salt and poured over a couple of charcoal briquettes. Sally had concocted it to illustrate to their younger son the wonders of chemistry. For a day the lumps of charcoal lay in the bowl, sluggish islands surrounded by an inky inert sea; the next morning a tiny white thread appeared on one of the black lumps. For days now the garden had been growing wildly, sprouting, piling up crystal on crystal; and as its coral-like fronds sprang from the charcoal and crept up the sides of the bowl, Lucas and his son eyed it uneasily, for it seemed to threaten to engulf the bowl, the rim, the counter, the entire kitchen with its voracious growing; but Sally hung over it absorbedly, with no apparent thought as to what she might have released in triggering this abandoned growth. Such things were, to her, imbued with a coded beauty.

To John Lucas, raised in a flat city in the firmest center of the flat Midlands, the only entirely trustworthy order was embodied in the Architectural Code, or perhaps the Bill of Rights. He put his confidence in what man could build and therefore control.

While his wife was uneasy in tall buildings — they *leaned*, she claimed — she would go unafraid into forests, feeling beneath her feet sinewy roots gripping the earth as Nature meant it to be gripped. It was she who had persuaded Lucas of the joys of wilderness camping. They were hard-won. City boy, more lover than fighter, he had been aghast that first summer in the Sierras when he had had to prove himself to his young wife. In an utterly foreign and savage realm, with what bulging muscularity he had driven himself to a raw, sunburned, charley-horsed state! He had lain wakeful under the glaring stars, listening for animals prowling the sinister brush, waiting for the pounce; while, in the blackness of the blackest nights he had ever encountered, she — his lovely Sally, his bride, for whose flesh he was so appallingly responsible — slept deeply and tactlessly beside him. How dangerously close they had come then to aborting a marriage just begun. But because he loved her more than pride they somehow survived his tenderfoot days. When the second summer came he found he was eager to return, this time as much for pride as for love. Eventually he came to enjoy it, with the ease of the familiar and the confidence of safety.

Sitting on his bed John Lucas suddenly stiffened. *Safety!* What, in all his hard-earned woodsmanship, his boy-scout craft, had he averted? What chances had he lost? Surely someplace in all that wilderness there might have waited for him — around a bend in the trail, behind a rock, hidden among the high huckleberries in the sleepy noontime heat of a mountain meadow — a she-bear ferocious with young. He might have faced her as she reared up before him, huge, terrible, howling, brandishing her claws. Was it by chance or cunning that he had avoided her?

Oh, he should have gone out to seek that bear! Or a cougar,

or a rattler, or — he remembered it now with a wry grin; *that* would surely have fulfilled the Gorilla Clause — Bigfoot.

Three years ago they had packed with the children back into the Trinity Alps, that region of northern California which rose not far behind the coastal town of Sequoia, where they lived. It was a high country of timber, scrub, and granite; from the top of the pass could be seen the towering complex of the Siskiyou Range.

Among the Indians in the area was an ancient legend, resurrected that year by the appearance of an enormous footprint across the fresh earth of a logging road, concerning the existence of a local Yeti. This creature — described by elderly members of its sponsoring tribe, the Hoopa, as being eight to twelve feet tall, entirely covered with hair, and sporting the muscular structure of a giant gorilla — had never been seen by a white man. But the footprint was unmistakably there. It was photographed by newsmen, cast in plaster, studied by scientists from the University of California, and pronounced by them "not ungenuine." It prompted a brief flurry of national speculation and a great number of local jokes. One prominent lumberman arrived at the Sequoia Country Club Inaugural Ball attired in dinner jacket and black tie, with huge pink rubber feet flapping from his ankles. The story faded at last back into the limbo of myth; but the Sequoia Chamber of Commerce still sponsored an annual Bigfoot Week featuring Hoopa dances and an acorn soup feed, and the Stump House down on Highway 101 still offered to tourists a Genuine Redwood Burl hand-carved into a replica of the Not Ungenuine giant foot.

The Lucases had taken only their two younger children that year. Chris, at fourteen and the beginning of contempt for family activities, had chosen Y-camp instead. Mark, who was eight, complained of perpetual thirst, cramps, and the weight of his pack. Four-year-old Cissie, on the other hand, was magnificent. There was a mountain to climb, she climbed it; there was a stream, she drank; it got dark, she went to sleep. It occurred to Lucas that this earthy wisdom of his daughter's might be part of some dark womanly instinct for resignation, an instinct that Sally shared in her acceptance of the natural world. It was simply there . . . Mark fought on, hopelessly, against a system whose superior power he must have sensed as hostile. Even mosquitos seemed to prefer him. He lay awake in his sleeping bag and stared uneasily at the fire, insisted that his knee was swollen, and asked if Bigfoot could see in the dark.

"Why, Mark. You know there's no such thing as Bigfoot," Sally said.

Mark eyed her dolefully, scratching. *She* was never attacked by mosquitos.

Deep in the middle of the first night Lucas awoke to his son's voice. "It's coming!"

He reached over and felt for the boy. Mark was huddled far down in his sleeping bag, whimpering in anesthetized gasps. Lucas peeled back the muffling folds. "It's coming," Mark said thickly.

"What's coming?"

"Dad — *do* something," he pleaded, and fell asleep again.

In the morning Lucas asked Mark what had scared him. "Did you think Bigfoot was coming, or what?" he asked, kidding.

The boy didn't smile. "I'm not scared of anything, for gosh sakes. And besides," he said, with a bleak honesty, "you're here." He went back to rolling up his bag.

Lucas gazed at his son's back, at the skinny shoulders humped doggedly over the task, and was flooded with the most astonishing sense of his own use and purpose. Here he was responsible, in the simplest and most primitive way, for them all. Here in the wilderness he was like the granite peaks around them; he was their shelter and their shield.

This then was why a man does not go out to seek bears.

Rronk.

He had been drifting off. His hide crinkled, his nape stiffened against the pillow. The sound came again, unmistakable this time: *Rronk.*

It was the snore of his wife.

His hackles limpened. His apprehension sagged. Even as it did he knew that once again he had been visited: in the instant of alarm the revelation had reappeared. It had not been tranquilized. Rationalization would not kill it. It would remain.

R-ronk, Sally said. With her snoring she woke him, taunted him, while she continued smugly wrapped in her own self-contained sleep.

He lay stiff with fury and exhaustion. The snore fluttered, gentle, ladylike, content, mocking. *I am serene*, it said. *I have no self-doubt. I do not waste the useful hours in outlandish regrets.*

I will wake her, John Lucas thought. That would shake her from her self-containment. He would go to her bed, separate her from her sleep, impose upon her, by God, his essence. *But no*, he thought morosely; after twenty years, twice in one night? She would think he was still drunk.

They had been to a dinner party that evening and he had had more to drink than usual; cocktail time had gone on a full hour too long. Driving the baby-sitter home afterward, he had almost strangled with the effort of exchanging the few bleak pleasantries necessary to convince her he hadn't passed out (she was a teetotaler), and that she was not being driven through the night streets by an insensate corpse. He spoke out of the left side of his mouth, attempting to blow the vapors of Scotch out his wind-wing. She sat as if she were an uncrated egg, and gasped frequently. He opened the window. She bravely tweaked her collar together — cold to the bones, this woman was, she traveled as if in a tumbril. He closed the window. They arrived at her little cottage and she tottered up the walk toward her valiant little porch light, his five-seventy-five clutched in her purse, her back unforgiving; guarding her from the car he had felt himself coated with a gross film of alcoholic esters. He whizzed back to his wife, who was still in the bathroom, but after a long time of secret silences punctuated by the noise of lipsticks and mascara wands being dropped back into drawers, and much running water, emerged in her best negligée, glowing with innocent lust. He was hugely sleepy but he had obliged her, with the usual pleasure and only a slight sense of duty.

— *Duty?*

Slowly he raised himself on one elbow. He leaned, staring through the dark toward his wife's bed. He listened to her breath, to the sough of blood through her body; he believed he could hear the faint chink of vitreous bone as she stirred, the crackle of hair follicles, the drip of cellular fluids, all the sturdy processes of replenishment within the warm organism he had long since committed to memory. Then he heard, for the first time, a tiny experimental tick of possibility. From this, separated. A separate, duty-free existence.

He gazed motionless into the core of this possibility. The short distance between him and the other bed thickened, took shape, became recognizable: a bond. Unseen stresses, the pressures of time and habit, the shear and erosion of cohabitation — could these ever cause a sudden rupture of the bond?

But I love her, he thought. *She is my wife*. He even whispered it aloud: I love you, Sally. You are my wife.

But there was no revelation here; only possibility.

II

Lucas awoke with the feeling of having traveled a great distance, all of it on foot. Plugged with sleep he thought he had returned to his adolescent bed; *something great*, he sensed, drifting, *is going to happen today* . . .

"Daddy!"

He was dragged unceremoniously back to the familiar shore. The voice summoning him was his daughter's. "Daddy!" she screeched, bouncing upon the foam rubber which for a moment there had been his frail raft, "Daddy, Mother says to get up and take me to Sunday school, Mark's sick —" She flung herself across his chest. "Ah Daddy, I love you," she whimpered. She lay relaxed and warm upon him. "Pew," she said presently. "You smell. Come *on*, Daddy. Mother said —"

He staggered to the bathroom with cracking knee joints and spinning head. The shock of cold water on his face awoke him. He remembered last night's thoughts; before him sharp as an ice sheet lay the revelation and the possibility. Struck with morning light, its dazzle was blinding, impossible. *I must have been loaded*, he thought, appalled. He had a roaring headache. That proved it, certainly. As if to sustain this proof he ignored the aspirin bottle, but as he dressed an aura persisted.

A blat of music down the hall made him wince. He went into Mark's room and turned down the TV. "Let's keep it down to a roar."

Mark lay in bed looking hollow. "I've got a sore throat," he said sternly. He drew one hand, which had been cupped for consolation over his groin, out of the covers and gestured wanly. "I can't *hear* it now."

Lucas went over and put his hand over his son's forehead. He did it as a vague gesture of acknowledgment; his children's heads always felt medium to him, fever or not. "You feel okay to me," he said.

"Well, I'm not. I'm sick. And I can't hear the TV."

"A sore throat doesn't make you stone-deaf. The TV blasting like that, it'd give everybody in the house a headache. You want me to get you some orange juice or something?"

"I can't swallow, for gosh sake! And if I can't even hear the TV just because you've got a headache — I'll bet it's a hangover." The boy had a white defiant ring around his mouth. "*That*'s why you can't stand any noise, you —"

"You may be sick, Mark, but don't think you're going to get away with being sassy." Lucas stalked over to the TV and snapped it off.

"That's why you're in such a bad mood, you went out and drank up a whole bunch of liquor last night!" Mark cried hoarsely. "I'm going to buy my own TV set, and then you can't come in here into my own private room and turn it off! I'll pay for it out of my own money!" He struggled up. "You think I can't get my own money, well I can, I know this guy who'll sell me his paper route, and Cissie owes me fifty cents, and I can mow lawns —"

As John Lucas stood looking down at his eleven-year-old son, he recalled with sudden clarity that the rental of the biplane — pilot, helmet, celluloid goggles and all — had been a dollar a minute. He said gently, "Mark, do you have any idea what a TV set costs?"

"I don't *care!* I'll earn it! You *owe* me," he said shrilly, "you didn't pay me for washing your car last week which is money I legally *earned* out of my own hard *labor* —"

"Mark! What on earth —?" Sally swept like an avenging angel to the bedside, administered palms and benefactions upon the thundering brow, handed down the Tables of Law and Order. "For heaven's sake, child, what are you screeching about with a throat like yours? Here —" She flipped the covers as if they contained an attacking asp. "— here, darling, get right back under here, I'll get you some aspirin —"

"He turned off the TV," Mark whimpered.

She shot the offender a Medusa look and he clumped heavily after her, the stone man. "What are you thinking of?" she hissed in the hall. "He's sick, why on earth you'd go in there and bother a sick child, honestly, John —"

Looking down at her face distorted with motherhood he remembered — totally out of any context — her face of last night when she had come to him clad in her negligée, and convulsed with pity for them all he stalked wordlessly past her.

The paralyzing brightness which seemed to wash St. Luke's Episcopal Church each Sunday came, Lucas knew, from an uneasy sense of sin, that residual heritage of his Puritan ancestry with which his agnosticism had long since come to intellectual terms. Still as he delivered his children one by one for their instruction (they had a right to come to their own terms) the crash of steeple chimes always seemed to him an intemperate reproach. A gray, gritty unshaven blob, he hulked behind the wheel as he opened the car door for Cis. On her knees, she kissed him lingeringly, longingly, lovingly, one eye on a prospective sidewalk audience. Pious Child Bids Farewell to Sinful Smelly Daddy. "Run along, Cis," he pleaded, scrunching down. "You don't want to be late."

She backed out on her hands and knees. "Goodbye, Daddy, goodbye . . ." Her rear encountered assistance to the curb. "Oh hi, Mrs. Shaw."

He said, "Cis, goodbye. Mother'll pick you up after."

Sarah Shaw dropped her music books on the seat and leaned in. She surveyed him. "The total effect is stupefying," she said. "All those vast areas of gray — T-shirt, face —"

He blinked at her. "You'd be stupefied too if you'd spent the night the way I did. Did you feel the earthquake?"

"No. Was there one?"

"Yes. Am I the only person around here who can detect earthquakes?" he said irritably.

"Maybe you've got a built-in seismograph, feel tremors other people can't. Some people can tell it's going to rain when their joints ache. They'd be in constant pain here."

"You live in a rain forest, you've got to expect rain."

She peered closely at him. "You sound blue."

Under her gaze — worried, affectionate, open with old friendship — he wanted very much to tell her of his unease. He could think of no way to put it to her. He could think of no way to put it to himself. He said, "I am gray and I am blue because I didn't get any sleep."

"Reviewed your life and wrestled with your conscience?"

"Sort of."

"You know what I wrestled with last night?" She began to

sing in a contralto of rich, eerie clarity, "*How much is that doggie in the window, the one with the waggily ta-il? How much —*"

"Sarah," he pleaded, scrunching down. Her voice was exuberant and powerful.

"Yes, and then there was an episode of the "Volga Boat Song." Did you know that tune works itself in behind a Bach passage, the one I'm playing today? I lay there it must have been an entire hour, humming and drumming my fingers on my stomach. Howard said I boomed in my sleep."

She was trying to cheer him, but the notion of forty-year-old Sarah Shaw booming lustily in her sleep, warding off doggerel rhythms, touched Lucas strangely. She had once confided to him that popular music — except jazz and certain recondite explorations — caused her the most grievous torture simply by remaining with her in fragments she could not dispel. "The one thing that truly scares me is that some day I might be very poor, and have to take a job where they play music over a PA system. It's everywhere. Supermarket, dress shop, dentist's — God, to hear 'September Song' over the grinding of the drill! How can I go out in the world and expect to escape it?" This fear of hers was very real. It seemed to be the only unpossessed thing about Sarah. She was a woman sufficient unto herself, sure of her powers, without airs.

He had been drawn to Sarah Shaw from their first meeting — was it ten, twelve years ago? His instant dislike of her husband may have had something to do with it. Fifteen minutes after they'd met at a party Lucas had him pegged for a windbag and a fake. Howard Shaw was an instructor in the English Department at nearby Sequoia State College and it was said he was writing a book. This fiction had been sustained so long that Howard had come to be considered by the community a real-life *ipso facto* author. When asked how "the book" was coming he answered with a shrug and a rueful grin intended to convey all the pain of the creative mystique. "Work," said Howard with a toss of his handsome head, "is hell. If you could just communicate by punching buttons." He spoke frequently of communication. "All the loneliness and misunderstanding in the world," he declared, "comes from people's not being able to *communicate*," and he would gaze bruisingly into some woman's eyes until she gasped, "Yes, oh yes," and then he would transfer his gaze to her décolletage and murmur sadly, "— but *you* understand this, don't you?" Most women, including Sally, "understood" Howard. They considered him deep and tragic. They wished — if Lucas got this right — to take Howard's head and place it on their motherly bosoms and console him for the mystic agony from which he so attractively suffered. Did Sarah so comfort him? Even after he knew her well Lucas didn't know.

At that first party, as her husband moved off among his coterie of women, Sarah stood sipping her drink with an abstracted air as if she were unaware she'd been left alone. She looked rather dowdy — a big woman, even then beginning to go gray, with a pleasant mobile, intelligent face: nothing here of placidity in spite of her *hausfrau* appearance. She had, Lucas noted, very fine long legs. A lacy edge of slip hung down slightly under her skirt. The sight of this pricked him with a peculiar sympathy. (It was most endearing to him, this secret sign of a woman's urge to femininity; years later when he caught Cis trying on her mother's bra, so hopeful of beauty, he had had the same feeling.) He went over to Sarah and rather abruptly told her a joke. She laughed. At that sudden burst, a veritable roar of genuine mirth from the belly with none of the small repressive mannerisms women employ to stifle their laughter, Lucas was enchanted. There could be no pitying a woman who could laugh like that.

Later, as the party decayed to a few intimate groups — Howard at the core of one — Lucas wandered into an empty room and found Sarah standing at the piano. On an impulse he came up beside her and with his left hand struck a few bass notes from the only piece of music he had been able to retain from a childhood series of lessons: the *Moonlight Sonata*. She smiled at him and went smoothly, lightly into the melody. It was so lovely he faltered, forgot where he was; she slowed too, and as he fumbled with his big stiff fingers laboring over forgotten bars she guided him with the music alone. They came to the end and he stood, helpless with embarrassment and pleasure. "I never learned the second movement," he said. "Never mind," she said. "We'll play the first one again." They sat down together on the bench and an hour later, when Sally came to find him, they were still there, shoulder to shoulder, playing the first movement of the *Moonlight Sonata*.

After that at parties, while Howard held court among his ladies Lucas would drag Sarah off to wherever the piano was and together they would play the *Moonlight Sonata*. "You aren't tired of it?" he would ask anxiously. She grinned. "Of course not. It's music, isn't it?" It was the only piece they played; it was enough.

Now as Sarah stooped over his car seat, chatting, trying to cheer him, he thought of the pleasure she had given him over the years — four hands at the piano, laughs, talks, friendship — and with the deep brimming of affection there rose within him an intimation that she, too, had lain and wrestled with revelation. How many times? Were there things this woman, this friend, could tell him?

He leaned over in the seat to ask her, and could not. Instead, he said, "Sarah, give me your hand."

Unflustered she held out her hand to him. It was broad and square and strong, faintly liver-spotted. He shook it solemnly. "Sarah," he said, "you're a good kid."

"Thanks," she said. She returned his squeeze warmly. She straightened, gathered her music. "I'd better go in now. There's just twenty minutes to warm up the organ."

"I wonder how the *Moonlight Sonata* sounds on the organ."

Came her full-bodied laugh. "I'll tell you how it sounds; it sounds like a selection by Korla Pandit, goony eyes below the turban and all. But you're welcome to try, sometime when I'm practicing."

"Today, after church?" He had the dim feeling he might be able to tell her then of his unease, roaring it out over the noise of the organ.

"Can't today. I'm taking Marina up to the Safeway lot to practice parking. She wants to get her license." Marina was Sarah's sixteen-year-old daughter and only child; she looked exactly like Howard. She was very beautiful and Sarah doted on her. "But maybe next week. I'll call you when I go over to practice, okay?"

"Okay, Sarah," he said. "Next week."

"I kept the coffee warm and there's bacon in the oven. Mark's temperature is one hundred and two."

He touched Sally's arm. "I really wasn't harassing him, you know. He just got all wrought up when I turned down the TV."

"You can't expect to enforce *every* rule when a child's sick." The smooth moon of skin beneath her eyes was smudged. The mascara she had applied in the bathroom last night lay on her cheek and encircled her gaze. She had awakened to a sick child; the negligée lay crumpled now on the bedroom floor; here in the kitchen she stood straight and dark before him in her old red flannel robe. With her huge stained eyes so ludicrously tragic, her weariness seeping from the austere folds of robe along with the aroma of bacon, she was Wife in her two warring incarnations: Lover and Mother.

He took her suddenly into his arms. "Ah Sally," he muttered into her warm breakfast-smelling neck, "Sally."

She gave him a ritual peck on the jowl as she moved out from under his armpit. "Sorry I snapped," she muttered. "It's just with Mark and all — Do you want me to scramble you an egg?"

He reached for her again. "In a manner of speaking —"

She moved away behind that stoutest of barricades, the kitchen stove. She rattled the frying pan. "One egg or two?"

"Sally —"

Every household should have a gong, a huge brass warning gong to be sounded in times of sudden peril, when it was very dangerous, for instance, to say *no* to one another; he would at this time pick up the hammer, swing it with all the power in his shoulders, and as the great single warning crash shivered the timbers of the house and lifted the lids from all the pots, she would understand and the household would remain secure.

"Ah, Sally, honey —"

She turned to him, cradling the egg in her hand like a schoolteacher with a piece of chalk ready to explain a formula she has just written in huge letters on the blackboard. He saw what was written there: NO. It filled the entire board.

"Mo-ther . . ." came the cry, hoarse and pathetic, down the hall.

Off she went to attend the needy.

III

I T was dark in his office, close with the smell of cigarettes and the musty odor old blueprints give off. Lucas opened the window to air the outer office and went through to the drafting room. He pulled back the louvers at the window by his desk. For an hour or so on Sunday afternoons he had the office, the whole building, to himself; he did his best work then, hard creative work, without the interruption of his two young draftsmen, his secretary, clients. All was quiet and deserted. In the street below an occasional car pulled up, waited at the stoplight, and was gone; the steps of a lone pedestrian might be heard, a solitary sound that gave him a fine sense of immunity.

On one of his drafting boards were roughs for a new office. It would be built when he had the time and money, on a small lot he owned out near the East Sequoia Shopping Center. He had already planted young pear trees there, and a large, fantastically expensive Mount Fuji flowering cherry, and a row of Monterey pines across the north line to blot out the pink stone and gingerbread shakes of George Wingluff's new laundromat which George's wife had designed all by herself. Once or twice a month Lucas would go out and walk around his lot with his hands in his pockets, and occasionally he would go next door south and walk around Bud Hansen's Nursery, eyeing the delicate limbs of little Japanese maples, surreptitiously pinching plump rhododendron buds, copping feels of young white-bark birches whose boles were slender as a virgin's thigh. Lucas was passionately fond of trees. He usually got an azalea or something in a five-gallon tin and staggered back to his lot with it, and planted it in a corner. The corners were filling in splendidly now, and he reflected each time that if he didn't get that office built soon he wouldn't have any space left to set it. When he arrived home muddy and satisfied Sally would say, "Arbor Day again, eh? Sometimes I think you don't really want to build an office out there, you just want to plant trees."

This was a sore subject, but she was probably right. Every man should have a park of his own. Then, when spring came, he could go out there and lie down on the new grass under the spreading Mount Fuji and let the pale blossoms drift down on his eyelids.

Bending now over his office plans, John Lucas scowled. Forty-two years old and his dream of bliss was to lie under a tree? A fine thing, when his prime was just approaching, hard and firm in him as a ripe brown nut. He stripped off the plans, rolled them up, and taped a tracing to his board.

He was working on the design for a church, a small one for a tiny congregation in an outlying community. They had almost no money but they had enthusiasm, need, the donation of some farmland, and the good sense to come to an architect. It was this last that had persuaded Lucas to take on their job in his overloaded schedule; and although they didn't know it he was charging them a fraction of his usual fee. The countryside was smeared with blots of ugliness because most people in Sequoia had long believed that beauty was inutile and to pay good hard cash extra for it was frivolous. It was an ugly town. Once he had hoped to change it.

Tucked away at the cold wet end of California, straggling up from a muddy bay whose shallow waters bred the fog which hung like webs from the eaves, Sequoia even in its lusty days was never comely. Back of it great ranges rose, dripping their wealth of forest; at its coastal elbows the Pacific ledge spread its hem on glistening rock; back from the mouths of the coastal rivers ravines hung padded with fern — but Sequoia's streets were straight and bald, her bay vista stark, her outskirts gouged with abandoned excavation. Beginning in a no-man's-land of slums, rotting wharves, secondhand shops, the town climbed a gradual slope from the bay in a grid of telephone poles. The downtown streets were built over a mat of redwood bark, the slag heap from early mills. When the tide was unusually high the walks seemed almost spongy.

Tourists came in the chill summers to stand on the crab-fleet dock; shivering in the wind they took pictures of the gulls and the bay and the thin strip of Rober Island, which was populated only by a lonely stand of cypress, hundreds of white egrets which nested like lint in the dark trees, and the gaunt ghost of a lumber baron's mansion. All the physical as well as historical color seemed to have been leached out of this coastal place. Nothing was left but the cold grays and cloudy whites of a climate which had been as harsh to the ambitions of men as it had to the paint of the waterfront shacks.

Three hundred miles from anywhere and shrouded in rain forest, little Sequoia's only claim to fame was the size of its redwoods, the lowest mean average summer temperature in California, and an article in some magazine a while back proclaiming it to be the Safest Town in the USA, bomb and fall-out-wise. Even the state freeway engineers had avoided it.

Lucas had come to Sequoia because his wife had been born here and loved it, because there was no architect, and because it had seemed to him that this remote place offered a personal challenge. In the exuberance of his untried craft he thought that one man could, with a vision of concern, transform this gaunt community into a back-country oasis — one of those small historical gems like Monterey or Mendocino. The inheritance and the history were here. Once, robust generations of individualists — fishermen, loggers, sawmill men — had flourished here. They had left their expression of vigor, buried under neglect, in a fine assemblage of carpenter's Gothic: that jumble of buildings on First Street, now housing used-furniture marts and motorcycle shops, bore under its crumbling countenance moldings and dentils and corbels, oriels and brackets, primitive elegance unabashed. What if these were to be brought erect, restored, painted? He had had a vision of blazing white louvered windows, tall khaki-green doorways . . . And the lumberman's mansion — with its bronze railing around the widow's walk, its cupola shingled with hexagonals, its stained glass set not in lead but in redwood strips — brought back to life as a museum, perhaps, housing all of local history and artifact, something to draw the focus of a town's new pride . . . ?

And trees. Lucas's enthusiasm bounded ahead by decades. To line these uncompromising streets not with telephone poles but with maples, maybe, and dogwood which glowed so warmly in the woods! "Imagine," he had said to his young wife, "imagine these streets with trees! Why, in ten years that alone could transform this place. Don't they know what they have here? Take the few good old buildings, the ones with character, and instead of tearing 'em down fix 'em up and *use* them — the Recreation Department maybe could maintain them for activities, youth group stuff, women's club — And instead of flattening a corner lot to put in a kids' playground, why not use these old grounds, clean up around the old houses, turn 'em into real parks —"

She had listened to him adoringly. "All it takes is someone like you," she said. He had laughed modestly. He had believed her.

If he had been gifted with patience: if he had had the patience to sit for hours on end while his seat numbed and his voice grew hoarse; if he had not grown older and considerably wiser in the process, John Lucas might now have been able to spot, among the telephone poles on the horizon outside his office window, a few tall maples. But sixteen years had not been enough; or perhaps it was that as you learn patience, you lose ardor.

"Now, what would we do with a gussied-up First Street? Why, it'd scare the winos out of their remaining wits." Old Mrs. Foster squinted at Lucas down the length of the Council table. Behind this wenlike slab of highly polished redwood burl she, five other Council members, and the mayor sat arrayed in the full musty odor of their authority. Young John Lucas returned her gaze cautiously. Old Mrs. Foster, for all anybody knew, lived here behind this table in the basement of City Hall. "Sequoia, *c'est moi*," she had been heard to say.

Under the veil of her hat her gaze traveled up and down John Lucas's black knit tie with urbane contempt. She was the only woman in Sequoia to wear a hat downtown. She *respected* downtown. Was not Foster's Department Store — founded 1904, the Largest Dry-Goods Emporium Between San Francisco and Portland — its very kernel and cornerstone? While the Council members fidgeted and peered cautiously at their watches (it was lunchtime) the sere presence of old Celeste Foster kept them riveted in their chairs. She had not finished with Lucas. She seemed to have taken an interest in him; she may have considered him an authentic oddball (*wants us to plant trees!*), or perhaps she had never seen a black knit tie before.

"Furthermore that block of buildings down there isn't worth the money to restore them," she said. "It's out of the business district. Paint," she snapped, rapping on the table with a huge emerald ring, "costs money. So do trees. Taxpayers' money."

"What do you want the taxpayers' money to buy?" Lucas asked. "Besides schools and sewers? This town could be made very, ah, beautiful." He had the uneasy feeling that this word, used so routinely in the University architectural department, might be considered suspicious here. "It has history, I mean. From a point of civic pride —"

"How old are you?" Mrs. Foster said abruptly.

"Twenty-six."

"You serve in the war?"

He reddened. "I was in the V-12 program. I got over to Okinawa before it ended, though. I was with the Seabees."

"You met my grandson Harry, here? He was a Navy pilot."

Lucas reached across the table to shake with the indicated Councilman, a plump young man who gave him a cautious grin, rolling his eyes slightly to indicate sympathy. Lucas was heartened.

"And you're an architect?" Mrs. Foster bore in again.

"I got my degree in 1947 and my California license last year. I'm married," he added, emboldened, "to Sally Welton, whose father used to be a lumberman here, and I've got a son who's a year old." *That* ought to take care of the nosy old girl.

She regarded him unamused. "I knew your father-in-law," she said. "He was here a long time. *You're* new. You may know that Sequoia has managed to bumble along so far without a, um, beautification program — and, if I may point out, an architect. I suppose we can use one." She leaned forward, and with her thumb she twirled the giant emerald on her finger. "What you have to offer, what you have to *sell*, in effect, is yourself. Not trees. Yourself, that's your commodity, and before you can sell your ideas you've got to sell yourself. With this in mind I advise you to start first things first. If service is what you're itching to give to this community why don't you join some of the service clubs? Get to know people, get the feel of the town, know the other businessmen, Kiwanis, Rotary, the Downtown Merchants' Association —"

"Mrs. Foster, I appreciate your advice, and I'll certainly take it into consideration," Lucas said, controlling with difficulty the first surge of what was eventually to become tidal. "But I'd like to point out that I'm trying to introduce before this Council ideas to improve not my own, uh, business but the town where we all live." He straightened, feeling this rather well put.

"That's right noble of you," she said coolly, "and we appreciate hearing what newcomers think of us. In view of your interest I think you'd better join the Downtown Merchants' Association, in case you haven't got around to it yet. The dues aren't much — one hundred dollars a year — considering what you as a merchant benefit from the activities of the association. Because of their parking-lot campaign the Council just last week passed on a motion to acquire an acre and a half of prime downtown off-street parking."

Not surprising, Lucas thought, in view of the fact of Celeste Foster's permanent presidency of both Council and Merchants' Association. With three months' residency in his office — a dim hovel between the Credit Dentist and the Betty Merriwell School of the Dance above Quill's Hardware — he was not yet ready to consider himself a Downtown Merchant, and almost certain that off-street parking would have no effect on his career as an architect. He bowed slightly to acknowledge her offer but in no way to obligate himself. He could see in old Celeste's eyes that she understood this, and the beginning of a grudging respect.

"Every tree planted downtown takes up a parking space," she informed him, and delivered of this Holy Writ she pulled down her hat. "Okay, boys, lunch." The Boys scattered in a flurry of basement dust.

The next time John Lucas was in Foster's Department Store he saw, under a sign which said LATEST FASHION FIND, an array of black knit ties.

But a battle had been launched. For seven years Lucas fought, and there were scars on the polished burl table where he pounded his fists and old Celeste Foster banged her ring and where forgotten cigars smoldered over the lips of ashtrays as the Boys of the Council sank their jowls into their collars in the effort to duck the cross fire.

"Mrs. Foster, God damn it," Lucas roared, "you know very well that Rossi property's too far uptown to be of any use as parking! It's halfway up to Jefferson School and that's an R-2 district, not commercial! It's a perfect location for a Recreation setup — and that old house is a beauty, really a great one. Lord, the portico itself should be preserved at all cost —"

"Rubbish. You're talking nonsense again, John. Any time you've got land that Safeway wants, you know you've got valuable land. If the value's in Commercial then it'll be rezoned Commercial. Safeway wants the whole block and they won't go in without guaranteed parking space. Wherever Safeway goes the business is good. It'd bring people nearer downtown to do their marketing . . . What's the matter with Safeways anyhow?" She scowled. Lucas could see she was disturbed at his strong feeling. "Architecturally they're kind of imposing, aren't they?"

"Architecturally they're imposing only to people interested in the price of hamburger," he said coldly. "That old Rossi house you call rubbish is worth several dozen Safeways. If you tear it down it'll be gone. They don't build that kind of thing any more."

"When I go I'll be gone too, and what's the loss?" She spoke harshly. "The only thing that's ever left is heirs."

Harry Foster shifted the cigar in his mouth and examined his fingernails.

"So you rezone for old man Rossi's heirs," Lucas said.

"We're rezoning for Safeway! Safeway's business. And business is the town."

That time Lucas lost his head. "How'd you like it, Mrs. Foster, if Macy's wanted to put a branch store in Sequoia? Macy's is business — big business. And business is the town."

There was a stunned silence. Everybody knew that the only fear, the only real horror, scratched on Celeste Foster's flinty old heart was the chance that someday a large chain department store might cast its eye on Sequoia.

"How would you like it," she said presently in a voice like a glacier sliding over a bed of boulders, "if the city was to go to a San Francisco architect for the plans for the new City Hall?"

Lucas's mouth went dry. The City Hall commission, of which he had been tacitly assured, was his first big chance in Sequoia. With its fee he planned to keep his wife, his son, and himself from starving. He stared down Celeste Foster's anodized-steel gaze as down a long sword. He saw his wife and child, wrapped in rags against this bitter edge. He saw himself bent over another man's drafting board, limning with poverty-stiff fingers another man's designs. He saw himself bent before old Celeste Foster, one of the Boys, his jowls tucked into his collar —

"If you want another architect, fine. If you want another puppet, find another man. Nobody threatens *me*, Mrs. Foster," he heard himself say. He walked out of the Council chambers.

He continued doggedly with the preliminary drawings for the City Hall. When he presented them a few months later for the first hearings Celeste Foster said nothing. The preliminaries were approved and his work went on. Although her respect for him may have increased, he had badly dented her affection. He became aware of this when a short time later she created a Civic Beautification Committee and appointed Lucas to head it.

"You've had it easy up till now," she told him with a malicious glint. "You've been a loner. All you've had to do was waltz in here and pound the table every time you felt thirst for Beauty and Improvement. We've tolerated your foolishness for a long time, given in on some of it. Now if you want to fight for your own way you can fight in public. See if the town really wants what you want."

"You think I might make a public fool of myself?"

She ignored this. "You find four men — or women if you want — to serve on that committee and see what you can get done. Don't say I didn't give you the chance. Maybe they can

help you convince the town it wants to spend its tax money on
fancying itself up."

They were alone in the basement room; the Boys had
scrambled off to their lunchtime booth at the Steak House,
where for two hours of the working day they held court, allowed themselves to be stood martinis, and dispensed petty pa-
tronage. Celeste was sipping cold coffee disinterestedly. She
rarely left the Council chambers now during the day. Eve-
nings around six o'clock after the store was closed Harry came
to drive her home to her big old house — once central and
impressive, now behind its overgrown grounds all but absorbed in the downtown sprawl, surrounded by a gas station,
the Ford agency, and a mortuary. She ate and slept there, attended by a handmaiden almost as ancient as she. Her real
home was the basement of the City Hall, surrounded by pa-
pers, files, spittoons, and the odor of stale cigars. Harry drove
her down every morning at six-thirty, opened the doors with
her key, and made her the first of the many pots of coffee on
which she seemed to subsist.

"Fancying up," Lucas repeated. "After all this time, knowing what I'm really trying to do, you call it fancying up."

"I've heard your speech on environment. Don't waste your
energy caviling with me on words. You think it's going to last
forever, that energy of yours?"

"Longer than yours, Celeste."

Her old fingers, yellow bones now, were steady on the Dixie
cup. The great emerald glimmered. It seemed to him that she
was as impervious as that green flame. She grinned without
humor. In that antique skull, papered so delicately in folds,
the grin was a reckless act; it could have ripped the parch-
ment. "We'll see," she murmured. And contemptuously, "You
— all of you. You none of you know."

"Know what?"

"Know how to use your will. The power to get your own way. I could tell you in one word if I'd a mind to."

He was silent.

"Oh, you're getting smarter, John. Getting older, too. Won't ask me, know it wouldn't do any good to press me. In that case I'll tell you." She leaned forward. "*Certainty*. That's what powers the will."

"You mean certainty you're right?"

She snorted. "Right or wrong hasn't a thing to do with it. *That*'s where weakening comes — standing on one foot and the other, wondering what's right, trying to see all sides, hemming and hawing — wonder you aren't all walleyed from trying to see it all." She shifted her voice into a cracked mimicry of the Boys': " 'Well now, we oughta consider the other side here, they may have a point here, we gotta look into all aspects —' Rubbish! Does that sound like *will?*"

Her eyes glittered. "You see this stone here, this emerald? Do you think it's an heirloom, handed down or maybe given to me by my husband?" she said softly. "This ring was given to me by nobody but myself. I bought it. I mortgaged everything short of my mortal soul for it." She stared down at the ring. "It was in 1907; I was a young woman. My husband and I were on a buying trip to San Francisco. All we had in the world was a dinky little dry-goods store in the backwoods. We had barely enough cash scraped together for a new spring stock of ladies' wear . . . San Francisco'd just started pulling itself to after that earthquake and fire. An older woman I knew had to pawn her family goods because her husband's business hadn't been insured. She offered me the ring at a fraction of its worth — but still a fortune then. One look at this stone and I had to own it. There was no question of right or wrong, I tell you! Only the certainty that this emerald should belong to me. The *certainty* . . . I won't tell you the various ways I got the money to pay for it. That's beside the point. I got it. And I've worn this emerald for over forty years."

She leaned back. She seemed abruptly to have lost interest in him. "Get your committee together," she said irritably, "and when you've come up with some kind of plan, present it to the town. Convince *them*, Lucas, not me."

This Lucas had never been able to do. In ways which he only now was beginning to understand, he became something of a public fool, a buffoon. He served on the Beautification Committee, the Planning Commission, eventually the Council itself. He served well; he received credit for many innovations and improvements; he became a respected and liked member of the community; but through it all his prime vision — of leafy streets and venerable architecture and a historical identity for the town — became bogged down in a burlesque hassle. At parties his friends made good-natured jokes. "Watch it, Lucas'll appoint you to the Beauty Drive." "Every day is Arbor Day." "Hey John, give me a Good Citizen's Certificate. I planted a rosebush in my yard." "Say Lucas, there's this old Victorian outhouse —"

"Funny, funny. Great little kidders," said John Lucas. But at home he fumed. "Christ, I feel like Young Arrowsmith! Standing up there in front of the PTA suggesting a Class Day tree-planting ceremony! I thought in the middle of it, *What the hell am I doing here?* All I ever wanted to be was an architect. And now I've become — my God — a small-town politician."

"Oh John," Sally said sympathetically; he noticed she didn't protest, or urge him to keep on with it. But he did, doggedly, for a while.

In 1955 a severe earthquake struck Sequoia at noon. Lucas was standing at the Steak House bar with Harry Foster, avoiding the Boys although they knew they would eat with them. As Council members they were Boys too, but Lucas felt apart because he was usually the dissenting member. Harry felt that as Celeste's grandson he ought to dissent as a matter of form. There was no warning quiver. The bar rose up slowly, hung vibrating, and then with a furious twisting shudder slammed down again. A woman next to Lucas toppled from her stool. He saw her legs come up, her naked thighs between skirt and stocking tops.

Sally, Chris, the baby. His single need was to get to them. He lurched toward the door. The quake, unbelievably, was continuing; roll after roll of heavy shocks thundered around them, there were cries and the shatter of glass. Unable to remain upright he fell to his knees and like a swimmer writhed toward the outside. Harry crawled alongside him in the tangle of struggling bodies.

Sally had been outside gardening and was okay; Mark was still asleep in his crib. He drove to the school. Chris was on the playground eating his lunch. "I saw the flagpole wiggle," he remarked. By some miracle nobody was badly hurt. A piece of plate glass just missed slicing off a woman's arm; a man at the Country Club bar was knocked out by falling bottles.

Down in the old City Hall, surrounded by clods of plaster and lath, bolt upright in the rubble, old Celeste Foster sat staring down the length of the scarred burl slab. Plaster dust whitened her felt hat, her eyelashes, her hands resting on the table, the great ring. She was untouched and there were no bruises. She was dead. A stroke, the coroner said. But the town knew what had had to occur before Celeste Foster would leave the City Hall. The huge old windows were boarded up and warning-signs posted on the tilted walls, and eventually they got around to leveling the old building. It had been sturdier than they thought, and only after repeated batterings by the wrecking-ball did the first wall topple.

The new City Hall was erected on the site, and a handsome building it was. Lucas had put everything he had into its design. When the last floor-polisher had left he went over to Bud Hansen's Nursery and handed him a plot-plan for the landscaping. "Do this just as it shows," he ordered. "Put in every tree, plant, lawn just as I drew it."

"Well now," Bud Hansen said with the weary patience Lucas had come to dread in such matters, "you know the budget for landscaping the Hall is still under consideration. It don't look as if —"

"Bud, you're dead right. But this time it's going to *be* as if." He took out his checkbook and wrote out a check for two thousand dollars, which was considerably more than they had in the Holy Fund for the boys' education. "Tell 'em you're donating this, tell 'em anything you want, but if you mention my name, as my last official act before I resign from the Council I'll personally see to it this property of yours gets rezoned R-1. Now get going. I want those grounds like a park, Bud, lush and green. Green as an emerald."

He told Sally that night that he would never again hold an office, serve on a committee, press his convictions on indifference. "It's their town as well as ours," he said, "and they're the majority."

Still, it was too bad he couldn't see the City Hall maples from his office window. It was usually too foggy.

Dust motes drifted up with the motion of his rule as he brushed it over the paper. His pencil rattled in the Sunday quiet. Restless, he turned on his stool and leaned on the windowsill. Across the silent intersection a whole block of Foster's Department Store windows poured forth their Technicolor into the empty downtown. Imbedded in the sidewalk in front of each window was a huge gray cylinder of concrete, which was supposed to look like a redwood stump but which resembled an umbrella stand made of a fossilized elephant's foot. In each cylinder was planted a shamefaced liquidambar sapling, denuded early of its few disillusioned leaves. His friend Harry Foster, astraddle public issue versus loyalty, sacrificing not one inch of parking space, had Led the Way. Blinking down at the elephants' feet Lucas reflected that it was perhaps fortunate the other Downtown Merchants had not taken the hint.

. . . Well, if he had been unable to do much for the official image of Sequoia there were private oases of green for which Lucas was responsible. There was the City Hall and its grounds. There were a few public buildings, houses, a church or two, with unity and grace and air in them. Whenever he passed them he thought: there is a part of me. He did not know who lived in some of his houses now but he believed those people dwelt in a certain felicity because of him. To design a house is to create an environment; you become a household god even if your name is never invoked. In this small town, this corner of the world, this place in time, specks of himself were here now and would continue after he was gone (and in the Safest Town in the USA, why not?). Could he ask more of life than that some part of him continued?

Standing at the window on that Sunday, that desert in every week, Lucas's restlessness suddenly balled itself like a fist, and began a slow astonishing pummeling of some vital part.

*   *   *

A clump of youths appeared around Foster's corner, ambling with that disjointed looseness that spells out boredom — hands in pockets, shouldering each other, stumbling off the curb as if it were too much effort to exert their leg muscles. The noise of their bickering drifted up on the faint rhythms of rock 'n' roll from a portable radio. They paused at the corner to light cigarettes. Yawning and blinking, they lolled against Harry's planter boxes. Their eyes slid up and down the street, their hands twitched in their pockets. One of them flicked his glance up momentarily, unseeing; in it was an edginess so recognizable, so familiar, it hooked like a sharp barb into the watching Lucas. He knew him, that nameless boy; he knew his boredom and hopefulness; he remembered the taste of those first cigarettes in the mouth, he understood how restlessness raced like a nerve across the muscles of the shoulders. The memory of long empty Sundays, of awakening believing that something was going to happen that day, something — *anything* — to break the tedium, to give him a chance to use those muscles — this memory stretched like a wire between that boy, the whole faceless group, and Lucas. He could have occupied their skins at that moment as easily as he occupied his own.

From his high window the watching man regarded the boys and felt the unseen wire vibrate tightly, unpleasantly. He knew what they wanted: the exercise of their full powers. Lately in his encounters with his own son Chris this same tension sometimes sprang. Lucas sensed in his son a challenge, a testing, an itching of horns; he would lower his head and seem ready to butt, egging, pawing, rubbing the irritating velvet against him, bucking his supremacy. At first this had amused Lucas. There was something pathetic, almost endearing, in the boy's helpless struggles with his own rage and illogic

which made Lucas sad for the man-child who so recently had
been a baby. But lately the butting had become more cunning.
The young horns had sharpened and sometimes they found
private places. These places which he had thought so secure
were suddenly opened, and beginning to feel raw with repeated pricking. At the height of a man's own maturity it is
not pleasant to be so gouged. In his inner ear Lucas occasionally sensed the full noises of approaching battle, the paw of
hoofs and clang of horn, the harem cowering on the far side of
the meadow. It was this premonition which could cause a man
on occasion to forget that what he wanted most for his sons
was their full manhood, and to exercise contempt upon them,
and to ruin the dinner hour. Lucas scowled down from his
window. It was not an easy thing to see the juices rise in the
young, while feeling within oneself intimations of the first hard
frost. *Frost?* He shook himself irritably.

Something happened down on the street. The wire between
them jerked.

The group became motionless. The aimless roiling stopped.
They paused in an attitude of attention, pulled as by a draw-
string into a tight knot. Even the music from their radio was
chopped off. They hung, frozen, listening to something which
Lucas could not hear.

In the core of silence there began an eerie thing: a pulse
which seemed to emanate from them, a beating, a throb barely
perceptible at first, sensed not in Lucas's ear but in his skull-
plate. It climbed to the threshold of audibility and exploded.
The knot flew apart.

Hollering, roaring, plunging against each other, they
streamed across the street. Lucas had the impression of
twisted faces flashing momentarily like the reflection from
mirrors. In a sensation of pure fear he thought that they were

coming to attack him. But they had not looked up. Below him the awning of Ralph's Sporting Goods blocked his view, but he could hear them. They were smashing the store windows. He heard the crash of glass, the hoarse scream of their voices.

Lucas leaned far out the window. He heard his own intoxicated voice: "*Hey!*" he bellowed insanely, shaking his fists. "*Hey hey hey!*"

They came out from the awning with guns in their hands. They went up the streets in full cry, brandishing weapons.

"*Hey!*" Lucas called after them. "*Hey, hey* —"

In the following echoes, in the fallen silence, he slowly pulled himself back from the window. He thought quite clearly: *I knew something great was going to happen today.*

IV

. . . urging that all-out measures be taken immediately. To repeat: it has now been officially confirmed that the two top Chinese leaders have been assassinated. The militarist faction, led by high-ranking Army officers and supported by underground elements in the Soviet provinces, has seized control of the Peking government. It was the violent opposition of this faction, the self-styled voice of old-line communism, which succeeded in wrecking plans for an international disarmament agreement last year, and which since that time has forced the leadership to back down from any further peace overtures . . . There is growing speculation that the new government may attempt to force an immediate showdown between the Communist and free worlds, through demands for immediate withdrawal of UN bases and security forces throughout the world, and a repudiation of testing and disarmament treaties. Informed sources emphasize that the full implications of the threat cannot yet be evaluated, but the first shock has been followed by attitudes of extreme tension everywhere. While there is as yet no outright discussion of possible pre-emptive tactics, it is well known that — Here is a bulletin. The President, now closeted with his advisers, will address the nation within the hour. To repeat —

J OHN Lucas drove home through streets as empty of life as a body siphoned of blood. There was a strange station wagon in the driveway; he swung in past it and nearly ran down Cis, who was skating in the carport. He could feel as if it were his own skin the fender brush her skirt. He lunged from the car, swept her up, pressed her head to his shoulder. He bore her into the house, her skates banging against his knees. She began to cry and kick. She slid out of his arms and fell with a clatter to the kitchen floor.

Sally appeared. "Cissie! What on earth —"

The shock of pain in his bruised knees was so severe he could not speak for a moment. Sally and Cis rocked in each other's arms. "He strangled me!" Cis howled. "He almost killed me with the car —"

Sally swept her off. He hobbled after them. She plunked Cis in a dining-room chair and knelt to take off her skates. "There, there. You're all *right*, darling, you're not hurt —"

"Sally," Lucas rasped, "my God —"

She looked up at him blankly.

"Don't you know? Don't you *know?*"

She had not known; but seeing his face she then knew. She crouched over Cis's feet; her hands slowly went around the child's ankles, held them. She stared at Lucas. It was a weighty thing that she had understood immediately from his unarticulated cry: *It has happened.* Each era had its unthinkable *it:* beast, elements, plague, flood, the gods' wrath.

Cis began to whine like a puppy; perhaps she knew what *it* was, perhaps she only smelled it on them.

Sally said flatly, "Oh God in heaven."

"John?" Somebody stood in the doorway.

Lucas blinked at him.

"Hey," the stranger said. Uncertainly, he offered his hand. "Hey there, John," he said.

"Joe," Lucas said.

Joe Anderson was a lumber wholesaler who came up from San Francisco regularly to talk to the sawmill people. He had been a friend ever since Lucas had designed a branch office for his firm out near the plywood plant. Every time Joe came to Sequoia he stopped by. When the Lucases went down to the City they always had dinner with Joe and his wife Barbara.

Now, shaking hands, Joe Anderson stared and he too knew. "Christ," he muttered. "If it's bad, tell us."

At this, inexhaustible Motherhood resumed its function; the motor could almost be heard to spit, catch, begin its powerful hum. Sally removed Cissie's other skate, stood up briskly, and hauled the child to her feet. "Cis," she said in tones of fantastic ordinariness, "you may get yourself a bottle of Seven-Up if you'll go outside and play. It's too nice a day to stay inside a stuffy old house."

"Seven-Up! Yay!" Cis cried, and went off to claim the bribe.

. . . so willfully and maliciously, in the course of so few hours, have torn a great hole in the fabric of hope over which the world's peoples have so painstakingly and so lengthily labored. This hope, this peaceful intent, these struggles cannot in the name of humanity be allowed to —

The face of the President slid slowly up the TV screen. Up and up it wafted, the mouth moving sternly, the chin firm; and then it was swallowed and at the bottom below the dividing bar appeared again the President's hair, and then his brow, and next his gaunt and angry eyes, and again the mouth. It did not occur to them to adjust the picture. They stood in Mark's room and barely breathing watched and listened.

. . . and particularly in the murder of their trusted leaders, we share with the people of China and the Soviet provinces this sense of betrayal. But we cannot ignore evil. We cannot seal it off. The fantastic success of a few men, operating so traitorously with the connivance of an outlaw power, indicates that this evil infection is already entrenched. We must face the fact that it may well be in command of China's military resources and striking force. Therefore, with full awareness of the danger, with full —

Sally went over and snapped off the TV. John Lucas regarded her back dazedly. Behind him Joe Anderson made an involuntary movement.

"Get back under the covers," Sally said crisply to Mark, who was crouched near his bed with his face flushed and his mouth gaping. "You have no business being up, young man. You have a fever. Try to take a nap."

Lucas made a lunge for the TV but she blocked him neatly. She turned to him, her eyes glittering strangely; then she bent and jerked the plug of the TV and began wheeling it toward Mark's door. Pieces of an old Erector set with which Mark had been building scattered under her feet, nuts and bolts scrunched into the rug. She gave the TV a push toward the men and herding everything out into the hall she said, "Go to sleep, darling," in tones shimmering with calm, and closed Mark's door.

The harrowing sounds of a frightened world came through on the TV Joe Anderson attended in the living room, while in the kitchen John Lucas faced his wife. "Do you know what you cut off?" he said. "Do you think you can punch a button on a TV set and cut off that boy from the world? Is that what you were trying to do?"

Her face was washed clean of color, of mascara stain, of blood; under her eyes the skin was bruised. "I don't know what's happened but I know it's terrible, and I know I'll hear about it in a minute or two. I just wanted a minute or two." She made a stretching, painful gesture of the neck, as if she were offering it up to him: long, exposed, sacrificial.

He put his arms around her and held her as if to warm them both. She sagged against him for a moment.

They walked together into the living room and listened with Joe to the concluding words of the President. The sound of them was like the sound of bricks being laid, each set tightly into its mortar so there would be no possible chink, and through which there might never again be a glimpse of the other side.

"I can't seem to get through on the phone," Joe said. "They're holding the lines."

"Oh?" Lucas said. "Well . . ." How could he say to him, how could he come right out and say, Joe, your family's sitting down there in San Francisco, a prime target area, and you're up here in Sequoia three hundred miles away —

The Safest Town in the USA.

Despite the rejoicing of the Sequoia Chamber of Commerce at the publication of that magazine article, despite the happy cries with which it had been greeted in the local paper — Oh how the citizens had laughed, even unto the Downtown Merchants' Association, and kidded among themselves! Nowheresville, they had said, even fallout would not drop in here, this was *news?* — despite this, Sequoia was taken seriously for a while. A few families had straggled in from places like Detroit and New York and Miami, seeking "Security in Sequoia" as the C of C had put it. A small order of Fundamentalists had set up homesteads in an outlying district, seeking there to reserve an encampment against the Coming Doom, which according to their calculations would take place in December 1969. Some of them had found it difficult to secure gainful employment and were now swelling the ranks of welfare beneficiaries. Several families had moved back to Miami, saying they'd rather be bombed than bored to death. "Obviously," a local lawyer said, "they weren't members of the Country Club."

At all this John Lucas too had been faintly and contemptuously amused. Now, regarding his friend Joe Anderson, who had a wife and three children sitting down on that peninsula, and remembering how impossible it was to get through the five-o'clock traffic on the clogged freeways to the south, or over the Bay Bridge to the east, or the Golden Gate to the north; remembering the signs, EVACUATION ROUTE, as he sat cursing in his car in the middle of the crawling traffic-sea, remembering the vast trap any city is, and particularly San Francisco, John Lucas could think of nothing to say to this man which would not reveal his pity or, most of all, the wild sense of reprieve which had jumped in him remembering: the Safest Town.

"Of course," Sally said, pouring coffee into their cups, "this may turn out to be just another scare, like Cuba or Berlin or . . ."

Joe watched her as she talked, absorbedly watched her lips move as if they were an idle pattern of leaves in a gentle breeze.

"I mean, it may be settled tomorrow, or next week." As if conscious of their gazes she shaded her eyes with her hand and got up to draw the curtain over the kitchen window. She pulled it open again and stood looking absently into the garden. "Oh for heaven's sake," she murmured, "Cissie's got her Barbie-doll clothes scattered all over the deck."

Joe Anderson said politely, "It might. It might be all over tomorrow." He was a tall man, almost as tall as Lucas but much lighter, almost skinny. He sat hunched over his coffee cup at the kitchen table, staring into it with a mild, puzzled expression. He looked like a dazed stork.

"Well, you know, world tensions and all," said Sally with effort. "You're going to have — there's bound to be periodic crises. I just can't believe that these — these new people could manage to keep the whole world upset for any length of —"

John Lucas stirred. Was she trying to make light of things? He wished she would stop talking.

She sensed his irritation. She gave him a crippled look. "Maybe Joe would like some more coffee. I'll make more." She continued to stand by the window, as if paralyzed.

"You want a drink, Joe?" Lucas said, because he had nothing else to offer.

"We had this plan," Joe began slowly. "I wonder if she took it seriously. During the last — situation, we decided that if things got really bad, what we'd do was we'd pile the kids in the station wagon, and take these cases of Metrecal. We thought, Metrecal being a complete diet, it'd be good for emergency supplies —"

"We put in a few boxes of that dehydrated food along with some canned stuff during the Cuban crisis," Sally offered. "In case there was a — interruption in transportation or anything. We never thought of Metrecal."

"—and some bottled water, in case we couldn't count on a pure supply. So we decided we'd toss everything in the station wagon and head out, up this way probably —"

"A lot of people here did the same thing, you know — stock up on foodstuffs. We're so far away from everything, once when there was a strike and the trucks didn't come through for a few days there was a shortage —"

"Sally," Lucas said.

"I was only explaining, she said. "I just didn't want him to feel alone in this. We're in it too." Into her face came a look of wonder, the almost ludicrous surprise sometimes seen on a boxer's face when he is hit very hard indeed and not expecting it. She came over to the table and sat down. She sagged forward on her elbow and curled her hand around her eyes. She took a sip of her cold coffee and shuddered.

As if there had been no interruption Joe continued doggedly. "I remember once I was up here and there was a lot of joking about Sequoia being a good place to be. It kind of stuck in the back of my mind. We figured if we could get out far enough — say the Lake County area maybe — if we had enough supplies we could hole up there for a while. I stashed an ax and some rope and a gun and fishing equipment in the car under the spare tire place. I told Barb to keep the wagon gassed up, full tank all times. I don't know, though. It's been so long, we kind of stopped worrying." He spoke carefully, frowning down at his folded hands.

There was a silence. John Lucas thought of the station wagon in his driveway. He thought of Barbara Anderson getting her three small children together, lugging cases of Metrecal into her own car — a Citroën — was the tank full in that little car? She would close the door of their Pacific Heights ranch home, and when the children would ask where they were going she would say brightly (she seemed like a cheerful girl, Barbara), *I thought it would be a nice day for a drive, children.* Lucas tried to concentrate on Barbara Anderson doing that, but all he could see of her was a well-stacked little blonde in Chinese hostess pajamas who had given them sukiyaki the last time they visited the City. She had cooked the sukiyaki in the living room on a hibachi and they had sat on cushions at a low coffee table. Lucas had got a cramp in his knee and had to stretch his leg out under the table, and his foot had encountered Barbara's bottom. Before he'd had time to joke about it she turned red and got up on the pretext of getting more saki. When she sat down again she'd inched her pillow over toward Joe's. Lucas had looked over at Barbara's face and realized that she was young, very young, almost a generation younger than Joe. Their children were all very young, two little girls and a boy who was barely toddling. Joe must have married late; he was Lucas's age.

"The only thing is," Joe was saying, "I'm wondering if she's remembering the plan."

And Joe had forgotten that he had the station wagon, packed with the survival kit. Lucas got up and took out a bottle of scotch and poured them both a drink. Joe took his glass and looked around the kitchen. He looked carefully, as if it were part of a ceremony, at everything: the lunch dishes in the sink, the empty coffeepot on the stove, the arrangement of oranges in a glass jar, the bulletin board with a grocery list and Cis's school coloring of the *Mayflower*, the bowl of growing salt crystals, the pot of ivy climbing the window, the Sunday comics on the stool. He nodded once, courteously, in a ritualistic gesture Lucas had seen before but could not remember where or on what occasion. Maybe a cornball movie: *Beau Geste?* They drank in silence.

Lucas went with him to the car. "Falcon, eh?" He opened the car door for Joe. "Thought you had a Chevy."

"Traded it in," Joe said. "I get terrific mileage out of this one . . . Well, see you, John." He put his hand out the window and they shook.

"Take her easy, Joe. Traffic's apt to be lousy, and you know that damned Redwood Highway."

"Yeah . . . Funny thing."

"What?"

"It's Sunday." He cleared his throat and stared out the windshield. "Jennie — that's the oldest girl, she's seven — she came to me the other morning, I was in the bathroom shaving. Jennie gets up and sets the table in the mornings and then she comes in and talks to me while I'm shaving. Anyway, the other morning Jennie was sitting there on the can and she says to me, 'I don't like school days sometimes,' and I said why, kind of surprised, because Jen's bright, you know, a kid that's always got a bang out of school. She said, 'I like school okay, I just don't like some school *days*.' I said what days, and she said the days they had air-raid practice and had to get under their desks. Then she said, 'Daddy, if a bomb is coming would you come to school to get me and take me home?' I thought, God. You know? There's some things you don't think about any other way. A seven-year-old kid . . . So I said sure, if I knew a bomb was coming I would come to school and get her and take her home. She said, 'Promise?' and I said yes, I promised."

He started the car. "One thing good. It's Sunday. She's at home. She doesn't have to worry about if I'm coming to get her."

He backed out of the drive and Lucas watched until he had turned the corner.

Sally was still sitting at the kitchen table, drawing circles with her forefinger around the rim of her cup. Without looking up she said, "I didn't know what to say to him. Driving three hundred miles back there into that place . . ."

"He had to go. His family's there."

"I know, oh I know . . . John. If it were us there, the children and me, would you hesitate to come back?"

"Hesitate?"

"He could die there. They could all die there, and he couldn't help them."

He stood by her chair and touched her hair, the back of her neck under it. "I know."

She leaned against his belly and he felt with his thumb the delicate knobs of her spine in her bent neck. "I might hesitate a moment, but I'd come."

As he stood there with his wife's neck under his hand he remembered all at once how huge his father had looked to him as a boy. He remembered his father's hands, stubby and square, as he stood at the table carving the meat; the freckled wrists flicked deftly as with one powerful stroke he sliced off the outside cut and laid it aside on the platter. Lucas remembered with clarity how his father had portioned out the slices, balancing them surely on the slender blade, neatly slipping them off on each plate. There was a fineness, a nicety, an inexorableness of justice in the apportionment; each had received the exact amount that was good and right for him to have. All things were dispensed in this way to them, and it was a sure, certain, and comforting life John Lucas had had then. His father sat at his place at the head of the table, and as long as that imperial figure remained the household and the world were secure.

He was my age then, Lucas thought. How old he had

seemed, how knowing. Whose knowing face, whose wise old eyes watched over this household? Was it possible, was it credible, that these must be his own?

V

"Bᴜᴛ nobody's phoned us even to ask. Wouldn't you think they'd at least check with us?"

"Why should anybody check with us?"

"We're the chairmen. You haven't heard a word I've said." She came in a silky slither of slip and sat down on the lid of the toilet. "I wish I knew what to do."

Slowly he sloshed his bruised knees up and down in the water. Enfolded in steam, he was held by a strange lassitude. "Do?" he said. "What can anybody do?"

"Don't talk like that," she said sharply. "It — sounds panicky."

"I'm not panicky. I just can't believe that a bunch of people would meet tonight out at a country club for a buffet supper to discuss the decorations for a dance."

"That's what I'm trying to find *out* — whether we should go or whether we shouldn't." She sat smoking nervously, in her slip with her legs crossed. Lucas gazed down at himself awash in the tub, knees rising like volcanic cones, penis floating laxly. He looked unreal to himself, distorted peculiarly; as in some gaseous element this unreality billowed slowly out to include the tub, his wife, the house, the quiet wooded cul-de-sac with its streetlight shining down at the corner. He, all of it, seemed to be lying flat against the earth like a possum play-ing dead. He sat up abruptly, the water streaming off his shoulders. "I need to think," he said.

"Then think about what we ought to *do*."

"I don't know what to do."

There was a silence. The smoke swirled up and mingled with the steam. She usually hated the odor of smoke in the bathroom, which smelled of her soap and her perfume. "It's supposed to be safe here," she said. Her voice caught. She wrenched it free. "I don't think any place is safe. I mean the kind of safety you don't think about, the kind of — sort of cushioned feeling you have when you're young. I guess that's one of the things you lose when you grow up, anyway . . . I think I'm babbling," she said carefully. "What I should be trying to do is act as normally as possible. After all, there're the children. If we panic, it rubs off on them. They — they're so *hopeful*, John." She stopped abruptly, rose, lifted the lid of the toilet and dropped her cigarette in. She stood looking down at it, hugging her naked arms.

Thinking of her and of the hopeful children he pulled him-self slowly out of the tub. It was a tremendous effort; he seemed to weigh 20 gs; the water sucked at him. When he gained his erect stature, dripping, he was dizzy from effort. She handed him a towel. "Okay," he said. "We act normal. We go to the Country Club and we eat our dinner and we discuss the decorations for next week's dance."

"What if nobody's there?"

"Then I guess we have to decide alone what the decorations will be," he said. "And eat up all that goddam creamed shrimp."

"Shrimp Newburg." She touched his wet arm wonderingly, as if its size and hairiness were new to her.

She turned and opened the drawer and out came utensils of maintenance and reinforcement: Madonna foundation, Cover Girl lotion, Silver-Blu eyeshadow stick, Erace Tan #2, the magic mascara wand so loyal and indelible. Clutching his towel he watched as she applied a plastic face which was almost as beautiful as her nude, real one. It was a pleasure to him that she had more than one. With the years a woman's infinite variety was the rarest pearl, for which any husband would pay the highest price.

"I'm getting worried about Chris," she said, dabbing Erace on a pigmented spot. "He's not home yet. He knows he's supposed to baby-sit tonight."

"Where did he go?"

"He left right after lunch; he was going to play tennis over at the school courts and then go over to Paul McKnight's —" She opened her eyes wide and over this astonished expression stroked mascara. "Do you want to call McKnights' and find out if Chris is still there? Tell him to come home *immediately*." The mascara was dropped back into the drawer and another wand brandished. He watched, fascinated, as her mouth became a stiff wizened O, as she dabbed at it, using only a picking motion of her fingers, the heel of her hand resting on her chin. "Ah*eey*eeuhly," she repeated, rolling her eyes sternly at him in the mirror. She finished and smacked her lips briskly. She had applied the full-power face, usually reserved for Club dances and the Military Ball.

"I have to shave," he said.

"Oh. Well. I'll phone McKnights' then. Hurry and dress, will you though?"

He stared after her neat, round rear, bustling with normalcy, and the sense of unreality returned. He toweled a clear circle in the mirror and peered at his image. He drew water into the basin and began to shave. He shaved steadily and methodically. As he was preparing for the final strokes above his mouth he paused, his razor lifted. There was a disturbance there in the mirror, an imprisoned glint.

McKnight?

One of those kids in the downtown street had been the McKnight boy. He had not known it then, he had not focused on any one of them. He had seen them as a unit. There had been no time for recognition. But now three hours later an image, which must have been silvered only an instant on his retina, detached itself; and with a clarity like Sally's face as it had grown under the wands one boy's face seemed to grow in detail, an eyebrow here, a mouth there: Paul McKnight's. Chris's best friend.

Where was his son this afternoon?

Sally moved about the bedroom smoking restlessly and complaining of Chris. He had no sense of responsibility. If he hadn't learned it by seventeen she did not see how he was going to be taught. It was about time that boy realized life wasn't a playground. He could rebel all he wanted against authority but she had noticed he was only too willing to accept the benefits of being a dependent but when it came to accepting some of the *duties* in return — "Where are you going?" she demanded.

"To look for him."

"Now really, that's silly, John. I *told* you I'd phoned everywhere, checked with everybody, there's no place you'd *know* where to look, you'd just be wandering around —"

On she went in her irritation, no fear such as his, which was grinding now with such severity he found it difficult to think. He went into the bathroom and closed the door. He

stood fighting his fear. He tried not to imagine Paul Mc-
Knight or the boys in that group who had gone down the
street with stolen guns in their hands. He tried not to imagine
what they had done with those guns. But he saw the tops of
the boys' heads and heard their roars, and now he believed he
recognized a head, a voice — He put his hands over his ears
as if this might stop the eye of his mind. *Fool*, he thought
furiously, and burst out again into the bedroom, scooping his
car keys from the dresser. He heard Chris's voice in the
kitchen.

He moved in, shoving the scolding Sally aside. "I'll handle
this. Chris, in your room."

Chris raised his shoulders and spread his hands. "If somebody would just *tell* me," he said in a high unsteady voice. "If
somebody would just tell me why all the fuss! A little thing
like coming in late — crissake, I've been late a thousand
times!"

"— responsibility," Sally overrode, "when you knew you
were supposed to be home at five o'clock! And today of all
days —"

"I don't remember any orders that I have to come home
every time the President makes a speech."

"*In your room*, Chris."

"I don't see why I have to—"

"Do you want to talk about it out here?"

He looked at his father. John Lucas thought: *There is a
mark of guilt on him*. Sick with recognition he stared at the
boy across Sally's head. Chris turned wordlessly and walked to
his room. He didn't even give his usual shrug of contempt.
Lucas followed him, walking as if his knees were made of
glass. He closed the door behind him.

Chris sat on the bed and folded his hands.

"Chris," Lucas said, "you've got to be honest with me now."

The boy said nothing.

Lucas took a deep wavering breath. "You've got to tell me who you were with this afternoon and exactly what you did." The boy's knuckles tightened. Guilty he was, guilt unmistakable . . . "Were you with Paul McKnight?"

"Sure, I was with McKnight. What's wrong with that?"

"How long were you with him?"

"Couple hours maybe." Was that wariness, cunning, in his son's eyes? "Why? All of a sudden there's some objection to McKnight? You think he's a bad influence, or what? You never seemed to think so before," he said in a stronger voice.

Lucas fought nausea. "Did you go downtown with him? Were you downtown at all? *Answer me*, Chris."

"I — I may have been. I don't remember."

Carefully, breathing with difficulty, John Lucas took hold of his son under one armpit and drew him up slowly. It took a great deal of power. The boy was tall, almost as big as he; but still not a man. It was necessary for him to understand this. "You will remember," Lucas said thickly.

The boy's features coiled, as if his father's breath had singed them. He swelled, jerked from Lucas's grasp, and surrendered.

"All right! All right! What'd you *think* I'd be doing?" His voice rose, cracked. "What'd you and Mom think — I'd be playing some kind of game, or what? Bawling me out just as if everything was normal, I come home and everything's the same, the same old cruddy *batch* — Did you think I could just keep on playing tennis, go back to McKnight's and drink Cokes? Did you think I could just shrug my shoulders or stand around sucking my thumb saying, Oh gee whiz, there's

going to be a war, well let's go to the movies? Do you actually
think I'm still a *kid?*"

"Chris —"

"You think you can go on hiding facts from us, you think
we don't know what things *mean?* You think we're so goddam
young and dumb you've got to protect us? *Protection!*" Spittle
from the word flaked his lip. "Just who do you think's supposed to furnish us protection — *you?*"

The full gale of his son's anguish had snuffed out Lucas's
own rage. The raw sounds of the child's cry in the man's body
were suddenly unbearably piteous. Sensing how his youth
burdened him, Lucas reached out, but the boy drew back his
battered dignity into a stance of contempt. "I'm not a *kid*," he
repeated furiously.

"I want to know what you did with the guns."

"I don't know what you're talking about."

"The guns you and McKnight and the other boys took from
Ralph's Sporting Goods after you broke in there this afternoon."

"I don't know what you're talking about." He looked at his
father as if from a great height.

"I was upstairs in the office, Chris. I saw it all. You can't lie
about it. What did you do with those guns?"

Bewilderment broke through the stony contempt. "Why do
you keep talking about guns? I don't know anything about
any —"

"Are you telling me you weren't with that group downtown
this afternoon, with McKnight? Careful, now!"

"Hell, I didn't even *go* downtown! I was —" He stopped. "I
was not downtown and I did not break into any sporting-goods
store and I sure as hell didn't steal any guns." His voice rose

again. "Why should I want to steal a gun? They'll probably be *issuing* me one."

The burst of relief was like a clip behind Lucas's knees. They buckled abruptly and he sat on the bed. "Issuing you a gun?" he said harshly. "Christ, what good would *guns* do now?"

"If there's going to be a war —"

Lucas rubbed both hands over his face. "We both better calm down here. In the first place, nobody's at war. Talk like that —"

"*You* were the one talking about guns, not me."

Lucas stood up and jammed his hands into his pockets and thrust his nose into his son's face. "Okay. Then let's just examine another question. If you weren't with that gang, just where were you? That outburst of yours looked pretty damn guilty, boy. Now let's have it. *What did you do today?*"

Their faces were so close that the boy's eyes almost crossed as he regarded his father. Like a braced cadet his chin was jammed against his neck, his head was drawn back, he stared down the short slope of nose. It was as if in his refusal to squint he had lost sight of Lucas, the speck at the other end. His voice issued from the same far slope.

"I won't tell you."

VI

A NURSEMAID sits on a park bench, beside her a baby carriage in which is sprawled a large striped tiger. It blinks menacingly out from under its frilled baby bonnet. If the nursemaid knows of this — knows the occupant of her buggy is a monster feline around whose jowls she herself tenderly tied the bow; or instead knows that the animal escaped from a nearby zoo, leaped upon her infant charge and devoured it, sparing only the bonnet to which it has presumably taken a fancy, and is now lolling satedly in a surge of peristalsis; or if the nursemaid is aware but simply doesn't care, servants being what they are nowadays — she gives no indication, for she is buried behind a copy of the Philadelphia *Bulletin.*

There are passers-by in the park but they too take no heed, for they too are rapt behind their editions of the same newspaper. Only one little skinny man has seen, believed the evidence of his senses, and is jumping up and down in a frenzy. He points his finger and calls wildly upon the citizenry to take note. But he is ignored; his babble of alarm goes unnoticed, for deep within their journalistic trance everybody in Philadelphia is reading the *Bulletin.* Everybody, that is, but the little man, who has somehow been deprived of his copy. Uninsulated, he is exposed to fearful sights.

The Country Club parking area was packed. "Oh what a relief," Sally said. "Everybody's decided to act normal." At the door she loosened her wrap, took a deep breath, and disappeared behind her copy of the *Bulletin*.

Bledsoe the Club manager nodded gravely as he floated by. Sally went to the women's lounge to leave her wrap, and Lucas wandered to the bar. Fixing his eye firmly on Ernie the bartender's red vest he ordered a double scotch.

There was this about Ernie: upon that sly Irish visage rested the same holy light which emanated from prophets, touts, and tax investigators — savvy brought to full blossom. Like a tuning fork Ernie vibrated to that music which sings around any given society. He could hear the supersonic whistle only dogs are supposed to catch. As he polished his highball glasses in the corner he would cock his head to one side, humming under his breath, and you knew he was picking up blips. It was not that he merely heard and passed on local gossip; this was the kind of brokerage all bartenders conducted, and he was not above obliging with a wink and a chuckle. It was only the *face* which issued bulletins, scores, temperature and humidity.

On this particular Sunday evening Lucas, himself vibrating with intimations, could not bring himself yet to consult the Oracle. He turned his back and leaned against the bar. There were a dozen men lined up as he was, with their backs to Ernie. They were arguing about whether or not the Club should again approach the stubborn farmer who owned the land abutting the fourth hole. The Club for years had wanted that land and for years the farmer had held out for a fantastic price.

"Maybe he'll sell now," Henry Rice boomed. "This might be a helluva good time to approach him."

Lucas attempted to reflect on why the Club would want to buy now, but he found he was so dizzy he had to turn around and lean both his elbows on the bar. He thought with astonishment that he could not be drunk, certainly not after one drink. As he turned he unintentionally caught Ernie full in the face. Even as his glance skidded by, he saw it. There was nothing on the man's face: nothing but skin.

The Oracle had been shut off. Fuse blown? Shorted? Lucas stared into the aspect which was now nothing but a regular bartender's face, and as he watched an invisible edition of the *Bulletin* materialized before it.

Onto plates which were eight inches across Lucas spooned out: bleu cheese, jellied aspic, artichoke hearts, garbanzo salad, macaroni and pimiento salad, creamed shrimp (Newburg), pickled beets, California salad with sour cream, raw salmon, olives, pigs' knuckles, guacamole paste, anchovies, and cole slaw. About eighteen inches above the buffet table ran a shelf of glass through which he watched his hands serving himself. Ahead of him a Mrs. Patricia Hue, who was extremely short and very nearsighted and too vain to wear glasses in public, strove to perceive through the shelf what to her must have been an array of formless jellies. She left a smear of frustrated and presumably germ-laden steam on the glass. Lucas took his plate over to the committee's table and then went off to find the manager.

"Look here, Bledsoe," he said, "what is that glass shelf you've got there above the buffet?"

"Why, that's the sneeze-rail, Mr. Lucas," Bledsoe said.

"A sneeze-rail. And what is a sneeze-rail supposed to do, Bledsoe?" Lucas asked courteously.

"It's been there for several years, Mr. Lucas. I'm surprised you haven't noticed it before. It's for the protection of the public. To protect the food from being breathed on. It's a health law, you know." Bledsoe rattled the menus impressively. "State law. Bureau of Health."

"I see." Lucas scowled. "I suppose we ought to be grateful we've got people down there in Sacramento looking out for our health."

Bledsoe darted a look at him. "Certainly, Mr. Lucas."

"On the other hand it could be looked on as an infringement of our civil rights. An attempt to legislate where and how we *breathe*, Bledsoe, which is one of the few individual liberties and personal decisions still left to us."

Murmuring bland apologies Bledsoe slithered by him and made his way, clucking and frowning busily, toward the kitchen.

Again Lucas thought: But I'm *not* drunk.

The committee were well into their pigs' knuckles and their plans for the garnishing of these halls. Lucas regarded the gold-leaf wallpaper which had been applied between the rough redwood beams he had specified for the dining room and lounge. He had not approved the wallpaper — had barely, indeed, managed to keep from threatening to rip it off piece by piece if they applied it. But who could bulldoze the wife of the Permanent Chairman of the By-Laws Committee? She was an amateur Glorious Home buff, this Tinker Bell of the Country Club, a woman splendidly endowed with everything but taste, charm, and reticence. Her spoor was everywhere, in the houses of friends, in this perfectly honest shell of Club buildings Lucas had designed; she had left her mark in puff-draperies, in rubbed-white antique finishes, in gold-leaf wallpaper. Gazing at this impetigoid ceiling, Lucas again felt dizziness, and with it a sense of nausea. For a moment he was convinced that it might fall on him, and infect him with an incurable disease which might flay off his skin and reveal all the organs underneath.

"You don't have to look quite so bored," Sally muttered. And louder, "Eat some of that shrimp, darling, it's awfully good."

"How are your children?" Mrs. Patricia Hue asked him. "How's that cute little girl of yours?"

She always asked him that. He did not understand why Mrs. Hue should be so interested in his children. He regarded her closely, seeking to pierce some veil he had hitherto been unaware of.

Sally nudged him to indicate he was being rude. She and Mrs. Hue rolled their eyes humorously at each other to indicate that he must have had too much to drink and therefore could be treated with tolerance, like the village idiot. Lucas arose and left the dining room and went into the bar. Except for Ernie it was empty; everyone was at dinner.

"How many drinks have I had, Ernie?"

"I never count, Mr. Lucas."

"Reach back into your memory. You served me exactly two scotches, didn't you?"

"I guess that's about right, Mr. Lucas."

"Well, fix me a third one, and make it a double. If they're going to roll their eyes at me and be tolerant of me I might as well capitalize on it. Right, Ernie?"

He chuckled obligingly, served Lucas a drink, and picked

up a glass and started polishing it. He blew on the glass and polished it some more, and held it up, balancing it on his fingertips and gazing at it critically. His wrists were competent and delicate.

"Ernie," Lucas said carefully, "I've got a question for you. If I jumped up and down and pointed my finger out the window and said that I saw a tiger out there, would you pay any attention to me?"

He eyed Lucas slantwise, the knowing old bartender's eye. "I guess. If there happened to be a tiger out there, Mr. Lucas."

"And if there were one out there, what would we do about it?"

Ernie had ducked down behind the bar but now his head rose slowly. Behind the horizon of knobs, tubes, bulbs, maraschinos, toothpicks, and bottles he surveyed Lucas with the mournful expression of a wizard whose implements have suddenly ceased to function.

"Do, Mr. Lucas?"

"Do, Ernie. There ought to be something we could do about it personally," Lucas said.

"Personally," Ernie repeated. He cocked his head, chuckled vacantly, picked up his polishing rag, and retired behind his *Bulletin*.

Lucas drained his drink and lurched off.

"I know this boy who's an art major at Sequoia State — really terribly gifted, he *may* be a genius, he makes these marvelous sculptures, he uses practically any medium, he goes to the beach and makes these perfectly fantastic sculptures out of wet sand, he uses his bare feet, he says he can *feel* the *roots* of the form that way — anyway, he did a perfectly marvelous little sculpture in ice for the Medical Auxiliary Ball last spring, a three-tiered fountain effect with blue champagne, he used food coloring, it was absolutely fantastic and quite beautiful really, spilling over this fountain with three disks of ice the edges carved out in scallop-shapes —"

"With his toes?" Lucas inquired. "Gripping the ice pick?"

Tinker Bell lifted her coffee cup, flashed her baguettes, and informed him coldly, "Sand, Mr. Lucas. He only uses his feet in sand."

Wafting a feather-duster laugh Sally came on tidily. "Ice statue, sounds like a wonderful idea! It could express the theme. Anybody got any ideas on this? What the statue should be of? I really don't think sand . . . Oh, and we'd better find out how much he charges."

"Toes gripping the ice pick," snickered Mrs. Patricia Hue, inclining toward Lucas. "Tee-hee. Toes gripping —" He gazed at her bleakly. She subsided.

A pretty youngster named Mrs. Hannibal said eagerly, "I don't know. Seems to me the idea of scarecrows sounds, well, less formal. Gayer. I mean gee, if the theme's going to be Autumn Daze —"

"I'm not at all sure we've decided on Autumn Daze," Tinker Bell said severely. "The theme's still actually up in the air."

"How about the Normalcy Frolics?" Lucas said. "That'd be in keeping. Have everybody come dressed as normal people having normal fun in good old normal times —"

"*John!*" A tendon stood out delicately along Sally's neck. Lucas transferred his attention to this tendon. It made her look older. He turned his eyes from his pretty wife, whom he did not wish to see growing old.

"— communication," he heard, and he saw Howard and Sarah Shaw at the next table with the Fosters. Howard was leaning forward on his elbows talking with scintillating intensity to Betty Foster; Harry was eating doggedly; Sarah was just sitting there. She lifted her eyes and encountered Lucas's gaze. She looked squarely at him and he had the sense of a sheet of grayness — gray Sarah, gray suit, gray eyes — a flat gray Sarah sheened with shock. She sat there stolid and dumpy and gray as concrete, and Howard's voice licked about her like a flame, rapt, suave, "— this thing, a thing like this, is very basically and in *essence* a problem of communication. You see this, don't you? All human misunderstanding is precisely that — a lack of understanding, and understanding has reality only within the limits of *communi* —"

Lucas tried to fix Sarah's eyes, to impose upon her his own solid reality; but he seemed to be reflected off that stunned gray brilliance as from the surface of sheet steel.

"The scarecrow idea would be fun, though — you know? We could make great big huge ones out of real straw, and dress them up in crazy costumes — a boy scarecrow and a girl scarecrow maybe —"

"Well, of course, whatever the committee decides is best is perfectly fine with me," said old Tinker Bell, bending the full wattage of her baguettes upon the pretty Mrs. Hannibal, who was serving on her first real grown-up committee. "The only thing is, scarecrows might seem just a teentsy bit, well, high-schoolish, and I have to let Hammond know. I mean he *is* terribly busy, as an artist he barely has time to *ruminate*, you know, and if we're going to commission him to do a piece for us —"

"I guess we wouldn't want an unruminated ice statue," young Mr. Hannibal muttered spunkily.

"For that matter," said Al Hue, who had finally completed mopping-up operations on his parfait and coffee, "how're you gonna tell a boy scarecrow from a girl scarecrow? Heh. Heh-heh." Mightily pleased, he wiped his mouth on his napkin.

"We could have both," Sally said. "I mean, how about having an ice statue carved in the shape of a scarecrow?"

"— the basis of semantic difficulties," Howard boomed.

Lucas got up and went over to Sarah's table. "Sarah," he said, bending over her courteously, "would you care to come and play the *Moonlight Sonata?*"

He had been away a thousand years, and during that time had visited exotic countries, toiled up mountains, from their towering summits gazed down on valleys of indescribable lushness. He labored back, laden with wonders. He came to flat on his back on what felt like sand. He was also — passing his mind's eye like a feeler over his body — totally naked except for his garters, socks, and shoes.

He moved gingerly; sand gritted; a bare toe encountered his shin. He recoiled in horror and collapsed again.

Helpless in his nudity, only his calves and feet sheathed, he divined with tremendous intellectual effort that he was recumbent upon a sand trap on some fairway of the Sequoia Golf and Country Club. And *she?* Dark, silent, this direly felt presence, even more naked than he (what with the bare toe) — she of the gray suit, friend, valued, organist —? Oh enormity!

He groaned.

There was a stirring beside him.

"Sarah. Oh God."

"Don't —"

"A friend, a perfectly good —"

"Don't mind," she said faintly. "Quit that now."

"— a perfectly good piano player. A *friend*." There was a pause. He wanted to reach out to her so that he might know what had happened to her, but he did not dare. "I wanted to —"

"Never mind."

"— comfort you —"

"I know." What was it that muffled her voice — tears, disgust, betrayal?

"God, Sarah. Please don't cry."

"I'm not . . ."

Again a silence. The blackness gaped and goggled. He moved; sand gritted in his mouth. "Forgive me," he said, and reached out to her. His hand fell on very soft flesh — the unmistakable and instantly recalled thigh. He drew it back, scalded.

"Oh John," she gasped, and he heard the edge of laughter. "For heaven's sake, you didn't rape me. I consented . . ." There was a touch on his knee, light and warm. "It was shared, a shared thing," she said. "A good moment shared." The dark lapped around her words. He lay there dumb with gratitude, and began to heal.

Presently he heard her scrabbling slowly about. There was a soft flap of some garment being shaken; sand sifted into his face.

He turned his head and spat contemplatively.

"Sorry," she muttered. "Can't seem to find my slip — feel around over there, will you?"

He sat up. His back was scaly as a lizard's with sand and sweat. "Sarah —"

"Mm?"

"It *was* a good moment," he said formally.

"Found it!"

"What?"

"My slip."

He got up on his hands and knees — thank God for the impartial dark which hid beauty and ugliness alike — and shedding sand like lice sifted around for his clothes.

He heard the snap of something elastic against skin. It was a nice sassy fleshy sound.

When they were dressed they stood together on the grass. A light mist was falling. The ground seemed to undulate under his feet. He tried to anchor on Sarah's face, but it was lost in the dark. He tried to remember what she looked like, this strange Sarah of the darkness; but he could not couple her with the old Sarah, the other good gray Sarah his friend. Closer recollection stirred, of flesh, ample and warm and sweet-smelling; of abundance, release, giving, and joy; of the long dream in the strange country. He felt a fearsome sense of loss.

As he stood there swaying Sarah felt for his hand. She said softly, "I'm still a perfectly good piano player."

He walked away from her blindly. Up the hill the remote lights and sounds of the Clubhouse bobbed like those of a lone ship far out on the ocean.

VII

ERNIE the bartender continued to impale maraschinos and orange slices on three-inch plastic golf clubs, lining them up in neat rows on the bar. Dinner was long over, the bar was deserted, and the sale of old-fashioneds after one o'clock in the morning seemed an improbability; but Lucas watched closely. Perhaps this arrangement of cherries and orange slices was Ernie's attempt to convey information to him. He brooded over the ranks as they grew but could discern no code. With the stub of a bar-pencil he sketched out a diagram of the array so that he might ponder it later. Omens were easier recognized in hindsight.

Presently a man came in and sat down at the bar. He regarded Lucas for a long moment and then let out an unspeakable bray.

There are persons between whom, without preliminary skirmishes, hostility arises full-blown. So it had been with this man, a pediatrician of diminutive stature named Max Kohner, who upon his first glimpse of John Lucas at a party eight years ago had exploded in hard, derisive laughter. At every occasion since, each time Lucas had come within range, the fellow had unleashed his hideous bray. Somehow this little man had conceived of Lucas as an enemy. This was astounding because they had never, within Lucas's memory, exchanged even a nod. As there was no reasonable way to deal with such random hostility — and as he was almost twice Kohner's size — Lucas ignored it, tabulating it alongside life's inexplicable assaults.

In what was their first genuine confrontation Lucas turned and stared full at him.

Kohner stared back. Hunched on the barstool, his feet barely reaching the lower rung, he squinted up behind huge horn-rimmed glasses of such tremendous magnification Lucas had the sensation of an audible clang as their gazes met. It roused him fully. In that aspect of unsheathed malice was the first naked countenance he had seen all night. It was as if he had emerged into clear thin icy air.

"The Fountainhead," Kohner said, "in glorious widescreen." He flicked his forefinger at an impaled maraschino. "Buy this man a drink, Ernie, and I'll join him."

Ernie's chuckle was brisk and vacant. "Sure thing, Doctor. Haven't seen you around for a while. How's everything with —"

"Great, Ernie, top-deck. There's been a fine measles epidemic, of the rubella type, some complications."

Ernie grinned in an obligatory manner and served the drinks.

Kohner cocked his head at him; the glasses gleamed. "Ah yes," he said in a diagnostic manner, "yes indeed, Ernie." He turned abruptly to Lucas. "What about you? You aren't here either? By God you *look* as if you're here, taking up all that space."

"I'm here," Lucas said. He swept the drinks toward them.

"Aah." It came out grudgingly, an aspiration that sounded like release.

Perhaps Kohner too had been searching for clues and had come up against the *Bulletin*. Perhaps in his desperation for a real face he saw in Lucas's a recognizable aspect — an enemy's maybe, blurred maybe, but real. Out of this intuition Lucas said cunningly, "Say a — large animal, a tiger maybe, was loose out there, what'd be the best thing to do?"

Kohner did not appear to consider this strange. "Shoot it," he said.

"Say you didn't have a gun. Say no gun could penetrate his hide."

"You aren't talking about tigers, chum."

Ernie retired to the farthest corner and resumed his orange-slicing.

"A gorilla then."

"Telephone the Humane Society and tell them to bring over their gorilla net," Kohner said.

Lucas scowled. "Just for the sake of discussion, let's do it my way. Say this animal — any beast, anything powerful, *vicious* — has you under siege. Maybe he's outside your own house. You've got your wife in there, your kids —"

"I don't have any kids." Kohner drained his drink. "But okay. I'll grant you the beast. Now you tell me what he wants. Does he want to destroy me or does he just want to get in? You'll have to clarify this, chum. You can't be sloppy setting up a problem of this sort."

"He wants to destroy you. Is that neat enough for you? Put it this way. A force — very strong force — you don't know what governs it or motivates it —"

"Strong wind. Hurricane. Blow off the roof?"

"No. It has to be powerful the way humans are, beat us at our own game, pry locks —"

"Seems to me you're goddam arbitrary about this, chum. Does it have to have a specific eye color too?"

Stung, Lucas said, "This is *my* problem, *chum*. I'm setting it up my way. If you want to discuss hurricanes that's something else." He added with dignity, "My roof's on tight."

"Is it now? How about that. You guarantee all your roofs, Lucas?" Kohner's tone was baleful.

"Why the hell should I have to defend my roofs to you? We weren't talking about roofs."

Kohner slowly removed his glasses and rubbed his eyes, then jammed the glasses on again. "Let's forget the roofs and the houses and the gorillas." He sounded suddenly weary. "I can't stomach games tonight. What you're talking about, you're talking about the situation. Let's face it, chum. The *situation*," he said harshly. "I wonder what they're calling it in Chinese. Ernie, for crissake will you give us another drink?"

Lucas moved heavily on his stool. "We can face it, but I can't figure what we're supposed to do about it. I never felt so helpless in my life."

"Never felt helpless?" His eyes traveled, measuring, mocking. "How about that. A guy your size, feels helpless."

For a brief moment, Lucas's mind cleared. Why had it not occurred to him before? *He is little, I am big.* As simple as that. "Is it that tough to be small, Kohner?"

He saw Kohner struggle with a spurt of fury. "Let me ask *you* a question, Lucas. You said you felt helpless. If you're right, if you really believe you're helpless — how does it feel?"

"It feels lousy," Lucas said with raw honesty. He put his head in his hands. "It feels terrible."

"Think about it harder. Really *think*." Kohner's voice was

closer. "Something's happening, Lucas. They're threatening us, everybody, you — they're doing something to you *personally*. It's dangerous. They're tinkering around with your life, against your will — How do you *feel* about this? Think!"

Lucas thought, hard, and between his hands his skull tightened. "It makes me feel mad." He lifted his head. "My God," he said with astonishment, "it makes me feel *mad*." He brought his open palm down on the bar.

"A-ah," Kohner breathed. "Now you are with it." He hopped down from his stool, dragged it closer, clambered up again, and began to speak, urgently, rapidly; behind the great lenses his eyes glittered with a holy light. "Now you know how it feels. All my life this same thing. Helpless, can't fight — what *right* have they, what right has anybody got, messing around with somebody else's — Listen! Somebody's got to listen, Lucas. Something's got to be done. We've gotta fight. Are we going to sit here on our asses and let them do it to us? That's our problem, Lucas. We can't just be *bystanders*."

"Point me at something I can fight, I'll fight it, Kohner. What do I fight?"

"The way things are!" He pounded his tiny fists together. "The setup. The power. Listen, what we've got to do, we've got to lay hold of some personal power."

Lucas stared at his own hands. "Us? You mean overthrow the government, like those Chinese?" His skull had begun to throb; his brain was soggy and tumescent within.

"No no no, *wait*. Let me explain. Haven't you ever thought that there should be some direct way of imposing your personal will on government? Some direct expression of personal choice on —"

"We have the vote."

"Indirect! We elect a man, a vague idea, a platform, a law

— filtered through bureaus and interpretations and political alignments — it's an indirect setup." All at once he leaped off the stool. "Go away!" he cried. "Out, sweetheart, out!" A woman Lucas dimly recognized as Mrs. Kohner had appeared by the door. She was a comfortable-looking cowlike creature with an enormous bust, a good head taller than her husband. As he flailed his arms at her she regarded him with the anxious expression of a farmwife surveying the weather.

"We're talking! Go away, sweetheart, go home!" She gazed down at him mournfully, then turned and lumbered obediently away. Kohner came back to the bar. "It's impossible to talk in here," he complained. He took up his glass and with the air of a statesman persecuted by cleaning women made for the men's lounge. Lucas dumbly followed him.

The dark of the lounge was illuminated by the eerie flickering of a huge 36-inch TV set whose audio had been tuned out. Its cold gray flames leaped at the walls like light from a fireplace. Somebody was sprawled on one of the leather couches in front of the TV. He lay with his face pressed against the couch back, his knees drawn up and his feet together as if they had been bound, placed precisely ankle to ankle and laid one on top of the other. His arms were crossed over his chest and the fabric of his coat was pulled tightly across his back. He was altogether bound in his sleep. He looked like a newspaper picture of a victim of gang justice. He groaned and clicked his teeth in his sleep.

Lucas lowered himself onto the other lounge and laid his head back. Kohner, pacing, resumed talking as if there had been no interruption.

"— in every house a special machine. You've seen these parimutuel boards — the computers that keep toting up changing odds? Or IBM machines — data fed in, and in an instant they readjust the score . . . In every house this kind of parimutuel machine, one for each member of responsible age. *Responsible*, this is very important, the key word — I'll get back to that later. There are these buttons on the keyboard. A whole console of pushbuttons." He laughed briefly, a jarring yip. Lucas winced and closed his eyes. "Can you think of a better symbol for the modern world? Every man with a button of his own. How would it be possible for you and me to feel helpless, the way we do tonight, if we could go into our houses and close our doors and with all the vested goddam powers of our responsible intelligence, push a button and thereby *take action?*"

He must have been pushed around a lot, this banty man. Lucas listened to the voice flow on; he tried to concentrate on the words but the steady pulse of his swollen brain thudded against his consciousness. He drifted off into a semi-trance.

". . . each individual machine goes directly to the Government Machine in Washington, and from there the results would go directly to the UN or some body set up to tabulate and put into effect the results from all the machines in all the countries — every goddam blip that comes in at every moment of every hour, forming the collective will of every individual in the world; a direct force acting directly on events — no, *forming* them . . ."

Lucas had fallen heavily asleep. He awoke suddenly with the sense that time had passed over him like a giant slug. He struggled erect. "Where is everybody? What time is it? *What's happened?*"

Kohner blinked as if he too had just come awake. He rubbed his eyes behind his glasses, set the heavy frame wearily back on his nose. "Eeh, so nobody listens."

"It's late," Lucas muttered uneasily. His head was cold and damp. "Gotta go home."

"So go home. Go home and close your door, and lie in bed and wait." Kohner's voice was rough, edged with a peculiar grief. "Everybody just waits . . ." He got up stiffly and walked over to the sleeping man on the couch. "Just lies around and waits," he said bitterly.

The man on the couch had flipped over onto his back. He gritted his teeth and groaned. The TV set was humming blankly, its white screen a panel of dancing dots. In its light the man's excavated face was like death; his skin appeared to be flaking off, growing whole again, flaking off.

"Hey." Kohner bent over him. "Hey. Wake up. Time to wake up and go beddy-bye, chum." He shook the man's shoulder. "Christ, he's out. Who is this guy, anyway?"

"I don't know," Lucas said. He rubbed his hands over his face; his head roared.

The man whimpered. Kohner adjusted his glasses and peered at him closely. "Geez, he looks comatose. We ought to at least get him on his feet. Hey. Hey fella. Come on, chum, let's wake up now. Hey."

Lucas watched him struggle with the drunk; it was like a child trying to lift a St. Bernard. The man was medium-sized but he was fat. Over his shoulder Kohner snapped, "Get off your ass and help! You think this's a spectator sport, or what?"

Lucas heaved himself up, staggered over, elbowed Kohner aside, and with one hand gathered a fistful of the man's lapels and lifted him to his feet.

"Goddam show-off," Kohner snarled. He pinched the man's jowls as Lucas held him upright, manipulated the face briskly from side to side. "Hey. Hey fella. Christ, I wonder if he's

diabetic. Hold him *up*, Lucas! No, no, not that way, you don't
have to choke him — *Stop that!*"

The man's entire weight had wobbled and sagged against
him. As Lucas clutched him, felt his weight heavy in his fists,
he suddenly became seized with a fantastic rage: how dare
this man lean against him? In a spasm of revulsion his
muscles jerked. The man's head jolted like a ball on the end of
a cord. Lucas jerked again, and in a charge of furious power
was mauling him — shaking him, pummeling him, lifting
him from his feet. This lunatic rage did not last for more than
a moment; horrified he let the man drop, almost threw him
from him. Kohner fell with him. He realized then that Kohner
had been clinging to them both, screaming and kicking, in an
effort to separate them.

Like a cat Kohner sprang immediately to his feet; they
faced each other, panting. "My God, I didn't mean —" Lucas
was stopped by Kohner's convulsed face.

He stood and watched as, without a word, Kohner bent to
tend to the stranger.

VIII

A HUGE weight crushed his chest. The fatal morning had arrived. At last his self-indulgence had caught up with him; at last the grisly malignancy he knew would come had reached a mass great enough to be felt; he had been warned; now it was too late; why hadn't he quit smoking ten years ago?

"Who's the man out in the living room? Daddy? Who's that man on the couch? Daddy —"

"Cis! Get off me!" He fell back strangled with relief and her weight. "Oh Lord, Cis, you're too big now to sit on me."

She slid off, nestled beside him on her elbows and knees with her rear humped in the air. She spoke directly into his ear. Her intimate whisper shivered along the filaments of his spine. "Okay, but who —"

He remembered then: yesterday. That day and that night were over, and all was still here. This house, this town, the world — surely they would have felt any distant thud of extinction? — all continued to exist. Praise the abeying forces, whatever they might be!

But as he lay living and saved on his bed yesterday's fear reformed and like the imagined malignancy lodged in his chest.

"Who is he, Daddy? Out in the living room —"

"How would I know who's out in the living room? Ask your mother . . . Cis, go get me the little radio. I think it's in Mark's room."

"*She* doesn't know. I asked her and she said to ask you."

"Cissie, *now*, please."

She returned with the radio as Lucas was dousing his head at the basin. "Bo-oy, you should see Mark's room. I could hardly get in there. He's building stuff and it's all over *every-thing* and he's got some stuff that's not his." She leaned against the counter and regarded him critically. "You never answer me. You just never do."

"You'll have to be quiet now, Cis, I want to listen. There's very important news."

"I know. Mother's cranky."

"Why don't you go into the kitchen and help her cook breakfast?"

"You hate me." She slammed the door.

. . . a meeting of the UN Security Council scheduled for eleven o'clock. There is still no official word from any source. The news blackout, in effect since the President's speech, has given rise to much speculation, chief among which is the persistent rumor that the White House, along with the other chief governments of the free world, is in receipt of a manifesto from the new Peking government, in which are outlined demands constituting an imminent showdown. Indications supporting this feeling are strengthening as here in this country strong rightist factions have begun to urge immediate pre-emptive measures . . . All diplomatic personnel are in seclusion and the White House Press Secretary has issued no statements beyond confirming that the President is still closeted with his advisers. There are very persistent rumors that the President may already have resorted to the "hot wire" in an attempt to communicate directly with the powers which hold Peking —
. . . There has been no word, official or otherwise, con-

cerning a warhead satellite said to have been launched somewhere in eastern Asia a few hours ago. Generally reliable
sources, however, say that the rumors of such a weapon are
totally without foundation and that there has been no report
of any new orbiting body from tracking stations. It is believed
that the rumor may have been started by terrorist agents operating according to prearranged plan. To repeat: there is no
official evidence to support rumors that a warhead of new and
radical design has been launched into orbit. Civil Defense au-
thorities caution all citizens to beware of such rumors and to
remain calm . . .

"Who is that man in the living room?"

"There's a rumor China's launched an orbiting warhead."

"*Have* they?"

"I said it's a rumor. They're denying it."

"There was a rumor at six o'clock this morning that the
UN'd been bombed. The reporter I heard was *talking* from
the UN. I haven't time to listen to rumors. I'm cooking breakfast." She stood at the bathroom door, with her apron like a
loincloth over her slacks, smelling of pancakes — Monday
morning they had pancakes. He dried his face on the towel.
The lump in his chest expanded. In a voice not one whit de-
creased in the hostility of its tone she repeated, "Who is that
man in the living room?"

Behind her Cissie said, "I *asked* him already, he didn't answer."

"Is there really a man in the living room?"

"There is. He's on the couch asleep — or dead for all *I*
know."

"He smells," Cis announced. "I just went into the dining
room and looked at him from there and I could smell him.
Ugh."

"Maybe he is dead," Lucas said. "Has he been there long?"

"You brought some drunk home with you last night, John, or maybe I should say this morning, and I'm sorry but I can't consider you particularly amusing now. After your performance last night —" She pointed the pancake turner at him. He sighted down it. *"Now, who is that man?"* she demanded.

"How do I know who he is? What does it matter?" He had wronged her; she should be more considerate of his sensibilities. "One drunk's the same as another. Unless it's Albert Schweitzer or somebody," he said, "in which case somebody'd better go put a pillow under his head and take his order for breakfast."

"You're still drunk yourself."

He considered this possibility with hope, but in honesty had to reject it. "I am not. I'm simply trying to adjust to the fact that I'm still living, if you want to know the truth." They stalked out, indignant of fanny, rejecting his candor.

He put on his bathrobe and shuffled out to the living room. Every step was a slow impaling on a rod driven up his spine into his medulla. It was dark and dense in there and did, indeed, smell. He opened the draperies. A gross stranger lay sprawled upon the couch as if in the terminal stages of a forty-year sleep. Pangs of awakening rippled over his face in agonized tics. He had an enormously black eye.

Lucas zipped the draperies shut and stalked back to the bedroom. He sat down on the bed. Presently he picked up the telephone, consulted the directory, and dialed.

Kohner's wife said he was at the hospital. Lucas called the hospital. After arguments with several starchy desk-denizens he had Doctor pried from his coffee cup in the staff room.

"It's all very amusing, Kohner," he said, "but what do you expect me to do with your sleeping beauty?"

He braced himself for the awful cackle but it did not come. Kohner's voice was mild. "*My* sleeping beauty?"

"You undertook to play Dr. Kildare last night. You could have taken that guy to a motel, or a hospital, or your place. Why dump him on me?"

"How do you feel this morning?"

"You're not my doctor." Lucas's voice strengthened with his temper. "But you're the self-appointed guardian of that drunk on my living-room couch, and I'm not sure he doesn't need medical care. He looks awful, and he's got a black eye —"

"Not too amazing, when you consider who socked it."

Lucas pondered. "*I* socked it?"

"Come off it. You weren't all that gassed. Oh, you got in your licks, Lucas. So it's only right he's on your couch."

There was a pause.

"Kohner, what am I going to do with him?"

"Give him some black coffee and some aspirin. Console him." Now the laugh came. It rattled like a shorted dynamo. "Talk over your troubles with each other, why don't you? Compare hangovers. Discuss the Situation —"

"Kohner, I'm warning you. I'm not the man — and this is hardly the time — for a joke."

"This may be the only time, chum. The last possible time," Kohner said, and hung up.

"More coffee, Mr. Moloney?"

"Moroney. No, no thanks, Mrs. Lucas. I've had a great plenty." He spoke as if every tooth in his head had just been extracted. His effort to smile was so revolting Lucas ducked his head to his own cup and took a painful swallow. Standing behind their guest, Sally regarded her husband with an absolutely immobile face. She loathed the expression "I've had a great plenty."

"More coffee, John?"

"I've had a great plenty," Lucas said.

She walked stiffly back to the stove, took off her apron, and left to take Cissie to school. Lucas watched her go as if she were a departing hospital ship leaving him ill and alone on a jungle island.

"Certny nice of you folks, taking me in this way," Moroney muttered faintly. "Sure embarrassing . . . must have got smashed last night."

"Quite all right." Lucas added with effort, "You weren't the only one."

The fat man's pain broke through, his face cracked into small fragments, a large gray cracked mosaic. "Whoo-ee, I feel awful." He groaned, put his face in his hands, recoiled. "Ah-h-aow! Eye. God, I've got a black eye —"

Lucas steadied his coffee cup between his palms. "Uh, looks as if you had a kind of rough night there, all right."

"Jesus. What did I do?"

"You don't remember?"

"I've drawn it, man. A blank, a real goose egg. I don't remember thing one. I was at the Country Club, I know —"

Lucas put his cup down. "Don't look at me. My memory's not too sharp either."

"I guess I must have run into a door, let's hope." Moroney laughed weakly, then drew in his breath. "*Ow!*"

"*What?*"

"My rib. Christ." He clutched his side.

Internal injuries . . . *Collapsed this morning in the home of John W. Lucas, well-known local architect. A rib had punctured his lungs. The autopsy showed that the man had*

been the victim of a brutal beating. . . . "Your rib —
hurts?"

"Only when I breathe." He laughed again. "Ow. Only when
I breathe. That's a good one." Moroney shakily lit a cigarette
and leaned back. "Well, I guess I'll survive, even if I don't feel
up to it. Like the guy who was seasick. Asked him if he felt
like he was going to die and he said he was afraid he wasn't."

Looking at the fat man sitting across his breakfast table
with his battered eye and his wrinkled clothes and his un-
shaved wattles, a sour dislike trickled into Lucas's stomach.
Moroney's face was round and pouched; his jowls sagged; he
had the faintly yellowed look of a man who had liver trouble.
He looked like the kind of man who would smoke rank cigars
and overtip waiters in expensive places and undertip wait-
resses in hamburger joints. His eyes — eye, rather — had the
peculiar, knowing, pimpish aspect of a man who sold musical
toilet seats or mink-covered shot glasses. He was gray and
wrinkled all over — suit, face, sparse hair, teeth even. His
breath smelled. Lucas imagined he smelled too, but it was his
own smell. This was *his* house, *his* kitchen. To be reproached
here by the presence of this man who was, all unknowing, his
victim — Lucas in a spasm of disgust felt his own teeth gray-
ing.

The man had a curious air of apprehension about him. He
kept running his tongue over his lips, glancing at his wrist
watch, smoothing his hair with his palms, shifting in his
chair.

"I guess everybody's sort of hung over today," Lucas muttered, "what with one thing and another."

"Yeah," Moroney said. "I guess."

There was a silence. Lucas longed, thirsted to get away
from him but responsibility rooted him.

"The thing is, I've got this guest card," Moroney said presently. "To the Country Club, I mean. Courtesy card from the company. I'd sure hate to of caused any difficulty. As a guest and all, you know."

"You're from where, now?"

"Seattle."

He waited for Moroney to volunteer more, but none came. Surely this was the kind of man who loaded strangers down with intimate revelations — photos of the wife and kiddies, details of ulcerous stomachs, fraternal affiliations, war record. "Seattle, eh?" Lucas prodded, vaguely conscious of guilt-and-masochism twinges. "You through here on business?"

"Pacific Coast Lumber. Wholesale," Moroney said shortly.

"You by any chance know Joe Anderson, San Francisco?"

"No."

"I suppose you'll be wanting to get back to Seattle right away," Lucas said hopefully. "What with the situation the way —"

"*No.*" Even the gray had left his face; before Lucas's eyes it had turned to an ashen skull. "I —" He seemed to be experiencing a kind of frozen convulsion; his mouth grimaced wordlessly.

Appalled, Lucas thought he might be having some kind of attack, that he had begun to suffer the effects of internal injuries, that the rib had pierced his lung. But as the man continued to move his mouth, as his hands flailed the air, as his eyes rolled, Lucas realized he was struggling against a seizure of panic.

"I — I don't think so," Moroney finally managed to say. Using both hands he got his coffee cup to his lips; he tilted it way back and his Adam's apple worked up and down as if to pump out liquid from the empty cup. Lucas looked away.

Moroney set the cup down. "I — haven't finished my business here yet, the company wouldn't want me to go back without finishing —"

"Christ, in a situation like this surely your company wouldn't expect you to stay away from your family! You do have a family, don't you?"

"Yes, I — have a family." He wiped his mouth with his wrist. With this gesture he somehow managed to repair himself, as if he had found a handful of invisible tacks — a lousy job, but holding together. "A wife and two kids. But they're older. They're very competent. We have a — shelter. I put in a shelter. They're as safe as anybody in Seattle," he said, and Lucas saw now what it was this man was afraid of. "I can't go running home at every — What good would I do them?"

Thinking of Joe Anderson, Lucas did not even try to conceal his contempt. "Just as a matter of principle, don't you think they might like to have you with them right now, Moroney?"

"Leonard," he gasped. "Call me Leonard." He scrambled up. "I better go. I got calls to make," he said frantically. "I got business to attend to —"

"While your family sits alone in a shelter up in Seattle?"

"You didn't have to say that. What business is it of yours?" He turned on Lucas. Like a trapped animal his lips pulled back; he swayed; he looked ill, ready to die. "God *damn* you! Leave me alone, will you? Will you just leave me alone?"

Lucas rose. "I'll be glad to," he said coldly. "Where would you like me to leave you?"

Moroney passed both hands slowly over his face. When he took them away he had a maimed expression, an arrangement hopelessly intended — Lucas saw with a shock of the first real pity he had been able to summon — to resemble a placating grin. "Ah hell," the fat man said. "I guess you must feel as lousy as I do. That's all, we're just hung over. Say what's your name, anyway? Geez, you do me a favor, I don't even know your name."

"John Lucas. I haven't done you any favor, Moroney."

"Oh sure," he hooted faintly. "No favors, you didn't take me in, let me sleep, give me breakfast — Say, thank that lovely wife of yours for that great breakfast, will you? Well, Johnnie, I'll tell you, I guess I'm not in any condition to go anywheres, not even to the hospital — too sick to go to the hospital, ha-ha." He closed his eyes and grasped the back of the chair. "I certainly can't bother you to — I guess the thing to do is I'll just call me a cab and drag this battered old carcass downtown to my motel —"

So great was Lucas's relief at getting rid of him he practically carried Moroney to the car. All the way downtown he had to listen to the fat man thanking him.

Only one of his draftsmen was in the office. "Where's Tommy?" Lucas demanded.

His secretary Karen was bent over a ledger. "I just talked to him," she said in a muffled voice. "He's not coming."

"Not coming? He's supposed to finish up those specs on the Chandler job today! What is he, sick or something?"

"No." Karen put her palm flat on her ledger and looked up. She was a plump, cheerful peasant of a girl, Sequoia farmland's sturdiest, just bright enough to be a fair telephone-answerer and by some aberrative quirk an exceedingly gifted bookkeeper. She and her desk were as tiny as the farm kitchen Lucas imagined to be her natural habitat; her little red and black entries simply snapped with precision, which was a valuable and fine thing for Lucas, who was severely bored with basic arithmetic. This morning Karen was in total, alarming disarray. Her face was streaked. Her blond hair straggled around her mournful neck. The roses all had left, alas, her cheek, or at least appeared to have dissolved and run down the buttery chin. "He — he's just not coming in today," she informed him tremulously.

"I was hoping," Lucas said, "that it would be possible to maintain a semblance of normalcy today."

She liquefied. She wept plump globules of buttermilk grief onto the neat rows of figures. "Oh Mr. Lucas, I don't know what he's going to do, he just sounded so funny and desperate!" Tommy was Karen's beau. "Oh, he was so *grim* —"

He hastily pulled the ledger out from the drizzle and sat down on her desk, and said in a fatherly way, "Ah come on now, Karen. He's only a kid. He's all upset about the situ — Chris was the same way yesterday. Christ, he thought —"

"You're taking the Lord's name in vain," she blubbered distractedly. "You shouldn't do that, Mr. Lucas, particularly now!"

Lucas wondered if He was any holier now than usual, but he said, "I'm sorry, Karen. I certainly didn't mean to offend your principles. Listen, you try to calm down a little, and we'll forget about Tommy, just give him the day off — Karen, quit that!"

She had risen from her chair, lurched around the desk, and thrown herself upon him. "Oh, I'm so scared, Mr. Lucas, I'm so scared! Tommy was talking all wild about everybody being blown up and the whole world coming to an end, and that awful bomb up there in the sky, that they don't know when they'll set it off or where it'll fall —"

She did not so much cling to him as engulf him. It was like being inundated in a great salty wave. Wrapped in her terror he fought panic himself, wrestled against it and her. "Quit that!" he panted. "Of course we aren't going to — Stop that, Karen!" He finally wrenched her away.

"Go home," he commanded her. "Go home, Karen. Take the day off." He became aware of his other draftsman, staring. "You too, go home. Get out! Everybody take the day off. To hell with it."

The draftsman slid off his stool, grabbed his coat, and was out the door. Lucas went down the hall to the washroom and stayed there until he heard the office door close and Karen snuffling her way along the corridor to the elevator. He waited awhile, then he went downstairs and around the corner and, at the Alibi Tavern and for the first time in his life, had a martini at ten o'clock in the morning.

With a strange, almost sleepy calm he went back to his office and surveyed its emptiness. He leaned against his desk, smoked a cigarette, and pondered. He picked up the telephone and called Sarah Shaw's number. He had no idea what he wanted to say to her.

"Howard Shaw here." He sounded as if there were a panel of dials in front of him in whose manipulation he had just been interrupted. John Lucas felt a sudden flabbiness in his knees.

Neither as a possibility on the other end of a telephone nor as occupant of any context, the idea of Howard simply had not occurred to him. Confronted suddenly with Howard, Lucas sensed all the accompanying implications leaping at him. Howard existed. He had existed last night. In the future, he — Husband, Wronged Party — would continue to exist. John Lucas was now inextricably linked with Howard Shaw.

Because of him, sprouting from Howard's immaculate and only slightly receding hairline was a pair of invisible horns. Lucas could almost see them, waving about like antennae, testing the air. Could hearth-despoilers be detected over telephone wires?

"Howard Shaw here," came again, impatiently.

Where else? Why couldn't he just say hello? Annoyance overcame Lucas's dismay. "John Lucas here. Let me speak to Sarah, will you, Howard?"

"Well he*llo* there, John." His voice was laden with meaning. Lucas's stomach lurched, even as he reminded himself that Howard always spoke in those tones, as if he had given a great deal of thought to the texture, color, and weight of each syllable. "She's not here."

"When will she be back, do you know?"

"Not precisely, but she might be back in —" Howard's watch, Lucas remembered noticing, was one of those mechanical marvels from which might be determined the position of the moon, the time in Hong Kong, temperature, barometric and hydrometer readings. Knowledge was power. "— about twenty minutes. She's over at the church practicing." His voice became intimate. "A rather wet party last night, no?"

"Ah —"

Howard chuckled. It was the most sinister sound Lucas could remember ever having heard. "I don't suppose you remember."

"As a matter of fact, I do have a lousy hangover," Lucas croaked.

"Well, maybe I shouldn't bring it up, but it is sort of amusing, you'll have to admit." He snickered. "Sarah said she was getting some air and she found you lying in the sandtrap over by the twelfth green. She said you were — heh; heh-heh — under the impression you were at some beach. She said you asked her if she'd like to take a ride in your Chris-Craft."

Lucas closed his eyes. *Friend and organist. Good gray Sarah Shaw.*

"I guess I wasn't communicating very well," he said to Howard, and hung up. He sat down at his drafting table and slowly unrolled a length of tracing tissue, tore it off, and taped it over the drawings of the church. He unrolled another length, and then another, and taped these over until he had built up a half-dozen layers. Then he folded his arms on top — it was smooth and crisp, like linen — and laid his cheek down, and slept.

The scream of the telephone awoke him. It was Sally. She was crying.

"They think it's true. Oh John, they think it might be true about the satellite. There's a boy on the TV news who says he's spotted it on a homemade thingamajig and he says everybody's lying, the government knows about it but they're hushing it up, he says he's figured the orbit over the West Coast and it's up there going around the earth, right above us, and — *Oh John come home.* I can't stand it alone. Please John come home."

IX

HE searched for his wife in the quiet house. He called to her, but she did not answer. He came upon her huddled in Cissie's room, in the rocking chair in which she used to nurse their daughter as the two of them crooned sleepily, the baby and she, in a soft warm wordless communion; the baby used to pat her breast and she looked down on it from her sheltering hair.

Sally was sitting now with her arms wrapped tightly across her breast, doubled over as if to protect what they held. She rocked fiercely and rhythmically, her feet lifting and thumping flat on the floor, like an old lady. He touched her. She looked up, and making no effort to protect her face she began to weep. She cried mechanically in grunts.

He knelt beside her and wrapped her with his arms. She sobbed against his shirt which was crusted with the salt of Karen's hysteria. Now his wife's tears dampened his shirt and warmed the skin of his chest; within him a dampening and warming commenced. It was as if the contents of his rib cage had long been dehydrated, and now with this rain began to swell. It had been a desert these past hours.

He scooped her up and trundled her to Cis's bed. She lay on her side still sobbing. He lay down behind her and pulled her back into the curve of his belly and knees. In this pocket of consolation he cradled her. Presently her sobs loosened. Her weeping died away and she lay unmoving. He could feel her gather about herself some invisible, housewifely garment; she had always been ashamed of crying.

His arm had gone to sleep. His fingers tingled. Cautiously he adjusted his shoulder under her head.

She rolled over on her back. The warmth between them seeped away. She stared at the ceiling. He watched the profile of her mouth. It was swollen, bruised, infirm.

"I'm afraid." She said it like a schoolgirl confessing a homely sin.

"It's okay, Sal. You're all right now. I'm here."

"I know, but I'm still afraid." She said bleakly, "I think Mark heard me crying."

"I looked in his room; he's asleep."

"Do you believe it? That they've launched that satellite, that bomb —"

"It's still only a rumor."

"But that boy, that teen-ager in Berkeley, he says —"

"Sally, a teen-aged kid! There's bound to be rumors. There've always been rumors." He put his face against her shoulder. "We have to trust, " he said against her skin.

"What do we have to trust?"

"I don't know."

She stared at the ceiling. "I had the TV on; I rolled it into the kitchen so I could get the news bulletins. First they had regular news broadcasts. There wasn't any news, really, just what they call 'official sources' and 'unconfirmed reports' — the wildest rumors. And then when they said something about the stock market plunging, I began to — everything started

seeming so weird. You know? The stock market! You know?"
She spoke wonderingly.

"I know."

"I mean, it doesn't seem to be *related* to anything. Then
after that some of the regular morning programs came on. I've
never seen them before. *Beloved for a Day.*"

She lifted herself on one elbow and gazed into his face.
"Did you ever see *Beloved for a Day?* They have these
women get up and tell about themselves, all these terrible
stories. Then the studio audience votes on which is the most
deserving. One woman told about her son and her daughter-in-
law who were newly married and the daughter-in-law had just
found out she was pregnant. They were so happy about it, and
then she got in an automobile accident and lost both her legs.
The daughter-in-law. She didn't win," Sally said, lying back
again.

" 'Win?' "

"Wasn't voted Beloved for a Day. If she'd won they'd have
given her a wheelchair. That's what the woman asked for — a
wheelchair for her daughter-in-law. If she'd won she'd have
got that and a bunch of other stuff too — a complete kitchen
with everything built in, the use of a Cadillac and chauffeur
for a year, a glorious weekend for two in Mexico City. The
woman who won got an operation for her husband. So he
could 'function normally,' she said. The MC asked her if they
had any children and she said no. The audience laughed." She
paused. "The MC kept mentioning that glorious weekend for
two in Mexico City."

She lay regarding the ceiling watchfully, as if there were a
message written up there. "I began to cry then."

"You could have turned it off."

"No I couldn't. I was waiting for the news." Her voice rose dangerously. "Don't you realize everybody's waiting for news?"

"I guess so."

"And then after that program was over another one came on, I forget its name — something about honeymoons. These young married couples come on and they ask them all sorts of questions, and if they don't break some secret rule — they set it all up beforehand with the audience — they get a chance for the Grand Prize. That was a kitchen too, I think, and a Lincoln Continental. I should think it'd be kind of silly for a young couple just starting out to keep a great big car like that in gas."

"They could sell it."

"I didn't think of that. Anyway, this one couple. The girl did all the talking. Do you know what she said?"

"No," he said drowsily.

"Well, first, the boy was very intelligent. He'd just graduated from Ventura High and had won a scholarship to Stanford. Evidently he was very poor and had worked hard for that scholarship — he had a job as a bus boy in some all-night place all through high school. He and this girl were going steady all the time, and she got this idea she had to have an engagement ring for her high school graduation present. He didn't have the money for a ring, he told her, he had to save it for expenses at Stanford. But she said if she was going to be engaged to him she had to have a ring. She didn't mind waiting four years she said but she had to have something to show for it. He tried to reason with her but she finally told him, no ring, no necking."

"Necking?"

"She said, 'I told Ray that until I got my ring he wouldn't

get any necking.' Everybody knew what she *meant* by that. She said it right on the show. I kept thinking they'd turn her off, but the MC just laughed in this awful chuckly way, and she stood there sort of smiling proudly. She was a heavy girl, with this very blond hair all poufed out, her head looked like a basketball. She looked huge next to that boy. They'd been married a week. That poor young boy, that intelligent kid who was supposed to go to Stanford — he just stood there looking embarrassed and sort of mad but *standing* there letting her talk about him that way on a national TV program!"

"Did he go to Stanford?"

"That's the tragic part. Ths girl stood up there and smugly went on telling how he pleaded and pleaded but she wouldn't neck him, and finally he gave in and got her the ring for graduation. Then she necked him, and it was so great — that's what she said, *great* — they decided to get married right away. He's working now in a supermarket. Naturally he couldn't support her and go to college both. I think she's pregnant. She *looks* pregnant. The MC asked if she was wearing the ring, and she said, 'Darn right,' and she showed it to him and he held up her hand for the audience, as if she was a boxing champion."

Sally was suddenly sobbing again, bitterly this time; fully aware, not hysterical, she cried, "People like that — they're normal people, John, they're considered normal and average! Is the whole world made up of people like that?"

"Ah honey, now come on —"

"We look at them and say *they're* selfish, *they're* stupid, *they're* ignorant and dangerous —"

"Sally, Sally, take it easy now —"

"Oh John I'm so scared! If we're all like that, who's going to stop us from — Who's going to save us? Who could *care* enough about us to save us?" She wrapped Cis's pillow around her head and howled into it.

"Sally! Don't be silly, come on now —"

But even as his hand pressed against her tossing shoulder, some knowledge sickened inside him.

Who was he to comfort her? Remembering what had emerged in him last night — Sarah; the fat man (let alone, would he have killed him?); the untethered violence which must have been his own brand of shock — remembering this John Lucas was sorely afraid. Lying with his wife on their daughter's bed he wondered if it were true, if they were all the same. Who indeed then would save them? What possible Power would find it worthwhile to rescue them?

X

I HAVE PLOTTED WARHEAD
ORBIT, FREDDY CLAIMS

Freddy Gates, of 1622 Hiland Avenue, Berkeley, claims to have postulated the course of the warhead satellite he maintains is in orbit around the earth, his high school science instructor confirmed today. In the face of official denials, rumors continue to grow around claims that the boy, using homemade tracking equipment, has evidence that such a satellite has indeed been launched. An honors program student, Freddy says that according to his computations the nuclear dreadnaught could have been launched into orbit from a space platform over Sino-Soviet territory. In an exclusive interview in his home today Freddy — a diminutive lad of 15 who sports a duck haircut — told this reporter that there is evidence the warhead carries steering-rockets of radical design which when activated could bring the satellite into a hovering orbit. "It's in the shape of a dumbbell, with twin spheres, and it has a slight axial wobble," the boy said. "I'm not sure, until I make some more readings on the next passes, whether the wobble is caused by a design or launching flaw or whether it's because of the positioning mechanisms. Either way, that's a pretty sophisticated piece of machinery they've got flopping around up there." When it was pointed out to him that the U.S. Government flatly denied the existence of the satellite and that nobody else had spotted it, Freddy scoffed: "Maybe no laymen have spotted it because of the cloud cover over the Western coast, and maybe the U.S. Government has some reason for its big fat hush-up, but it's there and you better believe it. It may be nervecity for one and all, but those Commies aren't just laying around playing nose-flutes. Which is to say, prepare to duck." . . . Alfred G. Weiss, the science instructor who has been guiding Freddy on the special term project which has blossomed into the light of world attention, has been at the boy's side at all interviews. "In spite of the attempts to discredit him, Freddy's genius will be vindicated. We have a new Einstein here," the teacher stated flatly. "I myself have worked hand in hand with him on this project, and the findings are indisputably accurate. Freddy and I are compiling all the relevant data in a joint paper which I am now preparing, and which will be published in Look *Magazine. While I cannot at this time reveal its contents, it will be clearly seen that the mathematical system employed is the same as one which I originated two years ago to postulate individual personality-integration-coaxials among computer auras, and which at that time received the highest acclaim from my scientific colleagues." . . . "Freddy has always been interested in science," his mother, Mrs. Alma Gates, said proudly as she served coffee and homemade cookies to newsmen. "Ever since I got him that abacus in Chinatown when he was two and a half years of age. His orientation adviser in kindergarten told me he tested right off the graph in empirical relationships." . . . In a later interview, a physicist from the University of California Nuclear Laboratory (who asked that his name not be given) said: "The whole thing is a publicity stunt. This Mr. Weiss has approached us several times in the past in efforts to gain publicity for his wild-eyed theories. He is evidently unwilling to submit these theories through the proper, though slower, channels of scientific publication and subsequent examination by his colleagues. So he has put the boy up to this and now it has gotten out of hand, which is too bad for Mr. Weiss but much worse for the gullible American public, which is willing to believe in any kind of witchcraft."*

. . . *California's Superintendent of Public Instruction has released this statement to the press: "While the explosion of ex-
cellence in the California public schools has been widely noted,
and while our Science Enrichment Program has pioneered the
advance of tomorrow-oriented skills in today's young, and as
we continue to successfully re-adapt technique-curriculums to
today's challenges and needs, these growth-expressions sometimes, in the process of knowledge-synthesis intake, may become distorted in the child's own indigenous response-mode.
Thus it must be noted that certain association-based programs
are subject occasionally to an interpretation-confusion, in
which individual instruction outside the curriculum-latitude
can, and indeed have, become radically disaligned with the intent of the program itself. It is such radical empiricism which
crops up occasionally, which is directly responsible for such
aberrative and random manifestations like 'l'affaire Freddy
Gates.' It appears Mr. Weiss may have been misdirected in
his zeal, and this department is the first to frankly admit it. In
a responsible choice-making society the program-orientation
must be toward the Whole. Revisionary procedures have already been taken." . . . Freddy's estranged father, D. P.
"Rusty" Gates, now residing in East Los Angeles, refused
to comment on his son's sudden emergence as a controversial
figure, saying only: "Leave me out of this. I been living in
peace for ten years. That kid already cost me this missing
finger when he started playing around with his first chemistry
set. I don't know anything about no bomb. All I'll say, if it's
Freddy's bomb watch out." . . . The governor of California
was closeted with advisers, but his press secretary said: "The
governor is astounded that there has been any public notice
at all given to such an irresponsible and obvious publicity
stunt. He has appointed a committee to fully investigate the
matter."*

. . . *While the world waits for news, any news, in this
most serious and historical of crises, evidences of the tremendous tension are appearing over the entire globe. In London a*

peace group is at this moment marching on the Prime Minister's residence. In Paris a huge pack of children, estimated by police to number well over 600 and ranging from 7 to 15 years of age, is roaming the outlying districts, breaking into and ransacking shops and homes . . . Here in the United States there appears to be a surge of religious feeling. In Kansas City, shortly after the President's address yesterday, even as the worshippers at the regular Sunday services were leaving the churches, growing numbers of people, mostly women, began pushing their way in. As the hysteria mounted and the churches became packed, those inside refused to leave. In many cases church doors were barred against the swelling mobs. Pastors and priests, who continued to conduct special services and Communions until the crush became dangerous, finally appealed to state troopers. Although the panic abated somewhat during the night hours, several churches are still jammed and barricaded, and mobs continue to clamor outside. . . .

XI

His feet were numb. They whisked dryly on the cold vinyl as he shifted his weight. The dark outside was crammed against the kitchen window like a solid body. As he smoked, the apparition of his face appeared above the sink, disembodied on the glassy black, flickering and fading balefully. Rooted from his bed by wakefulness, he had taken up his place here like a man on watch at a battlement.

How much later was it now? The bulk of dark had inched back. A faint and subtle graininess condensed at the far end of the garden; in the pre-dawn thinning he could sense the mass of the redwood grove. Once more he ponderously shifted his feet, and then paused.

A trigger of sound or movement had sprung him alert. In some far reach of the silent house something had come awake. The silence coagulated, swelled, and erupted into a noiseless thud. Lucas listened; something had begun to move. It came nearer, soundlessly. There was a waft of faint odor, a burrow-smell. The hair on Lucas's body became an erect pelt. The odor grew — fetid, sweetish; like decay, or fever; the smell of illness.

Mark?

If he sensed the presence of his father, the boy gave no sign. He crept past, unseeing in the dark. His passing was like that of a small night animal. The odor was so strong Lucas's throat thickened.

He had smelled fever before; but this stink now — there was another quality to it, an urgency, a biological signal he instinctively recognized: fear.

Shaken, Lucas hesitated. Was the boy asleep, walking in the grip of a nightmare? Such people should be awakened carefully. His joints creaking, Lucas shuffled after him. In the dining room he stopped, listening. He knew Mark was there because of the smell. There was a hanging silence.

"Mark . . . ?"

By the windows the draperies stirred.

"Mark? It's Daddy . . . Mark, do you want something?"

The draperies ballooned suddenly; there was a gasp, a thump and scrabble against glass. Lucas lurched blindly, reached for the form flailing behind the heavy curtain. The boy moaned. As Lucas tried to separate him from the cocoon a hook ripped; the skinny body struggled desperately. "No!" The odor blared in his nostrils.

"It's me, Mark! Daddy —"

"*No!* Won't let — you — *get me!*"

Crouching, Lucas clutched the boy against his chest. The sharp bones, the hard skull butted wildly. They toppled together. Lucas's elbow burned on the rug; he brought his knees up and clenched them around his son, imprisoning him rigidly against his body.

The boy suddenly went limp. Lucas staggered to his feet. The weight of the body which had seemed so sharp, fragile as glass, hung heavily from his neck. Lucas cradled him in, rocked him awkwardly. The boy's head rolled on his shoulder.

He seemed to be submitting himself not to protection but to implacable gravity. The last time Lucas had held a child this way had been to comfort Cis; plump and howling she had nestled into his arms and surrendered luxuriously to his consolation. This skinny length was unfamiliar; it dangled in his embrace. When was it he had finally surrendered the physical intimacy of this son's babyhood? In a voice rough with helplessness he mumbled, "Mark, you're okay now, there's nothing to be afraid of."

He carried him through the kitchen — faintly visible now, with the formless gray of flat surfaces — and up the black hall and into his room. The floor here seemed solidly littered with strewn objects. Lucas brought his bare foot down on something sharp. He stumbled. The boy's legs flapped against his thigh. Lucas clutched him desperately, but the body remained limp. He felt very hot. Lucas lowered him into bed.

Oh, he was ill, ill. Should he call a doctor? In the intimate conviction that no doctor could minister to this child's illness Lucas muttered a rusty, wordless prayer.

As he fumbled for the covers he sensed the boy's eyes on his face, the consciousness of some silent effort. "Mark, maybe if you could tell me what you were afraid of —"

He bent closer to the whisper, the sick breath. "I can't hear you, Mark."

". . . Bigfoot . . . got in the house."

"Bigfoot? Listen, Mark. You were having a bad dream. There isn't any Bigfoot, you know that. You know that's just a pretend thing, a myth, like a fairy story about giants, or Superman, or —" The boy was listening, but he did not believe. Lucas could feel the disbelief like a resisting force between them. "Please, Mark," he said, "try to trust me. Take my word for it, you just had a bad dream."

The boy's face was a featureless orb barely discernible against the white sheet. "Promise," he said.

"Sure. I promise you had a bad dream. I promise I'm not lying to you. Is that what you mean?"

"No." He lay flat and still. "Promise you won't let Bigfoot in. And if he gets in —" the voice wavered "— promise you'll kill him."

Lucas carefully drew the covers up around his son. "I promise."

The boy remained motionless, but his eyes closed. His face seemed to disappear, utterly sealed. Lucas sat on the bed with his hands hanging between his knees. Presently he got up stiffly and crept out.

Without any change in density the light in the kitchen had bleached. Outside, shreds of fog hung from the black clump of trees. Their mass loomed, hulking and silent. As Lucas brooded at the window it seemed to him that there was a shift within that bulk — a movement of branches, a swirl of mist, as if something were out there, among the redwoods, lurking —

Enough, this was enough! Cursing he reached out, light flooded on, and in the startling whiteness of this interior dawn the nightmare lost its power and was illuminated as sick fancy. With morning, the ill become stronger; fever abates; trust and reason return. In a couple of hours Mark would be better, as Lucas was now with the routing of night. With his forefinger he had cast out darkness. He had exorcised demons, conducted a miracle here in his own kitchen. He could go back and sleep now.

He turned, and his gaze fell on his bare feet.

They were ugly, they were utterly physical. They were bleeding slightly from the encounter with Mark's toy. Swollen with his weight the blue arterial ropes gnarled over tendons. The great joint was an angry red, the nails on the toes thick and scaling like horn, ravaged with parasitical sublife.

How was it possible to regard these obscene pinnings and yet believe that he was more than animal? That he possessed a transcendent soul? Between these feet and the seat of that soul — presumably imbedded somewhere in the braincase — what possible miracle occurred? Where, in all this plumbed flesh through which the current from ridiculous to sublime was presumed to flow, was the gland capable of converting such a current?

Will the real Bigfoot please stand up?

Lucas shivered. *Trust me*, he had said to his son. *There is no such animal.* Nobody here but us humans.

XII

"WHO *are* all these people? Where'd they all come from?" Harry Foster squinted anxiously through his cigar smoke. "I don't like it, not one damn bit. It's *spooky*."

John Lucas said, "Doesn't sound like you, Harry. Complaining about people being downtown."

"It's like a damn county fair out there. In the six blocks I walked between the store and here I didn't see one face I knew. Did any of you notice that? Who *are* all these —"

Dalton Fox said, "Harry, out of about twenty-five thousand people in this town there's bound to be a few faces even you haven't seen." But he took a couple of deep gulps of his lunchtime bourbon without his usual savoring appreciation. Fox was a big easygoing young Irish attorney, and the only times Lucas had seen him use bourbon without respect were those occasions upon which his wife was giving birth to another child.

They usually had Tuesday lunch at the Steak House, a loose group — Lucas, Foster, Fox, Fox's partner Roy McKinney, surgeon Dave Neale, any who couldn't go the Ladies' Day babble out at the Club. Today it was just as bad here — worse, because there was a lot of confused milling around.

The TV set high up in the corner of the bar was full blast on the news breaks.

Their regular waitress had saved them a booth in the back room. "If you hadn't of come I couldn't of held onto it any longer," she snapped. "People've been waltzing in and out of here like crazy ever since ten o'clock this A.M."

"Like I said, it's sure strange —"

"Christ, Harry, it's not as strange as all that," Roy McKinney said edgily. "You can't expect things to be normal."

"I don't expect them to be normal. I just can't see any reason for it, that's all. I know there's a crisis, but what's it got to do with everybody suddenly starting to swarm in the streets?"

Over his menu Dave Neale eyed Harry speculatively. Lucas had seen that look of Dave's before, once when he sat in his office preparing to listen to the biopsy report on a mole Dave had removed from his neck. The mole had begun to thicken and Lucas knew the Seven Danger Signs, so he had gone to Dave. He had had to wait two days for that report. He was certain that the look Dave was giving him from behind his desk was to size up his courage. Lucas had cracked bad jokes about "hearing the worst." The mole was benign. There had been nothing to indicate, Dave reminded him, that it would not be. Lucas realized then that the look had been merely one of mild contempt for his bravado. Now looking at Harry Foster this same way Dave said, "This is supposed to be a safe place. Remember?"

Harry's plump face quivered with incredulity. "You mean all those people are refugees? To *Sequoia?* Where'd they all come from then?"

"I'd guess mostly San Francisco," Dave said. "I was talking to a patient of mine this morning, a motel owner. He said they started coming in Monday afternoon, after that story about the kid and the satellite broke. He says there hasn't been a vacant room in town since last night."

"And I'll clue you on something else," Peggy their waitress said. "We're running out of steak and I can't save any for you unless you snap things up a little here."

They ate in silence. The steaks were overdone but Peggy did not apologize. "You want pie, you'd better let me know. We got exactly two left, last time I was in the kitchen."

"What *is* this?" McKinney flung down his napkin. "If a regular customer can't have his lunch in peace —"

"Mr. McKinney, you get people coming in here from ten A.M., you get them asking for food, you get families in here wanting to eat, you gotta serve them whether they're regular customers or not. What I mean, they pay, they got a right to eat too," and she flicked her napkin harassedly over the table-cloth and stumped off.

McKinney looked around. "They expect us to feed the entire city of San Francisco?"

"I understand there's a few people drifting in from as far away as Portland," Dave Neale said. "I guess people must be leaving the larger cities."

"They've certainly played it down in the news, then," Harry said. "I haven't heard a thing about it."

"Maybe they're trying to soft-pedal it, prevent a panic —"

"That's not the only goddam thing they're hushing up," McKinney said with some violence. "I don't know about you guys but I'm inclined to think that kid in Berkeley may just have a glimmer. All this secrecy — can anybody tell me exactly what *is* happening? All these goddam Red threats — what're they *doing* about it? Sitting there on their asses *conferring* and maybe *bargaining* — I tell you it smells of appeasement. They may be handing this country over to the Reds right this moment, without a fight, without so much as lifting a goddam finger! All this talk about warheads — well, we've got warheads too, we could settle this —"

"Roy, simmer down," Dalton said tightly.

"Simmer down, hell! What're they supposed to be doing, playing games? How long do they think they can keep us suckered like this? It's our lives. We paid taxes to build up that force that's supposed to protect us, and now that we need protection what're they doing? Waiting till our cities get bombed? *It's our lives!* When're they going to let us know what they plan to do with them?"

He lunged out of his seat, flung down some money on the table, and butted his way out through the crowd.

Dalton muttered, "McKinney's parents live in Portland. He's worried about them."

Dave Neale took a leftover cracker, broke it, then put the two pieces carefully on the tablecloth. "My father lives in Los Angeles. I tell you frankly I'd feel better if he was up here. He's stubborn though. I don't think he'd come. If I could get through to him on the phone, talk to him —"

Abruptly, as if somebody had flung a cape over his head, Lucas was smothered by the most pitiless longing for his own father. He missed him so desperately his mouth flooded. He needed him. He had to talk to him. He could see his hands, powerful and broad, grasping a bottle of beer, a golf club, pliers, Lucas's own shoulder — purposeful, above all, purposeful and knowing. There was never a tremor in his father's hands; in the articulation between forefinger and groin of thumb the muscle-pad swelled and folded surely. The light hairs on the backs of his fingers were stiff as a forest of scimitars. His voice was steady, calm, reasonable . . . but he was dead.

Fresh as if brewed just yesterday the gall of bereavement flooded back. His mouth and eyes filled with it. John Lucas sat at noon in a public place all these years later, silently bleeding his grief.

Peggy the waitress came and leaned her knuckles on the table. "I give up," she said. "It's the only sensible thing to do. You want to hear something crazy? The P-nuttiest? They're closing down the bar."

"Running out of liquor?"

"No." She was pale. Spots of orange rouge stood out on her old cheekbones. "They're cutting us off."

"What do you mean, cutting you off?"

"You're a lawyer, Mr. Fox, you tell *me*. You ever heard of a law says the state can close down all the bars in the middle of a regular day? It sure don't sound legal to *me*."

"The *state?*" Harry said.

"Just a minute," Dalton said. He leaned his elbows on the table, incredulity glinting in his blue eyes. "Let's see if I can remember . . . An Executive Order. Yeah, Executive Order 7 or 8 or something. States that the sale of alcoholic beverages shall be discontinued immediately if a state of extreme emergency shall exist in California. All licensees shall be prepared to comply with this order."

"You gotta be kidding," Peggy said.

"A black day for us Irish." Dalton's eyes were not amused. "It looks like the panic button's been pushed. The sovereign State of California, with its usual full-blown enthusiasm, leaving no stone unturned, allowing nary a single sparrow to fall, is getting into the Big Act. Well."

"I sure do like the way you lawyers talk," Peggy said. "Does that mean they're gonna call out all the cops, or what?"

"If necessary to exercise this particular idiocy, they'll find enough cops to enforce it. They won't be Irish, though," Dalton said bleakly.

"You mean some Voice down there in Sacramento can tell all the full-grown adults in the state we can't *drink?*" Lucas said.

"It's illegal!" Harry trumpeted.

"It's sure as hell un-American," Peggy said stoutly. "Next thing you know we'll have to sign an affidavit to go to the little girls' room." As if to defy the governor and verify her God-given rights she stamped off to the powder room.

"I never heard of that law," Lucas said. "Dave, you ever heard of that one, the right to stop the sale of liquor?"

"Maybe. I think I read it somewhere in a column or something. It was a joke." Dave Neale pushed back his chair. "There's a lot that used to be a joke," he said.

He hesitated, then put his hands down on the table and looking at them said, "I guess nothing's very funny when people are scared. I guess *I'm* scared. The thing is, I guess we've got to sort of take hold, and hang on. We've just got to hang on, that's all," he said and, coughing with embarrassment, left. Dalton Fox followed him out as if hearing trumpets.

"Hell," Harry said shakily. "Hell, he didn't have to say that to people like us. Sure we'll hang on. What else is there to do?" He lit a huge brown very smelly cigar. "Until we have to have an affidavit to go to the can. That's when I'll get *mad*," he said, and grinned at Lucas.

Lucas looked at Harry and, even though he could see those stupid cement-burl planter-boxes defiling the honest pavement in front of Foster's Store, finally forgave him.

I DON'T see how it could have happened so fast." There was
an edge of panic to Harry's voice. Coming out of the
Steak House they confronted a throng solid as a physical
blow. They were sucked into it; even Lucas felt himself
caught and borne along in the packed, jostling stream. He
grabbed Harry and they shouldered their way out to an an-
chorage at the corner.

There were crowds of children — kids who should have
been in school, babies, teen-agers. One little child in a pair of
footed Nitey-Nites was standing bawling alone in the pedestrian zone. Lucas reached out and hooked its collar and reeled
it in. He squatted down. "Hey fella, hey now there —" The
baby stared at him and redoubled its frenzy. All the juices of
its anguish flowed in ammoniac currents; its seat was soaked,
its nose streamed, it was unglued, undone. Somebody's knee
shoved Lucas in the back and he fell forward onto his hands,
skinning his knuckles. He scooped the child up. It straddled
him automatically, its legs wrapped around his kidneys.
Lucas put his palm under the soggy rump and tried to hold it
tilted away a little. Some woman came screaming up like a
pass-receiver and skimmed the child off him. It had a firm
clutch of Lucas's tie with both fists and all three of them were

brought up short, with the baby dangling in the middle. The woman ripped the child's fingers off his tie, glared ferociously at him, and disappeared in the mob. Lucas pulled off his ruined tie and balled it up and stuck it in his pocket. "You're welcome, madam," he snarled. "And we hope you enjoy your stay in lovely Sequoia."

Harry was gazing at the traffic lights. Everybody had a finger on the WALK buttons. The system seemed to have suffered some electronic fatigue and cracked. The lights kept flickering green to orange to red very rapidly. Nobody except the button-pushers seemed to care; the jaywalkers streamed on, and as far as they could see the traffic was stalled for blocks.

"I see it but I don't believe it."

"The dream of a lifetime, eh, Harry?"

"A nightmare," said Harry. They were carried across together on a surge from behind. "It wasn't this bad just an hour ago even! Where are the — oops, sorry — police? There ought to be some kind of traffic control." He raised his elbows and twisted pudgily along in the buffeting current of shoulders, bosoms, heads. "Somebody could get *hurt*," Harry complained. "It's anarchy."

"Look at them mobbing your store." Lucas pointed down the block.

Harry stood stock-still. He stared down the street at the throngs going into the store, his store, the Foster Department Store, Sequoia's Own, Redwood County's Biggest Home-owned with three full floors, twenty departments, a Beauty Shoppe and a French Room Salon and a Portrait Arts Photography Studio and a brand-new Gourmet Cellar in the basement. "Christ," Harry whispered. "I wish Grandma was here."

"Yeah. We've got 'em downtown at last."

On a rising tone Harry said, "You know something? I was

planning a big sale next week on Ladies' Playclothes . . .
Christ. You know what I've got down there in the Gourmet
Cellar, John? Talk about *supplies*. You know what I've got?
New items, exotic foods, taste treats, cocktail snacks. Cases of
them. Tins of pâté de foie gras. Smoked oysters. Jars of special French imported mustard. Pigs' feet. Piñon nuts. Fried
grasshoppers — did you know we sell that stuff? Great for
cocktail parties, all the rage. My wife suggested 'em. Locusts.
Rattlesnake meat. Fried baby bees. Oh, I've got supplies!"

Profoundly shocked, Lucas said coldly, "You better get
down there and mark 'em up then, Harry."

"Ah no, you've got it all wrong, John! What I mean, if we
do run out of supplies — Can you imagine a mother opening
a can of fried baby bees and saying to her kid, Eat it, it's
good for you?"

"Harry, I'm sorry."

"The thing is, if I'd known, I'd have ordered a lot of other
stuff. Nourishing stuff. Cheeses . . ."

"Harry, you're not a grocer. You couldn't be expected —"

"Hey!" His face lit up. "Champagne. I've got cases of it
down there. And some fancy wines too, you don't find much
better."

"You better sit on those. If this liquor law thing is going to
hold."

"Do you suppose that includes wines? Oh Lord. I just don't
know. Nobody's told me anything. Maybe I should stop the
sale of those wines. Listen, you want a case of champagne? I
can't sell it maybe, but I could give it away. They couldn't
squawk about that, could they?"

"Harry, I don't know. Maybe we'd better wait and see. But
thanks anyway." They could sit drinking champagne, he and
Sally, while the rest of the town struggled with the problem of

getting food? From the looks of things, it was virtually certain there would be trouble. Wine is a food, Lucas thought: it supplies calories and trace minerals and certain vitamins, it is used as a tonic for kids and old people . . . "I don't know, Harry. I just don't know what any of us should do right now."

At the entrance to his own building Lucas was suddenly caught up in a new press; it was very powerful and had direction. He let himself go with it and it swept him past the boarded-up windows of Ralph's Sporting Goods and halfway down the block. There it met with a compact jam. The mob writhed helplessly about. There were screams and curses. A doorway was under siege.

"Please," somebody beside him was saying in a high monotone, "please, pardon me, I must get in, please —" A bald shiny pate was weaving under Lucas's armpit, using it as sort of umbrella. He twisted around and Lucas saw a priest's collar. "Would you mind helping me?" the priest panted. "I don't like to push but I have to get in there."

Lucas put his elbows up, knocking off a screeching woman's glasses (sorry madam but you can see I am on a pilgrimage), and bulled his way through, the priest plastered against his back. Faces and bodies flattened against the inside of the big double plate-glass doors. He got a big enough wedge for himself, but the priest was amputated from him, caught in the forehead by the edge of the door. Lucas saw his naked head against the glass, a red welt down the side, his eyes stark with determination. Somehow he pulled the door open again and got the priest through. He managed to push out a clot of struggling bodies before the door closed again. He put his back to it and dug his feet into the carpet. He was in Pitera's Jewel Box.

The press was not so great in here; a couple of dozen people milled about but perhaps because of the carpet there was a hermetic muffling of the babble. A voice rose in pitch above the rest.

"Please, if you'll just be orderly, folks. Give everybody a chance. Please, just a little order, that's all I ask. No, that's not *solid* gold, lady, it's too soft if it's *solid* gold, it's gold plate. A very good bracelet, be very nice for dressy occasions. Please make a little room there, the girl can't see what she's choosing —"

Mr. Pitera the jeweler was sitting on top of a glass showcase in the middle of the store. He waved his arms, chattering, having a good time. He spotted the priest and held out both hands. "Hey, Father Walsh! Hey, I'm sure happy to see you. Maybe you can help me restore some kind of order here, eh? Hey you, let Father Walsh through now!"

The priest labored toward him and Mr. Pitera waited with a joyous expression. "Ho now, this is a fine thing," he cried. "Somebody here we need to calm everybody down, they'll listen to *you*." He patted the glass whereon he sat. "You sit up here with me, we can look out for things together." He stretched out his hand and the priest, after a moment's hesitation, hoisted himself up next to the little jeweler.

"How are you?" Mr. Pitera asked. "Say, you got a cut on your head there?"

The priest took out a handkerchief and mopped his head, examined the blood on the handkerchief. "Maybe if you can lock the door," he called to Lucas over the crowd. "Can you do that?"

"Such a cut," Mr. Pitera clucked. "Let's hope it doesn't get infected."

Lucas arched his back and felt behind him. It was a sliding

bolt set in aluminum sash. The pressure against it was squeezing a slit in the door. His fingers fumbled but he could not slide the bolt. There was a small boy leaning beside him — helping, he realized, to hold it. "I'm going to push as hard as I can and when I do you slide that lock over, quick," Lucas told the boy.

"I don't know. My mother's out there."

"You're helping me *hold* this door, aren't you?"

The kid looked at his sneakers. "I guess."

Lucas made another desperate lunge with his shoulders. If plate glass couldn't bend, break with the pressure, his neck could. "Well, the priest wants it locked. If you can help hold it you can bolt it, can't you?"

"I'm not a Catholic," the boy said.

Lucas made a strangled noise and again fumbled at the small of his back.

"Oh, okay," the boy said, and slipped his hand in behind Lucas and locked the door.

Lucas massaged his shoulders. The boy cocked his head, watching. "Do you suppose we could let just my mother in?"

"No. Not right now."

"Well, could we open it for a second and let me out?"

"*No.*"

The kid hooked his thumbs in his jeans pockets. "Are you a Catholic?"

"No. I'm a philosopher, like you."

"What's *that* mean?"

"It means I can't make up my mind what side of the door I want to be on," Lucas said.

"Mr. Lucas!" The jeweler was waving at him.

He pushed through to the small circle cleared around the counter where Mr. Pitera and the priest were sitting. Nobody

paid attention to them, but there was this space of the kind —
caution? respect? — people leave around somebody who obviously has a very bad cold.

"Mr. Pitera, I think you ought to reconsider," Father
Walsh said in a high, clear voice.

"Mr. Lucas!" the jeweler cried cordially, reaching over to
wring his hand. "Thank you, thank you for helping us out
here." Sweat poured down his pleated old face. He waved his
arms ecstatically. "Order, order is all we need here. A little bit
of calm and everybody will get his share."

"You have a sale going on, Mr. Pitera?"

"Sale, ho!" He elbowed Father Walsh in a transport of de-
light. "A sale, he says! Listen, Mr. Lucas, there's never been a
sale in history like this one. No selling! No money changing
hands! No slips to write out, no Charge-a-plates, no sales tax."
He touched his chest with his fingertips. "You want something? It's yours. I give it to you entirely without any obligation!"

"You're kind of excited, Mr. Pitera," Father Walsh said.
Under the immaculate dome of skull the slab of cheek and jaw
were an incredible extension. Never had Lucas seen a head
which appeared so long and narrow. It looked as if he slept
each night with it in a vise. The priest pinched his lips with
uncertain fingers; now that he was here, arrived after such
holy determination, he did not seem to know how to begin,
what ministrations might be called for. He took a package of
cigarettes from under his robe and, with a ritual air marred
somewhat by hesitancy, offered it first to Mr. Pitera and then
to Lucas. He carefully extracted one for himself, and as Lucas
held the match for him he inserted the cigarette between the
outermost lobes of his lips where it was barely secure. The

priest puffed a couple of times, the cigarette wobbled, he hastily caught it and tucked it back in, succeeded in starting it, took a jerky drag which he immediately exhaled, and then held it for the rest of the time stiffly between his fingers. Lucas held another match in front of Mr. Pitera's face but he did not seem to notice. He rolled the cigarette around between his palms as if to warm it, and it finally crumbled to the floor. So much for ritual, Lucas thought.

"Of course I'm excited, Father," Mr. Pitera cried. "This is an exciting event! You have no idea how wonderful I feel."

"Your wife is worried about you. She's afraid you're not well," Father Walsh said.

A shadow came over the jeweler's face but it cleared immediately. "Aw, she worries, Father, she frets over me like I was a baby," he scoffed fondly. "Women. You know? I woke up this morning and I said, Katherine, in spite of everything this is going to be a joyful day if I can do anything about it. You are looking at a man who is going to try to make it a joyful day. And she looks at me in that funny way — you know the way women look at you — and she says, Alberto, you don't look so good. Your color is too high. I don't like it. You have a temperature, I bet. And I kiss her and I say to her — One only, lady, please. You want that compote, take it and welcome, but one item only if you please. That's the only rule here, being orderly and one item only. We got to be fair. Otherwise no strings attached. Okay?"

Father Walsh furtively got rid of his cigarette in a glass bowl.

Mr. Pitera bent a charming smile upon them all, a philanthropist doling candy to eager greedy children. "I hate to deny anybody, but this is a small shop, there's a lot of people in this town. Mr. Lucas, what do you think, you're a businessman, should we let these ones go out now, they've had plenty of time to choose, let another batch in? Do you think we should manage it that way?"

"I'm not sure I understand what you want to do, Mr. Pitera," John Lucas said uneasily.

"What he is doing," Father Walsh said in his high concise voice, "is giving away everything in the store."

"Marvelous, isn't it?" Mr. Pitera said with great exuberance. "You have no idea the *pleasure*. Selfish pleasure, selfishness, I got to admit. I started out the day thinking, Well, so it's a bad day, everybody waking up to this same bad day, there ought to be *something* somebody could do. Helplessness I hate, it turns a man the worst kind of sour. So I tell Katherine, I gotta *do* something. Change the kind of day. Just one day only, change people's faces. Look at the happy faces! Satisfied customers." He chuckled, swung his feet like a child. "So it's selfish too, I freely admit it, Father. Such a release! It's letting go. You know? I feel a great weight off. All these years this weight, worry, planning, every day for thirty years I come here to this store and I sit here — over there at that desk in the corner — and I wonder who will come in, what I will sell." He laughed. His face gleamed merrily, its seams and gussets polished with perspiration. "I did okay enough. Why did I sit there and worry? Even when I was starting out repairing watches in that little hole up by the movie theater — that was before you came here, Father, long before, and Mr. Lucas too — even then we did okay, Katherine and I. With no kids we had enough to save, and move in here, and grow to the second biggest independent retail jeweler in town next to Cady's, who incidentally is a good friend, a close friend of mine, Cady. No grudges *there*, even competitors we stay friendly . . . I'm sorry we don't have any kids, though. Katherine says this store is our kids."

"Would you give your kids away, then, Mr. Pitera?" Father Walsh said in suddenly strong tones. "Would you divide them up and dole them out to strangers? This is your life's work, Mr. Pitera. You and your wife's. Hasn't she sacrificed too?"

The little jeweler felt about in his pockets, produced a handkerchief, and slowly passed it over his throat. His eyes wandered about, to the glass shelves, the polished displays now disarranged and gapped. The hands of strangers were everywhere, rummaging and reaching. One woman standing near them held up a ring to the light, squinting suspiciously, turning it this way and that. She slipped it into her coat pocket. As she did so she glanced over and saw that Lucas was watching her. She stared back defiantly, her hand still in her pocket. Then she turned and shouldered her way to the front of the store. Through the crowd Lucas could see her hunched over another counter, her hands shielding her cheeks.

"Maybe we ought to let in some others now," Mr. Pitera said faintly. He put his palms on the countertop and lowered himself carefully to the floor. He gazed around. He made a sudden dart toward a display table, lifted an enormous punch-bowl, and bore it toward Lucas. "Here," he cried. His face was indeed feverish. He looked very old, his skin was yellow, almost transparent. "Here, Mr. Lucas. You haven't picked out your gift yet. Take this, then. It's a lovely thing. Genuine etched Swedish crystal, the stand solid sterling and this rim here — feel the rim, run your finger along it! — silver too. Smooth as the glass itself, you can't even imagine the joint. You take it — take it please, your wife will adore it. Think of her face when you come in the door! Think of your wife's face . . ."

As if drained of their strength by the heavy bowl, his arms buckled. Lucas had to grasp it. "Thank you, Mr. Pitera," he said. "But I — "

The jeweler wasn't listening. He turned toward the priest, who was standing now too, regarding the little man with a gaunt look. "Hey," Mr. Pitera whispered, "I want to know something, Father. Just a little question, okay? Did she call you up and tell you to come here?"

Lucas carefully set the punchbowl down on the counter behind him.

"Your wife?" the priest said. "Well, yes, she did, as a matter of fact. It was only because she was worried about you, Mr. Pitera. You didn't look well, she said, and you didn't seem to listen to her. You really don't look well, Mr. Pitera. Maybe you should have a rest. Would you like me to take you home? You can lie down, and we can talk if you want."

"Why don't you let him be?" Lucas blurted. "It's his store, Father. He was happy. He said he was a happy man this morning."

"I know," Father Walsh said. "Don't you think I know?"

"I don't want to be happy at the price of other people," Mr. Pitera said. "Father, I don't mean to do wrong to my wife."

"Mr. Pitera, did I say you're doing wrong?" The priest's long face was pale; the red welt on his head stood out, strangely the color of an old scar. The deep cornices of his lips were pinched, as if within the heavy folds chronic pain were contained. "I don't know," he said. "I just don't know."

"Father, with all respect," the old jeweler whimpered, "Father, you ought to be able to tell me if I'm doing right or wrong."

The priest closed his eyes. Lucas had the notion that he was praying.

Somebody bumped against Lucas's back. He jerked around. "Quit shoving," he snarled. "The least you could do is to quit shoving!" Claustrophobia swelled in him. There was a tight pain in his chest. He could not breathe. He wanted to lash out, escape, flail his way out of there — away from the greedy crowds, from Father Walsh standing with his eyes closed, from old Mr. Pitera with his head bowed so humbly over the punchbowl. He felt like a man who had started to expand in all directions.

He plunged toward the door, scattering all those faces, those arms hugging treasures. One teen-aged boy, cradling a swollen jacket, grabbed something off a counter; as Lucas reeled by he knocked it out of the boy's hands; it crashed to the rug. Lucas swung at the lock of the door with his fist. More startled faces thrust against the glass; like fish they gaped at him. They swam toward him as the door burst open.

As he lunged through the crowds toward the street he saw Cady the Credit Jeweler struggling in — Cady with righteous rage bristling blackly, Cady the Competitor, the close friend, no grudges *there*. Over the heads Lucas shook his fist and roared, "Go back, Cady! Leave him alone, you —"

Nobody heard; nobody turned; nobody paused. The throngs continued to flow around Lucas, as he stood shaking his fist helplessly at Cady, who had disappeared.

XIV

PRESIDENT RUMORED IN SECRET MEETING WITH
WORLD LEADERS
— San Francisco *Chronicle*

MARKET PLUNGE CONTINUES
— *Wall Street Journal*

IMPEACH GOVERNOR, LIQUOR LOBBY DEMANDS
— *Bartenders' Journal*

IS FREDDY GATES A COMMUNIST TOOL?
— New York *Daily News*

SEQUOIA APPEALS FOR EMERGENCY TROOPS
— Sequoia *Evening Register*

"*— that until state militia can be sent Sequoia will have to fend for itself. Mayor Wingluff has issued an urgent call for all able-bodied men to report to the Veterans Memorial Building. Those who have experienced active service as commissioned or noncommissioned officers are particularly urged to help organize —*"

"John, that can't mean they want you to go back in the Army?"

"*— maintain law and order, enforce temporary regulations, aid in expelling undesirable elements.*"

He looked up from the paper. "Not the Army. A citizens' militia."

She picked up a head of lettuce and began distractedly tearing pieces into a bowl. "Does that mean they want you — men — to fight? Carry *guns?*"

"You can't talk mobs into being lawful and orderly."

"I think Sam Wingluff must be crazy! It can't be that bad! Asking decent citizens —"

"You haven't been downtown."

She stared at him. "You'd get hurt."

"Sally, take it easy. I haven't volunteered for anything yet. I'm still standing here in the kitchen and I haven't got my gun out yet. Do you think I'm going to go out and stride around like a resurrected Nazi, kicking women and kids out of my own city streets? I'm no gendarme and I never was. But I'm an able-bodied man and I have to at least go down there."

"Not tonight!"

"Tomorrow then."

"But we may need you here! If it's that bad, your own family needs you —"

"What's a gendarme?" Cis had wandered in.

Lucas folded the newspaper. "It's a large breed of dog, similar to the Great Pyrenees, French by origin, rough-coated, used for rescue work."

"Are you fooling me, Daddy?"

"Yes," he said. "A gendarme's a policeman, Cis. He —"

"Run *along*, Cis. Daddy and I are talking. I'll call you when dinner's ready."

"She must know more than you give her credit for," Lucas said as the child left. "You can't keep protecting her."

She stood rigidly, holding the lettuce in her palm like a balance weight. "What good would it do to frighten her?

What do you think I should *tell* her? That the world's —"

"She sees the people on the streets. She said she was scared coming home from school today, there were so many people. What do they tell her at school? Are they discussing it at Sharing Time, or Social Studies, or what?"

"She hasn't said. How can I ask?"

"Sal, you can't seal her off, not even here at home. And Mark —"

"His fever's down but he's still weak," she said sharply. "I just can't think it's sensible to *worry* him."

"Mark damn well senses what's going on, even though you won't let him watch TV or listen to the radio. What do you think he suspects? He knows he's not all that sick. I think he's having a quiet panic all by himself. All that junk he's collected in his room — that tower he's building — I went in there a while back and he's just sitting in it, surrounded by all that stuff —"

"Mark's always loved building things; he wants to be an architect like you," she said in a high voice. "He — if he enjoys building that silly thing and it keeps him occupied I think he should be allowed —"

"I'm no psychologist, but has it occured to you he may think he's building some kind of shelter?" At her struck face he said gently, "There's nothing more scary than to be vaguely aware something's going on and get only silence. Look at us. Nothing but rumors."

"If they're negotiating, they obviously can't let us in on everything! It's a delicate situation!"

"So, okay, we're adults and we're supposed to understand that. They're kids. They have to be able to trust us, and they can't if we don't level with them, Sal."

She turned blindly back to the sink, holding the lettuce

ceremoniously now in her two hands. "You — you can explain it to them I guess.

"I intend to." He touched her shoulder. "Have a drink with me, Sal? One before dinner?"

"There's only a half-bottle of scotch. You said we should go easy on it."

"I know what I said. To hell with Executive Orders. Besides, Harry Foster offered me a case of pink champagne. If things get worse, we'll take him up on it."

He should, perhaps, have accepted Mr. Pitera's punchbowl. He had held it out: his charity, his goods, his supplies. If he had accepted Mr. Pitera's silver-trimmed punchbowl he could have put Harry Foster's champagne in it and poured the rest of the scotch in too — what the hell, all the liquor in the house, the bourbon and gin and crème de menthe; cooking wine; sweet vermouth they kept for Betty Foster's Manhattans; brandy; bitters; the bottle of saki Barbara Anderson had given them last time they had had dinner together in San Francisco (it was to be used in the sukiyaki recipe Barbara wrote out, in childish script, for Sally). He could have put their entire remaining fortune of alcohol and memories into Mr. Pitera's charity punchbowl, invited all their friends in, and flung an End-of-the-World Punch Party. Mr. Pitera would have liked that. He understood the grand gesture. Going Out In Style.

With a flourish Lucas measured out the scotch.

"It says here the president of Sequoia State College will hold a conference tomorrow to see how many people can be accommodated in the gymnasium and swimming-pool facilities. The Post Office announces it is temporarily out of government pamphlets on fallout shelters. There has been a run on axes, shovels, guns, sand, gunnysacks —" He put down the newspaper. "Where did we stash those emergency rations? The ones we got during the strike?"

"I'm not sure. I think in the crawl-hole above the garage."

"We'd better get 'em out. And we ought to check what we have on hand. They say the stores are going on a half-day schedule, and only bona fide residents of Sequoia will be allowed to purchase foodstuffs. You have any trouble getting things from the grocery today?"

"I didn't go to the grocery today. I stocked up the freezer Friday as usual and I —" She had been tossing pots around with high abandon; she stopped, stood in the middle of the kitchen. "Oh John. I just didn't *think*," she said faintly.

What did it take to make a thing real to them? The mere shadow of an event — a strike, an interruption of daily convenience — had been enough to drive them to provisioning a crawl-hole; but when a real event arrived, when the tangible multitudes pressed at their very door, they neglected to go to the market. This morning he had told Sally that they would have to be careful with the liquor supply; even then he had not thought about food. Could he blame her? Lucas went over to the storage cupboard.

"Mushroom soup. Pickle relish. Catsup. *Why do we need to keep five bottles of catsup on hand?*"

"There was a sale — five for a dollar." She elbowed him aside, and began sliding things around defensively. "Noodles. Beans. Lentils. Tomato paste. Raisins. All good nourishing — Jello. Spaghetti —"

"What's this?" He picked up a small can. It rattled drily. *"Fried baby bees?"*

She snatched it from him. "Oh Lord. It was kind of a joke. I got it to have when the Roses came over next for a drink, I —"

She veered a shamefaced glance off his scowl. She made a semi-hysterical sound.

Lucas grinned. She tittered. They broke all at once into a gust of laughter.

"I can see Ted Rose grabbing a handful while he's talking, throwing them into his mouth —"

"And they *crunch!* They make this awful crunching sound —"

The laughter became a roar — full, released, past mirth.

"— I doubt if that'd stop him, he'd keep right on talking —"

"And Ellen! She and the *escargots* they had in France and the *locusts* in the Middle East, that's the reason I got them, they're so damned blasé —"

Cissie came in and eyed them with revulsion. "I'm hungry," she said. "Why are you crying?"

Sally pulled away and mopped at her face. "We — we're not crying, we're laughing — Oh dear, it's so totally *ridiculous* —"

"You're probably drunk," their daughter said flatly.

Sally fell into Lucas's arms and they were off again. It felt wonderful. They clung together, swaying. Cis put her arms around their knees and pressed her chin into Sally's hip. "Are you drunk? Are you? What are you crying for?"

They gathered her between them and wiped their wet faces on her hair. They were not drunk, they said — she had never seen her parents drunk, had she? — they were only laughing. "I don't like you to laugh that way," she said.

"Please, Mark, try to eat something?"

Mark shook his head and continued to play with his bathrobe tie, slumped in his chair.

"At least make him sit up, will you?" Chris said edgily. "It's nauseating trying to eat with him leaning on me like a smelly old dog."

"Daddy's going to be a policeman," Cis announced.

"He's *not* going to be a policeman." Sally turned a look of blank, glazed appeal to her husband. She had the aspect of a blind person who hesitates at an intersection, sensing against her skin the reverberating redness of the traffic light. *Get this over with*, she pleaded silently.

Lucas cleared his throat. "It isn't policemen, it's the militia we were talking about."

"What's a militia?"

"Militia, dear, are your *friends*. Like firemen, or —"

"Are all those people militia? There's whole bunches of them. I don't like them," Cis said.

Mark whined, "I'm not hungry. I want to be excused."

"No, Mark, wait, darling. Daddy has something to discuss with you children —"

Mark put his hands over his ears and screwed his eyes shut and sank down into his chair. Chris ate steadliy. Cis ducked under the table and fished around for her napkin.

"First of all, you don't need to be afraid of those people out there. And they're not the militia, Cis. They're people who've come here, most of them families like us, because they, um, feel safer here right now. They . . ." He looked around the table. He said sharply, "Cis. Come out of there."

She emerged with her napkin. "We played tetherball today. Susan Vickery wanted handsies and keepsies but the teacher said we had to play just handsies. Susan cried."

"Is *every*body in your class named Susan?" Chris said.

"Cis. Daddy wasn't talking about tetherball. You interrupted him," Sally said.

Cis said defiantly, "I didn't know he was talking to *me*."

"I was talking to all of you. I want you to listen."

"I want to be excused," Mark said. His face was flushed, swollen, frantic.

"Oh good grief." Chris released his fork, leaned back, and raised his fingertips to his temples. He massaged them with the air of one who suffers long and silently. "Do we have to discuss this at the *table*? Do we have to discuss it with *them*?"

"Yes we do have to discuss it with them," Lucas said tightly.

"You want to *worry* everybody, go ahead." Chris's face was suddenly pale. "I don't know what good you think it'd do, worrying everybody. Christ, they're so dumb they're scared of you joining the militia! I already *told* them you wouldn't get hurt, you could take care of yourself —"

"Chris, I wasn't talking about my joining any militia. That question hasn't been decided yet. What I'm trying to get at, if everybody'll quit interrupting, is the bigger question of the national situa —"

"Not *decided*? You mean if the mayor and everybody sees fit to call on people to go out and help protect the town you're not *decided*?" Chris's face was scandalized.

"Darling, they're asking for volunteers only, and your father doesn't feel —"

"Doesn't *feel*? You mean he's not going?" He turned to his father and repeated incredulously, "You're not going to *help*?"

"Of course I'm going to help," Lucas snapped. "In any way I consider right. If it becomes absolutely necessary, I assure you I'll go out and bash as many people as adequate for you to consider me a hero, Chris. Until then —"

Chris was slowly nodding his head. "Oh. I get it. I get the picture now." His face was sick and defiant.

Lucas balled his napkin and half rose.

"Oh please," Sally pleaded. "John, Chris doesn't think you're — he doesn't understand — Come on now, *please* let's not quarrel." Her voice teetered. "Please not tonight."

Chris dropped his gaze and blindly took up his fork. "Skip it, skip it," he muttered. "Crissake, can't a person merely inquire —"

They lapsed into silence. Lucas regarded his plate.

"Mother?"

"Yes, Cis."

"If you had to die . . ."

Movement, rustles, chewing, domesticity, all was suspended. Lucas had the sensation that the room — the entire house — had ceased to breathe.

Cis looked around; perhaps dizzied by what appeared to be unaccustomed respect she shouted, "It's a puzzle! Say you had to die, would you rather be bombed or swallowed by an alligator?"

"You're dumb!" Mark exploded. "Dumb! Dumb!" He slid all the way off his chair and crouched under the table. "I'm sick," he whined frantically, "I'm sick, I'm so sick —"

Mortified, Cis cried, "You are not sick! You haven't even urped! And I am not dumb, you are! You can't even answer my puzzle — would you rather be bombed or swallowed by a —"

"SHUT UP!" Lucas's roar shattered the confusion; the shards of it rattled away. They sat at the table in a throbbing stillness, and again the airless pressure sealed itself around them. Under the table he felt Mark's body press against his legs, the entwining of Mark's arms, hobbling him, Mark's head against his knee. Cis began quietly to weep, gazing with streaming eyes at her father's face. Sally sat stunned. He was ringed with stunned gazes.

"They're scared, Dad," Chris said. "They know." He got up and went around the table and picked up his sister. He put his hand on the back of her neck and drew her head down into his shoulder. "It's okay," he said. "It'll be okay, Cis. Quit it now." His face was creased with responsibility, like an old man's. Over her head his bleak eyes met his father's. It seemed to Lucas that at that moment they were one man, his son and he; that they drew mutual breath, occupied the same space and body, that all their parts were identical. "It'll be okay," Chris said sternly. "We're here, aren't we? Dad's here, I'm here, we won't let anything happen to you, for gosh sakes. Now quit that right now." He gave her a small shake. Cis's weeping declined abruptly.

He pulled his sister away from him and set her into her chair. "Now shut up. My sweater's soaked," he said severely. He stumped out to the kitchen. He came back with two dishes piled enormously with ice cream. He banged one down in front of her, the other at Mark's place. He reached under the table, pried Mark off his father's legs, and hoisted him into his chair, totally ignoring the child's limpness. He pointed at the dish of ice cream. "Eat that," he commanded.

Mark and Cis began slowly to spoon their ice cream. With a martyred scowl Chris addressed his parents: "As long as I'm up, would anybody else care for dessert?"

TO THE PRESIDENT, THE WHITE HOUSE, WASHINGTON DC (NL)

"Night letter? Why not send it direct?"

"You mean straight wire. Because you can say more in a night letter."

"But if it's important enough, it should go straight wire."

Cis hung on her father's arm. "It's nighttime. That's why it's a night letter."

"You're dumb," Mark muttered. "What do you know about it?"

"Now Mark. We're all doing this together, you know." Sally frowned over her coffee. "Isn't there something they call a Public Opinion Message? You can send it for a fixed rate —"

"The rate doesn't matter. Let's just get the message over." Lucas read again: "To the President, The White House, Washington DC." Okay, what do we want to say?"

"How about, 'We are a family of five who wish to —' "

"Say, I just thought. If it's seven o'clock here, it's ten o'clock in Washington," Chris said. "You think that makes any difference?"

"Let's not worry about that, Chris. He'll get the message in the morning."

"The President isn't alseep, is he? Would he be sleeping now?" Mark said anxiously.

Sally patted his wrist. "Of course not, darling. Don't worry about *that*. The President's working very, very hard."

"You ought to know *that*," Cis said.

"Maybe he won't get the message. I mean, we're not even sure if he's in the country," Chris said.

"The President gets all messages," Lucas said wearily. "He has a large staff working night and day just for that purpose. One way or another the President will get our message."

"I suppose," Chris said, and his voice split with the effort of stretching toward both belief and wisdom, "our wire'll go into a basket somewhere."

Carefully Lucas said, "It will go into a basket labeled

PUBLIC RESPONSE, if you want to put it that way. It will add to the weight of public opinion. That's the real function of sending a message, Chris. It adds its ounce to the ton of real weight, and that weight has force."

"Like a vote, I guess." Chris's sternness, his hope struggled on his face. *He is young,* Lucas thought, *he is a natural believer because he is young.* "Like a vote," Lucas said, and turned back to the piece of paper upon which he had printed, in his precise draftsman's hand, their salutation.

TO THE PRESIDENT, THE WHITE HOUSE, WASHINGTON DC (NL): WE ARE A FAMILY OF FIVE WHO WISH TO

be heard, Leader. Make ourselves felt. Say to you: we are here, we exist; we have faces; we breathe, walk, function, have self, even as you. We share with you the enormous intimacy of our fear, the appalling burden of our hope . . .

"Cissie, don't lean on my arm. I can't write when you jiggle me."

"You're not writing anything, you're just doodling."

"Well, what *are* we going to write?" Chris said impatiently. "We can't just sit here."

"I know, I know." A vote was indeed faceless, a little speck of power maybe but lost as a grain of sand on a vast beach. *What was it he wanted?* He thought suddenly of Max Kohner's crazy machine: to push his own personal button and have it go directly to the Powers that Are, and Cause — "Look at it this way. If the President were here, right here in this room at this table. What would we say to him?"

"Keep us from getting killed," Mark said.

XV

AT 1:45 Tuesday night Joe Anderson delivered himself and his family into John Lucas's hands for shelter and safekeeping.

Householders at the doorstep at night appear to be caught in adultery: laden with sleep and dismay, she clutching her gown over her breast, he pulling together the fly of his pajamas, they blinked out into the dark.

Joe Anderson's haggard face hung in the porch light like the dubbed-in ghost in a séance photograph. He held a wrapped bundle against his chest. He moved his head as if groping for an object to address. "Kathy's sick."

"She needs a place. A decent bed, a doctor, she needs a doctor." Barbara's face dangled near Joe's shoulder; two more faces; the porch was alive with clusters all turned up toward Lucas. They bobbed like unmoored balloons around Joe's central bulk. "I don't care how late it is, she's got to have the doctor, a decent bed, proper medicine —" Barbara's voice rushed along in an insistent monotone piped with hysteria, but she made no move. Nor did Joe; huddled in the middle of the intricate knot of his family he simply stood with them looped around him, the bundled child sagging in his arms, looking at

Lucas as if at a moving light. He was past any communication but the primary signal of his presence: *We are here.*

Only later Lucas realized they had hesitated, he and Sally. (How long? Had Joe been aware of it?) Hospitality was a sacrament. They were bound in it from the dimmest and most insistent of pasts. Why then, before the mute needy presence of these friends, had they stood blocking their own doorway? He could remember only a sense of threat, an intimation as he looked at these people that through their presence he was endangered, through that danger he was to be tested, and from that test he would emerge in a condition in which he might remain the rest of his life. They moved together for an instant and as he and his wife touched the decision was made. They stepped aside.

The Andersons rushed in together as if fearful of losing a moment's contact with each other. The corner of Joe's bundle brushed Sally's nightgown strap off her shoulder and a child's elbow caught a moment in Lucas's pajama fly.

Lucas took the child from its father's arms. Joe released her and his hands dangled at his sides as if they had been severed at the wrists and hung only by skin. The child was a heavy log of heat beneath the blanket, redolent with the odor of illness. Lucas set her down gently on the couch. Her blond hair lay against her face like wet feathers, her skin was the lurid color of a plastic flower, luminous, waxy, greenish. She looked dead. If it had not been for the heat in her Lucas would have thought she was dead.

Sally bent over the child. She sucked in her breath. "Oh dear," she whispered. "She really *is* sick, isn't she?"

"I told you." Barbara Anderson spoke in tones of high triumph. "I told you, she's very, very sick." She wore black stretch pants and a poppy-print nylon ski jacket and was carrying a large book. She hugged the book tightly to her chest, cradling it like a beloved toy. Lucas saw the title: GOURMET COOKERY. She looked even younger than he remembered. She looked like a child who had been up far past its bedtime and allowed to eat too many sweets and to sip at the dregs of adults' martinis; petulant, at the edge of nausea with fatigue, determined nevertheless to miss out on nothing, she had long ago passed that time when it might have been possible to yield to sleep.

With an effort so immense it seemed as if his bones might be heard to creak, Joe put his hand on his wife's shoulder. "All right," he said. "We're here now." He came toward Lucas, moving as if through water. He looked down at the child. "She's been sick," he recited in the careful inflections of one who is drunk and knows it, "for a couple of days now, but this afternoon she got worse. I forgot to pack a thermometer. Stupid. All that planning, forgot to put in a ther-mo-meter."

"Well, we don't need a thermometer to tell she's got a good high fever. Kids run fevers so easily," Sally said in the stout tones which were supposed to make everybody feel brisk and normal. "I'll just go get a robe on, and then we'll attend to everything. Barbara, bring the other two children and we'll put them in our beds for now. Joe, you look as if you could use a drink. John, pour him a drink."

Barbara blinked at Sally. "I could use a drink too," she said. "It hasn't been easy."

"Of course it hasn't. It must have been just hell. Come on, we'll just tuck these sleepy little kids here into bed and then you certainly shall have a drink." Sally smiled and held out her hands to the two children clinging to Barbara's thighs.

Barbara suddenly collapsed on the living room rug and began to cry noisily. Cradling the book she rocked back and forth. The two children immediately lunged for her lap and began to struggle for position, howling.

Joe toiled over to them and pulled the children gently away, and leading the older one and carrying the littlest went into the Lucases' bedroom. Sally knelt beside Barbara.

Lucas went into the kitchen and called their pediatrician's number. His wife said he was at the hospital, he had been at the hospital all day, he had been at the hospital half of last night too, he might as well be living at the hospital, she had had calls all day, she had four calls in the last hour, she had children too, they couldn't sleep because they were constantly being awakened by the telephone, did people think doctors' kids didn't need sleep like everybody else, didn't need their father home for dinner just once in the last couple of days, but no, people came to town with sick kids and expected —

Lucas hung up and called Max Kohner's number. He answered almost immediately. Lucas told him to come, there was a sick child in the house.

"I'm not your doctor, Lucas," he said. "And I just got in. Call your own doctor."

"It's not my child. I did call our own doctor. He —"

"I know." Kohner's voice was so weary it was bled of all inflection. "He's still at the hospital. I'll come."

"They won't let you camp in a state park now more than one night. Emergency measure, they told us. They're trying to get everybody to go back." Joe leaned against the kitchen counter. "You must have loaded this drink," he muttered. "I feel dizzy as hell."

"You're just pooped. Drink it, Joe. You want to sit down at the table?"

"No. Sitting in the car so long . . . The traffic, my God. We had to keep stopping to let the kids out. Mike gets carsick . . ."

"Joe, you should have come right up here, instead of camping out like that. With a sick kid —"

"She wasn't too sick when we left the City. She had a kind of sore throat, you know how kids . . . When I got back Sunday night — Jesus, was it only two days ago? — we just loaded up and left." He closed his eyes for so long Lucas thought he had gone to sleep on his feet. "I got back about midnight Sunday and we loaded the kids and stuff into the wagon and just took off. Funny thing. On the way down I remember wondering if Barb'd followed the plan, loading the car and so forth, taken off with the kids . . . She'd loaded it, *her* car, the little Citroën convertible. She was waiting. She didn't want to go without me, she said. That bug was so crammed with stuff she couldn't have got the kids into it."

Lucas said, "You had the station wagon, Joe."

He laughed suddenly, an arid cackle. "Hey. Hey, you're right! Me, the big planner! I —" He stopped and looked around as if he had forgotten what he was saying. Lucas poured him another drink.

"Christ," Joe said, "I'm keeping you up."

"Forget it. I'm not sleepy. And Kohner ought to be here any minute." Joe's children were in the Lucases' beds; Sally and Barbara were in there; for almost twenty minutes the commotion of crying had been stilled. What were they doing in there? Was anybody with the sick child? Had it died? Lucas looked uneasily at the kitchen clock: two-thirty. It was too quiet; the house boomed with quiet. Why hadn't Kohner arrived?

"Who's Kohner?"

"The doctor, Joe."

"Doctor?" Joe frowned, his eyes wandered, he resumed talking. On and on he talked. It had been rough at the state park. He knew rules were rules but with a sick kid . . . They counted Sunday night as an entire night but they had only got there around four in the morning. There was Sunday night and Monday night; that was when Kathy got worse, Monday night; they said they'd have to get out. He had told the ranger Sunday night shouldn't be counted. There hadn't been that many people there then anyway. The ranger said there were too many people to handle there now, rules were rules, he was really very sorry, but, etc., etc. Joe felt sorry for the ranger; he was a nice guy, young kid, only trying to do his duty; who really was to blame was whatever boy scout they had up there in some headquarters bossing things, some blind bureaucrat that couldn't run sick kids through his IBM . . .

A moth lay plastered against the black window, wings spread, speckled cream, buff, tan and brown, the colors and shape of a tiny hawk. It trembled occasionally, pressing its tissue body flat to the pane. Lucas pinned his eyes on it. Behind him Joe Anderson's voice reeled on and on like the slow uncoiling of a hawser trailing off unnoticed into the wake.

". . . so I finally told the ranger if he could find us a doctor we'd vacate our space in an hour. So the ranger took me over to another campsite and pointed to the white permit card they tack up on the post by the spaces; it said DR. FRENCH. So I ask this Dr. French to come over and look at our little girl who was sick, and he said he'd like to but he couldn't help, he was a Ph.D. at Cal, teaches ancient history. He said he was sorry my kid was sick, everybody in his family had a lousy cold, all five kids, and did I have any sherry. He said he has a couple glasses of sherry every afternoon and he'd be damned if he

didn't already miss that sherry even more than a decent mattress, although he hated camping and outdoor life and they
didn't have any equipment —"

The moth was flattened in speechless worship, spread-
eagled against the pane as if to bathe every possible surface in
light. Why was Kohner taking so long?

". . . so when I got back another family had driven up to
our site and were unpacking, so we moved on to another camp,
Redwood Grove I think it was, we just moved in on a family
like they'd moved in on us. God, I hope you believe how we
hated to do that. It isn't the sort of thing people like us do. You
know? We never thought we'd ever do that sort of thing.
Kathy was vomiting, she just kept on vomiting, we couldn't
stay in the car, we had to have a place —"

The doorbell rang.

Congested fury glistened on Max Kohner's face. He shoved
past Lucas, barely seeming to notice him. "I'm late," he
snarled, "because I stopped to watch the murder of a child run
over by that pack of madmen on the public streets. Now if
you'll show me where *your* kid is."

In the kitchen, Joe Anderson drained the last drops from
the scotch bottle and informed the moth that he had paid two
dollars a gallon for gas at a place called South Fork.

"You mean to tell me you didn't know that kid had
mumps?"

"She complained of a pain, she said it was in her neck. I
thought just a sore throat . . ." Barbara Anderson's gaze
wandered off on another tour of the kitchen. "Where's Joe?"
she asked again, petulantly.

"Mumps encephalitis is nothing to fiddle around with,"
Kohner snapped. "Surely when she started to vomit like that

— It's a brain involvement. You understand? The brain is inflamed."

"Oh, awful, awful." Barbara's eyes rolled to the ceiling, the window, the cabinets. "Oh, terrible. Where's Joe?"

"Come on, Barbara," Sally said, "Joe's on the living room couch, he's dead tired. And she's tired too," she said coldly to Kohner as she led Barbara out. "So if you don't mind, Doctor —"

"Stupid," Kohner muttered. He mimicked, " 'I thought just a sore throat.' That's a stupid woman, letting that kid —"

"These people are dead on their feet, Kohner. And it's not their fault the kid's sick."

"I'm dead on my feet too and it's not my fault their kid's sick, I just can't stand stupidity. Where's your phone?"

Lucas pointed. Kohner dialed, spoke, hung up cursing. "Why do we insist on believing what we know isn't so? I knew there wasn't a bed left in the hospital." He looked around quite calmly. He seemed to have forgotten Lucas was there. He clapped both palms to his chest, found cigarettes, lit one with an enormous flame-throwing windproof lighter. Squinting against the smoke he regarded the lighter's flame as if it were the Burning Bush, about to offer him counsel. Slowly he revolved his wrist; the flame bent, burned upside-down, devoured itself. He snapped the lid of the lighter, stuffed it back into his pocket, and telephoned again.

"Lundgren. Get off your fat Swedish ass and get over to this address I'm going to give you, and stop by at General and see if you can check out some i.v. equipment —" He talked some more and when he hung up he was grinning maliciously. " 'Semi-retired,' she says. That old harridan'll never retire. Too goddam bossy. That old Lundgren, she'll smart things up around here."

He wandered restlessly about the kitchen, poking and prying at buttons, dials, gadgets. He stopped and looked closely at the salt garden. "What's this?"

Lucas was lumpish with fatigue. "Salt crystals."

"Christ, I made one of these once when I was a kid." He humped over it. He poked at a frond; it crumbled to dust on his fingertip. He inspected the finger, rubbed his thumb against it, inspected that, and with delicacy put out the tip of his tongue and tasted the smudge of white on his finger. His tongue was long and pointed, blue-veined and skinny. He flicked it back inside his mouth; Lucas could see it curl against his palate. He leaned his elbows on the counter and blew gently into the bowl. A few dustlike crystals drifted up around his face.

Lucas looked at the little man's back. His skinny shoulders poked like twin humps through his child-size jacket. He would have had to go to the boys' department for that suit. Through his weariness Lucas felt a stir of pity. From the twist of those shoulders and the strain of cloth between them he saw how very small Max Kohner was, how desperately tired he must be, with what effort he sustained in that midget body the blast of energy inside. Even now, as he was momentarily so still, Lucas sensed the inner rumble of refueling, the stoking of engines.

He moved uneasily; there was a sense of imminent explosion in all this compression. "Kohner, why don't you go home? If a nurse is coming —"

"Home!" Kohner turned, jerked upright, flicked his cigarette off his thumb. It whizzed past Lucas into the sink where it sizzled a moment like an expiring meteor. "Why should I go home when it's so goddam homelike here?"

"I suppose," Lucas said dully, "that's some kind of insult."

Kohner crossed his hands on his chest and surveyed the ceiling. "God, you sensitive artists, looking for insults . . . Same beams, same module, same color. Way up there, high. Oh man, *high*. You always paint all your ceilings white, Lucas?"

"If you'd seen all my ceilings you'd know." Lucas was too tired to try to figure out this man's apparently aimless jabs; that he was under some kind of attack he was aware. "Yes, I paint most of my ceilings white. More light."

"I wonder if it's the same plan. You always use the same goddam plan, Lucas?" He rocked from side to side. "Plan SV dash 4, flip this one, disguise with outside trim? Oh, the dining room's larger I noticed, the living room's to one side —" He paused. "Lucas," he said soberly, "I live in one of your houses. Didn't you know that?"

"I never designed a house for you."

"That you did *not*, chum. But I bought it and I live in it. The Searle house," he snapped. "Didn't you know I was the one bought the Searle house six years ago?"

"No. Why should I care who bought the Searle house? I designed it for them, they lived in it, he was transferred away. They were very sorry to leave the house. They told me so. I did my job."

"Oh you did that, all right. Oh you designed hell out of that house, Lucas."

There are places in a man's pride in which no looting can be tolerated. Lucas said tightly, "The Searle house is a good house. I put a great deal of thought into that house."

"You did that, chum, indeed you did. All the cunning of your craft." Kohner's voice was high, hard. "Aesthetics. Engineering. The architect as God. 'Let there be light,' you said, and, 'Here I will set the firmament, there the sun ——' " He stabbed viciously with his finger.

Lucas was fully awake now. "Kohner, what's *wrong* with that house?"

"It isn't *me*," he mimed, posturing grotesquely. "It just isn't *me*, you know?"

"I said *what's wrong with it?*"

"Have you any idea what a fourteen-foot ceiling does to me?" He spoke with sudden savagery. "Or a room with the proportions of a —— a goddam cathedral? You may think you designed that building for the Searles, but it was for yourself. That place is scaled for giants, Lucas. No wonder you think it's one of your best! Let me tell you something, chum. A house like that, it's an environment. It can dominate an ordinary man. You live in it, it can lead you around by the nose. If you let it, Lucas. *If you let it.*"

Behind the great glasses his eyes glinted, watchful, embattled. Lucas perceived at last what this little man was: a sheath, a tough hide trussed around a sensitivity so keen it was close to unbearable. No wonder he battled him! In the way that Lucas was dwarfed in the mountains, this man was dwarfed in his house. He struggled with that pervasive sense of domination there. No wonder he had eventually to seek out the architect; he fought with giants under his own roof.

Sorely troubled, Lucas said, "You didn't have to buy the house. You don't have to live there. You could move."

"And give in?" And then rawly, flatly, he said, "It's a very beautiful house, Lucas."

Lucas felt as if, using a power he had not known he possessed, he had ambushed an innocent stranger.

*   *   *

Kohner lay the needle flat against the child's arm; the tip of it disappeared into the tiny blue canal of vein. The nurse Lundgren slowly lifted the plastic bottle, hooked it on a hanger device at the head of the bed. The needle was secured with strips of tape. The vein bulged gently. In her coma the child sighed; they could hear the click of her tongue against her dry throat. Kohner, murmuring, put his palm against her cheek, stroking it with his thumb. He sat murmuring to the child. The old nurse, standing over them, said presently, "Go home, Max. Go home and rest." She touched his shoulder. "Max, get some sleep."

. . . Huddled in mounds, in strange beds, on couches, the household slept at last. John Lucas wandered the rooms and listened to their breathing, with the insomniac's conviction that it is only his watchfulness which holds the resting world together.

XVI

SOMEWHERE an animal was singing. He could hear its grieved cadenzas, muffled embellishments of complaint, woebegone blubbers. Light was pale green against his lids. He rolled them back and it was morning. Filaments of a rigid reticulum soared above him. He gazed up through splinters and slats, cords and fibrils: a long blue drafting-pencil, JS STAEDTLER MARS-LUMOGRAPH F, bloomed like a naked stamen from a Tinker-Toy joint eight inches above his head. Knotted to the same joint by kite-string were two jacks. He was on the floor of Mark's bedroom. There had been poaching and prowling during the night. Mark had had another nightmare. The Yeti had brought him back and stayed to fend off horrors.

He shielded his face with his forearms and edged stiffly out from his nest. Mark must have woven him in later, much later, after he was finally asleep. Lucas did not care to reason why; he shut out a vision of oysters sealing off irritants. He sat up, scraping his ear on an Erector set beam. The entire complex tinkled dangerously. A few leaves of paper, folded like wings, fluttered down. An entire section composed of milk cartons held together with Scotch tape and rooted in a foundation of Mary Ellen jam jars threatened to buckle. Carefully steadying the jars, he tottered to his feet. His pajama sleeve snagged on an arrangement of spokes. A cornice collapsed. Cursing, he stepped back. His bare heel crunched on a recumbent pink celluloid Kewpie doll.

Mark watched silently from his bed. How long had he been lying there watching his sleeping father?

Particles of celluloid embedded in his heel, Lucas hobbled out. In the hall the animal's song was like the faraway sobbing of wolves. He followed this spoor of sound and found, outside in the driveway in the Andersons' car, a huge dog. The car windows were beaded with frantic respiration and saliva.

"Oh poor, poor old Fritz!" Barbara Anderson cried. "Out there in the car all night! We completely forgot him!"

Needing his clothes, he looked into his bedroom. "Coffee," Miss Lundgren croaked. She yawned hugely. Her long Scandinavian lip closed over her long teeth. She folded her arms and regarded him with the morose humor of the night nurse. "All systems definitely non-go without coffee. Hot, black, no cream but plenty of sugar."

"You'll have to wait awhile for breakfast," Lucas said. "I think they're going to feed all the kids first. How's the little girl?"

"Her temp's down a bit." She yawned again. "Lordie, you've got a houseful, haven't you?"

"They aren't all ours. We've got a family visiting."

Wise-old-nursewise she narrowed her eyes. "Refugees?"

"Visitors," Lucas said shortly. "And the sick child isn't mine, it's theirs."

"No offense. You look like you were up all night too."

"I might as well have been." There were noises in the

kitchen. "I'll just get my clothes from the closet and dress in the bathroom."

"Somebody's in the bathroom. Both bathrooms. It's like a zoo around here." She bared her orange gums in what Lucas recognized as a sympathetic grin.

She was a giantess, almost as tall as he; her broad white bosom was as flat and inviting as a clean-sheeted mattress. Lucas hesitated. "I wonder if you can answer a question for me," he said.

"Shoot."

"I haven't had mumps. What do you think are the chances of my getting them?"

"Depends on how much contact you had with the patient. You handle her at all?"

"I carried her from the living room in here."

She pursed her lips. "Well, mumps isn't *too* contagious. Not like measles, say. Measles is a whole lot worse to get, usually."

"But mumps — for a man —"

She grinned again, in a comradely way. "Aw, quit worrying. Chances are you won't get 'em, and if you do chances are you won't develop orchitis, and if you do chances are pretty good there won't be any lasting effect."

"Orchi —?"

"From the Greek *orchi*, testes. *Orchid* comes from that too. Appropriate, when you think of it." She regarded him with such ungainly coyness, aware she was the buffoon, her big old face drawn even longer into dry brackets of amusement, Lucas had to grin back.

"I'll take that as a compliment," he said.

"Do," she snickered.

He dressed in Chris's room, which was empty, the bed already made. Both bathrooms were still cloistered. He went outside and stood behind one of the redwoods, and watched with dour satisfaction as his urine steamed against the cold bark in the foggy air.

The incubation period for mumps was from ten to twenty-one days. Putting it this way he supposed he would be overjoyed to be guaranteed the worst case on record, with all possible complications. At least he would know what was incubating in those days.

"Ten people," Sally hissed to him, "and all we've got is six eggs!"

"Scramble 'em and put in a lot of milk. Here's some Rice Krispies. The kids can fill up on that."

"Three quarts of milk! How long will *that* last? John, we're just going to have to ask them about their supplies. Didn't Joe say he'd planned to take some?"

"Sure. Ask them."

"*You* ask them. You can ask Joe if you can help him bring in the rest of the stuff from his car, I thought I saw some —"

"Sally, you're not *afraid* to ask Barbara if she brought any food? Surely you don't think it'd *offend* her?"

"You're a big help." Her voice trembled. "Oh, you're just the biggest help. Quibbling over who's going to ask —" Her face was stained with weariness; her hands shook as she raised them to her hair in a vague tidying gesture laden with hopelessness: *I am ugly*, it seemed to say; *I am ugly at last, you might as well see it. There is nothing I can do now to repair the ravages time and homemaking have wrought to my youth and beauty . . .* It always made Lucas feel inexplicably guilty when she made this gesture. She had no makeup on and she was wearing Chris's old maroon plaid bathrobe. Its cuffs were turned back to reveal her wrists, brittle and pathetic beneath them.

Out of this mysterious guilt Lucas rasped, "What do you expect me to do? Before we've given them one single meal demand that they turn over their supplies? Let's get breakfast over with first before we —"

Barbara came into the kitchen. "Poor old Fritz. He just doesn't know what to make of that garage. He's just used to being in the house, that's all." Barbara had wanted to bring the dog in — dogs were not allowed to run loose in Sequoia — but Sally had suggested she would prefer the dog to be confined to the garage. Sally did not care for dogs.

"It's just that we don't have a dog," she said, "and the house is a little crowded." She spoke nicely but very firmly.

Now Barbara said, "Would it be okay if I scrambled a couple of eggs or something for him? Maybe if he gets *fed* out there he might not mind it so much."

Lucas said hastily, "I'll round up the kids," and got out of there.

Breakfast lacked graciousness.

Two-year-old Mike Anderson sat in Cis's old youth chair propped with pillows and emitting calliope howls. His face streamed like a squeezed orange. His mother sat next to him, her elbow on the table, holding a spoonful of Rice Krispies. "What a pill. What a pillbox," she clucked. "Come on, Mikie, just taste it. It won't poison you." She steered the spoon alluringly toward his mouth. He batted it away. Rice Krispies splattered across the table to Lucas's sweater sleeve. "Now look what you've done," Barbara chided fondly.

Cissie said, "But I don't want to go to school! I have a *guest*." She and Jennie held hands and looked at Lucas with terrible female solidarity.

"You have to go to school. There'll be no argument."

"Nobody else is going!"

"This isn't a holiday. We're not having a flower festival. Of course everybody else is going. Now if you're through with your breakfast get your coat and —"

"Jennie, you haven't finished your egg. Honestly. She eats like a bird. She's the worst child to get to *eat* anything," Barbara said. "Look. Look at all that good egg still on your plate."

"It's watery," Jennie murmured.

"Watery, ugh," Cis agreed. They squeezed hands, making faces to show how verminous and unpalatable were watery eggs.

"It. Isn't. Watery." Sally's face was dangerous.

"Come on, Mike, just a little teentsy bit —"

"But Jennie's not going to school! She's on vacation. And Mark's not going, and you hardly went to work at all yesterday —" Cis and Jennie moved closer together, they entwined; Little Match Girls, frail, buffeted, starved, they whimpered.

"Don't be ridiculous. Mark's sick, and Jennie's, uh, visiting. Why should I argue with you? Why should I sit here and take a lot of gas from a seven-year-old? *Get your coat*, Cis," Lucas thundered.

"Please . . ." Sally said faintly. She made the weary gesture. "Girls. I'll tell you what. Jennie can go with you to school today. She can visit school. Okay? And Daddy will drive you, because it's so late."

"Oh bo-o-y," they squalled.

"John, will you please tell Chris he has to get up now and have his breakfast, he's going to be late for school. He simply has to take some responsibility for himself, I've been much too *busy*—"

"He's up. His bed's made."

"*Up? I* haven't seen him. I've been out here for hours and I swear he hasn't —"

They stared at each other, and went together to Chris's room.

"His bed hasn't been slept in," Sally whispered. She turned tragic eyes to him. "Oh John, his bed hasn't been slept in! He's gone, he —"

"What a pot," Barbara crooned. "You're a pot, you know that, Mikie boy? Won't eat cold cereal."

"Maybe he's full, Barbara." Sally began clearing the spattered mess from the table.

"Not this one, he's a terrible piggy. Aren't you, Mike? He usually has an *egg*, and *juice*, and then hot Gerber's *ce*real, and then *ba*con, and then *toast*, and then *milk*, and —"

Sally set the dishes down. "John," she said with distilled articulation, "we absolutely have to start thinking about getting more food."

"Oh, we'll get it," Barbara said. "Let *us*. It's the least we can do. Make a list of what you need, Sally. Joe can run over to your market after he wakes up. Where do you get your —"

Sally pulled Chris's bathrobe tightly across her chest and turned to Barbara a countenance akin — at Lucas's closest guess — to that expression of Madame Defarge as the blade fell on an overprivileged neck. "The only thing *is*, Barb," she said sweetly, beautifully, "the local groceries won't be open today until noon. And when they are it will be for just two hours, and only Sequoia residents can buy supplies. You see, we're being rationed. So much for each person in the family. The only advantage is if you have a baby. Then you get an extra quart of milk. While it lasts."

Her mouth ajar Barbara looked incredibly stupid. *Kohner was right*, Lucas thought, *she is stupid*. Her childlike quality came purely and simply from a lack of mentality. She just didn't grasp. Like the children scurrying excitedly around the house, like the baby howling at the table, like the sick one in a semi-coma on his bed, Barbara Anderson's vision was turned inward to her interior needs, which touched her only as directly and as literally as the chair in which she sat. The whole perimeter of widening concern, those concentric rings which the adult must struggle so hard to ride out in the expansion of his life as a thinking, growing creature, simply did not exist for this woman-child. Her hysteria of last night, which Lucas had mistaken for the paralysis of fear — from the inkling of insight into their common plight — had been nothing more than fatigue and discomfort. Now in the morning, refreshed, her child cared for, she did not understand that the torment of possibilities still existed. As he looked at her a slow welling came into Lucas's chest, and he was afraid. The test had begun.

He put his arm around Sally's shoulders to steady her and remind her of this test. "Maybe you two can get together and help figure out the problem of supplies. The fact is, Barbara, that with people flooding in the town's pretty low on food. We'll all have to be careful for a while."

Barbara took the baby out of its chair and hugged it to her breast. "There now, Mikie," she murmured, "there now, there now . . ." as if it were the child who needed comfort. Sated, sleepy, her son gazed at her with wonder. Out in the garage the dog Fritz hurled himself desolately against the door.

*   *   *

"Jennie's wearing my skirt and I'm wearing her dress," Cis said. "You'll *hate* Mrs. Irwin. She's our teacher. She makes us do extra arithmetic when we —"

"Show Jennie how to fasten the seat belt, and quit bouncing around so much," Lucas said edgily.

Even out here in their residential district the traffic was unbelievable. Lines of cars crawled in both directions on every street, an apparently aimless stream simply *out*, as if to be cruising the streets were a purpose in itself. The aura of unease rose like gas in these normally serene blocks. Lawns, dotted with clots of people skirting the congested sidewalks, had already a ruined look. As he inched past in the smog of exhaust, his eyes smarting with morning light (amber now with hydrocarbons, just like in the real cities), Lucas saw that old Mrs. Hilwider's show of dwarf azaleas had been mercilessly trampled to a thicket of twigs. Mrs. Hilwider herself was out in front of her great old brown-shingled mansion (to Lucas's mind one of the finest buildings in town, and one which he had always been grateful he did not have to fight to save, Mrs. Hilwider being so firmly entrenched and apparently ageless), a wide-brimmed old straw hat not one whit diminishing the glare in her fierce old eyes, waving her scrawny old fists at the sky and heaping horrible old Victorian curses upon those living beings who had the temerity to move about on two legs rather than remaining chastely rooted where planted. As the traffic puttered, stalled, and finally expired, Lucas sat in the throbbing car and watched with morose sympathy as Mrs. Hilwider strode back and forth howling disaster and vengeance, her denim skirt flapping around her tough old shanks, her grass-stained bowling shoes pounding like the tread of an insulted deity upon the morning dew. He half expected snakes to spring from her instep. The traffic lurched and they crawled again in lowest gear.

"You girls'd get there faster if you'd get out and walk."

"We don't want to," Cissie whimpered.

"What's the matter?"

"We're scared."

"Scared? Why? *Why* are you scared, Cis?" He turned.

"Jennie says she doesn't like driving with all these cars."

Jennie sat straight on the seat, staring at him. He had not really looked closely at her before; all children but his own had always, like Orientals, looked the same to him. She was a skinny little kid with dark bangs cut straight across above her eyes. Next to her, Cis in her sturdy blondness seemed almost blowsy. In each others' clothes they were quite ridiculous. Jennie gazed silently at him with eyes so dilated they seemed to have no irises. The waiflike urgency of both gazes — one blue and one black — unnerved him. They held hands.

"Well, you could get out and walk as I suggested, then. You want to do that, Jennie?"

"She doesn't want to," Cis translated the silence. Jennie had not said a word since they had got into the car. "She doesn't know the way to school."

"Honey, *you* know the way to school, you walk it every —"

"There's too many people. They'd push us. We'd get lost. A bad man might come along in a car, and want to give us candy —"

"Okay, okay, girls. Calm down now. I'm taking you, aren't I? You don't have to worry about anything — *God!*"

A troupe of teen-aged youngsters had darted in front of him, squeezing between his front bumper and the rear of the car ahead. If he hadn't been going so slowly they would have been crushed. A delivery truck behind nudged them sharply as he braked. Lucas rolled down the window and yelled at the kids. They hooted back, waving their arms, and then tore off excitedly through the crowds.

Jennie had started to cry. Cis joined her.

In desperation, to drown out the crying and the surge of claustrophobia from the realization he was trapped in the stream of cars and could only float along helplessly in it, Lucas began to sing. "*When the Deep Purple falls, over sleepy garden walls,*" he roared, "*and the STARS begin to flicker in the skies —*"

The girls stopped crying and listened, fascinated. He leaned out the window and sang back to old Mrs. Hilwider as she slowly receded, "*— in the STILL of the night once again I hold you tight, though you're GONE our love lives on—*"

She shook her fists at him.

They were twenty minutes late reaching the school. Here the traffic was so choked he left the car in the middle of the street while he jockeyed the girls to the curb. Throngs of children milled around the schoolyard.

Cissie held back. "I don't know any of these kids," she whispered fearfully.

"Maybe some of them are visitors like Jennie." But he didn't like the looks of it himself. Some of the children seemed much older than grammar age. Grouped together in shifting clumps, they had an aspect of expectancy, a flux of restlessness; occasionally a ripple came from one of the knots and the sound was not childish laughter.

He gripped the girls' hands and moved with them into the crowd. Looming like a Gulliver, exposed, his charges pressed tightly against his thighs, wading through one cluster close to the steps, he felt rather than heard, like a shower of tiny darts, faint hostile jeers. The faces around him were blank and insolent. *Children*, he thought, *these are only children.*

A rock whistled over his head and crashed through a window. He felt the jar of air, the shatter directly in his ear. He ducked instinctively. As if at a signal the schoolyard exploded.

A barrage of rocks pelted against the building; high-pitched screams and shrieks became a ferocious caterwaul. A stone grazed his shoulder; another thumped, hard, into the middle of his back. The sudden clamp of pain staggered him. He swept Cis and Jennie in against his chest. Their heads banged and they began to howl and struggle in a panic. Crouching on the steps he pressed them closer; a shower of gravel broke against his back. In the writhe of kids' legs, blue jeans, skirts, socks, he hesitated: *But these are only children*, he thought in dumb astonishment.

The girls were struggling desperately now. He realized they couldn't breathe crammed against his chest. He eased his grip but kept them under the protection of his body. "Listen," he said between his teeth, "listen and do just as I say! Stay close to me —" Several kids lunged against them, bawling like calves. "Mama!" one little girl screamed. "Mama Mama Mama!"

"Hang on to me no matter what happens, put your heads down and just push, I'll get you out —" He wasn't sure if they heard him but they clung like cats. He lowered his head and lunged off the step. In a waddling semi-crouch he butted through the mob of children. They clutched at him; he glimpsed their frantic faces and he could not tell victims from attackers; some had rocks in their hands. He tried not to knock anyone down, but the crush was so violent it took violence to get through. One boy came clawing toward him, his mouth so wide and close and yelling Lucas saw rows of orthodontic metal, wires from a head-brace bent down along his cheeks; he put his head down behind his shoulder as the boy flung himself against him; the wire snagged Lucas's jacket but he lunged on. The jacket ripped, the boy screamed. "Ow-ow-ow!" he screamed. Lucas could not look back. The boy had had a rock in his hand. *Didn't he have a rock in his hand?*

At the edge of the schoolyard they broke and ran. A throng of adults, mostly women, carrying brooms and hammers, howling, demented, bore in. One woman swung her broom at his head as Lucas fled past, dragging his two weeping charges.

The car was solidly wedged in the paralyzed traffic. He did not even stop for the keys. He hoisted the two children into his arms and staggered off toward home.

Three blocks away Sally and Joe came running. They scooped the children from him.

"Oh God, my God," Sally wept, squatting and rocking Cis in her arms, "we heard about it on the radio, we were so afraid —"

Jennie's thin legs dangled down Joe's front like the ends of a shawl. She put her head in the crotch of his neck. "You said you'd come," she said wearily. "You said you'd come to get me." He bent his own head into her shoulder as if to join himself to her.

"Thank God, thank God, Daddy was there to take care of you," Sally cried. "Oh John, thank God you were with her . . ."

Lucas sat down on the curb. Thank God he had been with his daughter. They should be together. It was time now for them all to stay together. They needed his protection.

He put his face in his hands. He tried with all his remaining strength to believe that he would be able to protect them, that his missing son Chris was all right, and that the boy whose braces had been ripped from his mouth had had a rock in his hand.

XVII

THEY went forth to stalk food.

The friendly neighborhood breed of merchant was, they found, endowed with as much cunning, sagacity, and art as any ancient prey. A throng lay in ambush at the doors of Hackett & Son, Fine Foods since 1931. At ten minutes to noon LeRoy Hackett, Son, appeared from around the shuttered maw of the loading zone in back and bawled, "All right all right folks. We're openeen in a few minutes here as per accordeen to the instructions of the City Council and I am announceen that accordeen to our policy which goes into effect right now which will last for the duration of the emergency we can't sell to nobody except our regular cash-payeen and charge-account customers which are on our current books. We are very sorry to announce this but we are sure all of you folks who are not regular customers should understand our position."

There was a growling from the swamps.

John Lucas and Joe Anderson edged their way through the tossing boscage of hostile housewives. "Geez," Joe muttered. "Are you a regular customer?"

"In food alone that guy and his daddy take in about three hundred dollars of my income each month, and God knows

what in liquor, cigarettes, and comic books. Excuse me,"
Lucas said to a skinny crone in curlers.

LeRoy, who had known other moments of glory when as
"Hacker" Hackett he had for five years in a row been the
heart, sustenance and center of the Sequoia High School Loggers, blinked down upon them, shuffled his vast feet, and then
apparently catching Coach's whisper in his ear took a deep
breath and resumed his exhortations. He had a very high-
pitched voice. What should have been a roar of manly thunder
sounded like a squall.

"Now I'm gonna ask you folks who normally trade else-
where to please step back and to kinely allow those which are
regular customers to step forward. If you will do this in an
orderly fashion, then, uh —" he pondered "— everything will
be orderly. And now if you'll let me through here to the
front door —"

"If you're open for business you've got to let everybody in,"
a woman screamed suddenly. "The Council didn't say anything about preferred customers!"

"Our money's as good as anybody's!"

"This is a democracy!"

"— report you to the FBI!"

"Discrimination! Civil rights!"

Globules had collected on the broad steppe of Hacker's
forehead. His elbows up like flippers, he wallowed armpit
deep toward the door where his father's visage stared broodily
out. Hackett *père* was as shriveled and sere as Hacker was
mountainous and moist. All the father's juices seemed to have
gone into the making of the son. Arms folded, he lurked behind the single pane of door. Back of him Lucas saw the shad-
owy racks of impulse merchandise with which in less urgent
times their tots and wives were lured: hair spray; the Big

Golden Dictionary; Doris Day Sings for Fun Time; licorice cigars; Official Explorer Rocket Model; the Lennon Sisters Paper Dolls with MagneTized MagiStix Clothes; Hallmark Cards for Those Who Care Enough; Genuine Bird-Call (Crested Flicker); Disneyland pencil-box; paperback *Jurgen*. The kidney-spotted Purveyor in his lair.

Midst screams and buffets and accusations of intent to rob, defraud, subvert, and maim ("He stepped on my foot!" a fierce little old lady howled. "He broke my toe!"), Hacker fixed his eyes upon the glassy icon of his father's face and rowed mightily toward the door. Achieving it in a lunge he grabbed the handle. His father banged on the glass with a mottled fist, shook his head ferociously, and refolded his arms. Hacker turned in desperation.

"Now you folks just lissen here, if there isn't some order around here nobody's goeen to open any door. This is an emergency situation and if we can't have some cooperation —"

"Hacker," Lucas called, "why don't you just let us regular customers in first and then when we've all had our chance let the rest of 'em get what they need?"

"Discrimination!" A woman jabbed him in the ribs. Her head was a glittering arsenal of aluminum tubes, all set, cocked, ready to explode. "I've got as much right as you! I've got kids to feed!"

"We all have," Lucas said reasonably.

"It's your kind got us into this!" She jabbed his ribs again. Her elbow was very sharp. Lucas's face reddened.

"For crissake don't argue," Joe muttered. "She looks dangerous."

"Commie!" Somebody butted his back. A fight had erupted in the outskirts. Over heads Lucas saw a bunch of kids beating their way into the crowd. They had on green caps and uniform shirts he didn't recognize. They were using billy sticks.

The tension that had glued the crowd together came apart. The smell of it changed. An odor like ozone hung in the air. The cries passed abruptly from fury to fear. Lucas saw the woman with the curlers wrap her arms up over her head as she ducked cringing behind him. Chopping with their sticks the kids drove in.

A boy thrashed toward him, his face clamped in ecstasy, his teeth bared in a skull-like grin, his eyes screwed shut. His stick came down on the curler-lady's back ribs; they boomed like a drum. Lucas heard her gasp.

Lashing out, with the back of his forearm protecting his face, he grabbed the boy's club. The boy opened his eyes. His pupils were white-rimmed and feral. The rim faded instantly as he saw Lucas's face, saw Lucas's size. Lucas wrenched at the club; the boy's arm buckled but he hung on. With the side of his body Lucas shoved him out to the edge of the mass. Wrestling for his stick the boy was forced to his knees. His face changed from its blind, greedy expression to astonishment. "Ow," he whined, and as the pain hit him, "*Ow!*" He screamed. "Ow, ow, *ow!* He's broken my arm — Hey, hey, you're under arrest, you goddam — We're the *law*, you goddam —" Lucas flung the club far out and left him writhing, and grabbed the wrist of another club-wielder.

"John! You have a bruise on your cheek, an awful —"

"Never mind." He dumped the groceries on the counter. "Now listen. Get everything out, every bit of food we've got in the house. Get the stuff from the crawl-hole. Put it all here on the kitchen table. You too, Barbara. Get whatever you've got in the car and bring it in."

"Get it, Barb," Joe said harshly. "Don't just stand there."

"You're all banged up too! Joe —"

"*Get it.*"

Lundgren appeared. "Home is the hunter, home from the —" She stopped. She gave a low whistle.

"Lundgren, how long are you going to be here?" Lucas said.

"That depends." Her eyes were still, wary, the flicker of humor doused. "How long are any of us going to be here?"

The deliberate brutality of her words were, he saw, intended to match his fury. "Never mind that," he said. "What I am asking was how long you figure you'll be here in this house and on this case."

"Living here, you mean. Eating here."

"Yes."

She addressed Joe; her voice was uninflected. "Your Kathy's doing pretty well, responding. Her fever's still up but not as high as it was. Last night was probably the worst. I'm not the doctor but I'd guess that if everything goes okay and she continues to respond I ought to be able to leave in another few days. I'm calling Dr. Kohner this afternoon but you can check with him now if you want."

Joe said, "You're doing a good job, Lundgren. It's just that we have to —"

"Feed me. I know." Without the sustaining humor she was old. The fatigue of long dark hours, of waiting at bedsides, of remaining clothed, gartered, belted, in stiff uncomfortable chairs, had adzed this woman's big old rawboned face into a monolith of weariness. The dignity of the handmaiden, of one who serves without grudge, had given her weariness an austere grandeur. She looked rather like Abraham Lincoln.

Before this aspect Joe muttered, "Please understand that we're grateful to you. Kathy —"

She moved her shoulders. She did not smile but her face relaxed. "I know," she said again without rancor. "It was bad getting that stuff, eh?"

"I wouldn't go through that again for anything less than a situation where we were all starving," Lucas said. "I don't mind being roughed up but I don't like being turned into an animal." Feeling was returning. His jaw, the side of his face began to throb.

"I heard it on the local news. All over town they're fighting to get into the stores. And those local Volunteer fellas — you saw the militia?"

"*Militia*," Lucas said harshly. "They're a bunch of kids. They were beating people up as if they enjoyed it. I — I think I broke an arm. A kid's arm." He stood in the kitchen and thought about the fact that he had just returned from breaking the arm of a young boy. The boy had been the age of Chris. He began to tremble. He sat down. "He was banging a woman on the ribs. I could hear . . . What's happening to everybody?" He looked around the kitchen.

"Nothing that hasn't happened before," Lundgren said calmly. "Don't lose your nerve. Everybody's too nervous, is all. Just hang on and don't get too philosophical. Philosophy drains a man." Joe was staring out the kitchen window. She went over and touched him on the shoulder. "Come on, now, you're trying to get food supplies together, aren't you? Well, I've got some stuff over at my apartment. Not much but enough to feed *my* big mouth for a few days. You guys can walk over there when you want to get it, it's not far from here." She snickered faintly. "I always did figure I ought to go on a diet anyway. Now's as good a time as any."

Lucas said, "Lundgren, you're great. You're really great, you know that?"

"Thank you, Mr. Lucas," she said in awful, scandalized tones, and marched back to the bedroom.

"Christ. You offended her," Joe said.

"Yeah," Lucas said reverently.

Lucas understood that there were many ways to distract and please a woman. But he knew only one sure-fire way to make a woman bloom any time, whether it be in the middle of the night, during a swim in the Mediterranean, or (alas) while making love: ask her to make a list. To this task her orderly soul yearned as a saint yearns for chastisement. Something here made the welkin ring.

"— six, twelve, eighteen cans," Sally recited. "Okay, John, you can lift those down and put them over there with the others. . . . Seventy-two cans chocolate-flavored Metrecal."

"Butterscotch Metrecal twelve cans, vanilla Metrecal twelve cans," Barbara sang out. "Metrecal soup twenty-four cans. Total Metrecal, uh, twenty-four and twenty-four and seventy-two makes —"

"One hundred twenty cans. Where's the per-person column? Oh, here. I thought it should be at the bottom, below the totals." Sally tapped her teeth with the ball-point pen.

"How're we going to divide eleven into a hundred and twenty? I mean, it won't come out even," Barbara worried.

"Well, it comes to ten and ten elevenths cans per person, so we can put the extras into a special pile —"

Joe and Lucas obediently shoved around cases, cans, cartons, and jars. Joe turned a can in his hands. " 'Serve Willapoint Smoked Oysters once a week for increased energy and interest in life,' " he read. They exchanged glances. Lucas opened the can, and squatting on the floor they ate the oysters. "Cheers," Joe said. "To your health and increased interest," Lucas said.

"They're *eating* something," Barbara tattled. "They've opened a *can*."

"Where did you get that? What pile was it on? Honestly . . . Oh, never mind. All those little cans haven't been sorted yet. Now let's see. These cans of ravioli —"

"I feel stronger already," Joe said.

"I feel much more interested," Lucas said.

"I adore ravioli," Barbara said. "There's this place in North Beach you can get the best ravioli, real Italian homemade. They put it up in cartons to take out. We get it for Sunday night supper and take it home and I make a big salad and we sit around on the deck with the kids and Fritz, everybody simply stuffing on ravioli. Oh my goodness!"

"Hm?"

"We forgot Fritz! Poor old Fritzi out there in the garage. We haven't counted *him*."

Sally straightened and stood very erect and still.

"I mean, the poor creature's got to have his share of food too. Do you suppose he'd drink Metrecal? Joe, do you suppose a dog'd drink Metre —"

"No. *No*," Sally said.

Barbara was wearing plaid madras pedal-pushers. As he squatted behind her among the cans Lucas saw the backs of her knees, pink and plump between bracketing tendons, the cloth smooth over her buttocks. Part of her shirttail looped down over her rear. She had broad hips for one so young, broad maternal hips. He slid his eyes down and fastened them on her knees. It seemed a neutral point. There was no place to look but Barbara's knees. Lucas was glad he could not see her face. He wished he could not hear her voice. It was stubborn and drained of all childish inflection. "Well, Fritz has to have something."

"*No.*" He could not see Sally's face either; it was up there somewhere towering among her chattels.

"He'd starve!"

"One dead dog."

Barbara drew in a strangled breath. "We love him. He's a member of the family. I won't let him die."

"He's an animal."

"He's living! He's a living thing! He —"

"He'll die someday." There was ugliness in his wife's voice. He had never heard this particular, deliberate cruelty in the voice of anyone but strangers. Carefully he searched his memory; no, never had he heard this; for such intimate cruelty was impossible in a stranger. Perhaps he had been deaf all his life, and now he was not.

Joe Anderson was unmoving beside him. Lucas sensed that he, too, had just experienced a popping of ears.

The tendons of Barbara's knees began to quiver. "I don't care. I don't care what you say, Fritz is my dog and I love him and I won't let him starve! I'll give him some of my food."

"That's ridiculous. But it's up to you."

"Love isn't ridiculous!"

"In this case it is. It's sentiment. Taking the food out of your own mouth for a dog, an animal —"

Barbara's voice sharpened with cunning. "*Your* children are bigger than ours. They eat more. And Kathy's so sick she isn't eating anything —"

"Barbara." Joe got slowly to his feet.

"I don't care! It's terrible! I never heard of such a thing, deliberately letting a poor defenseless animal die of starvation! What kind of people are you anyway?"

She shook off Joe's hand. "You don't want us here. You hate us. Oh, it's plain enough, if you think I haven't *noticed*. Little things. Like when I asked about the egg —"

"We had exactly six eggs for ten people's breakfast," Sally said crisply, "and we did not and still do not know when and if we will get more."

Lucas rose. "Sally —"

Barbara's resistance collapsed. She leaned against Joe, shivering. "I always liked *you*," she accused tearfully. "We always got along fine before. We had dinner together. We were friends —"

"Friends? We don't even really know you very well."

He could see Sally's face now. It was gray. Her lipstick was a ghastly line around her mouth. She put her hands up to her hair in that vague tidying gesture. She said, "I don't know. I don't know anyone any more."

In the frozen silence Chris appeared. He closed the back door ostentatiously, as if it were quite fragile, and stood by it. He had on a green military cap, a khaki-colored shirt, a white armband, and from his belt dangled a billy club. "I can only stay a few minutes," he announced sternly.

He started to put his hands in his pockets, withdrew them, and hooked his thumbs in the front of his belt. He had a moment's trouble with the billy until he decided to cup his palm around it. The silence grew. His eyes flicked uneasily. "I can't stay," he repeated. "I was in the area and I thought I'd drop by to see if everything was okay."

"*In the area?* Oh Chris!" All Sally's tension and fury exploded. She flew at him. "Where have you been? We've been worried sick! Gone all night, at a time like this, with every-thing else on our mind, you come back and say you were *in the area!* Oh I could just *kill* you, Chris, for worrying us this way!" She stopped. "What's that ridiculous outfit you've got on?"

"Ridiculous. *Ridiculous.*" He drew in his chin and looked down on her. He laughed pityingly, his lips tight. "In case you don't know, Mother, this is a uniform. I've been on duty."

"Duty? Oh Chris, you haven't enlisted —"

"Not in the Army, Mother, for crissake! It's the local Vol-unteers. It's —" He licked his lips; he kept his gaze stonily upon her forehead. "Most of the old guys finked out on this call for the militia in town, so we figured somebody had to do something."

Sally half turned. "John . . ." *You handle him,* she used to say in despair of a four-year-old, *he's been a holy terror all day, you're his father.*

John Lucas moved stiffly to her side and faced his son. Clad in his uniform the boy stared back. It was as if he had un-sheathed his horns at last and stood before him in the full fig of glaring ivory, the tips pointed directly at his breast.

"One thing you'd better understand," Lucas said slowly. "It's right we have to do something. This morning I had to see that the family had food. That was my first duty. You un-derstand that, don't you? Does that clear it up in your mind about us old guys?"

"Ridiculous!" Sally shrilled. "Wearing a uniform, carrying a — a club, I never heard of anything so silly, a boy this age, a *baby*, why, it's dangerous! He might get *hurt* —" She broke into wild sobs. "Oh John, he might get hurt, he's only a —"

"No. He's not a baby." The boy had straightened, grown an inch or two in the light of his father's admission. He stood with his hand on his club, one hip cocked, loosed already in a kind of swagger. Seeing this, a chill seemed to siphon off every kilowatt of heat in Lucas's body.

"But let me tell you this, Chris," he said harshly. "You're not a full man either. You may have emergency powers, but you'd damn well better use them carefully. *Carefully!* Some of you guys are already out there throwing your weight around like Junior Storm Troopers —"

"John! You're not going to let him go! He might get hurt —"

"He's going. But Chris . . . watch it. *Watch it*, Chris."

The boy turned. With a stiff creak of leather — and no leather was visible on him — he left, carrying with him his full emergency powers.

XVIII

"WHAT do you mean 'structurally sound'? You think I'd design a building that wasn't structurally sound, Sam?" Lucas's voice had a hard edge audible even on the telephone.

Sam Wingluff protested, "You misunderstand me entirely, John, we're not saying — The thing is, we've got to find out, the question we have to explore, we have to know if the City Hall's *safe* —"

"You called me up to inquire if the City Hall's *safe?*" Lucas said ominously. "After seven years you want to know —"

"— for a fallout shelter," Sam bleated. "Will you let me finish? When I say 'structurally sound' I mean the, um, what the hell you call it, insulation —"

"Sam, are you gassed?"

He groaned. "I run a laundry, not a goddam engineering department! When I ran for mayor I sure didn't think I'd have to qualify for a Ph.D. in every goddam subject. I've been listening to this technical crud for an hour now — what it is, we're down here trying to see if we can't rig up some kind of shelter program. I got a hot flash from Civil Defense. The City Hall's about the only place big enough, we don't know, we need some *professional* advice. Can you get down

here, John? We're going over your blueprints and hell, none
of us are much good at figuring out what all these squiggles
are. Selzac keeps talking about maximum stress —"

"Oh *Selzac*, no wonder."

Selzac was the city engineer, a short squat man fresh out
of Cal who had parlayed a Middle-European accent, a meer-
schaum pipe, and a slide rule (he was never seen without that
rule, sticking out of some pocket) into a city job. Despite little
experience he had completely snowed the Council into believing he was some sort of *nouveau* Einstein. Lucas grudgingly admitted he was a competent engineer but he had
always been suspicious about the accent. Selzac made no attempt to hide his attitude that Sequoia was only a brief in-
troductory interlude in a brilliant career. He had caused Lucas
some inconvenience on several occasions when he had seen
fit to question the load-bearing qualifications of Lucas's spans.
(Once after arguing patiently for an hour Lucas had seized
the slide rule from Selzac's pocket, demonstrated in a few flips
that the span in question was capable of supporting the full
weight of a loaded logging-truck if necessary, and jammed
the rule back into the engineer's pocket. Selzac had turned
quite white, but only said, "Hm. So," and nodding very
thoughtfully walked away, his hands clasped behind his back,
stooped as if he had all this time been absorbed in pondering
arcane theorems and had only briefly been interrupted by a
yapping dog.) Lucas had seen Selzac once on a pack-trip into
the Sierra, an eerie encounter. He and Sally had stopped beside the trail for lunch when the apparition of Selzac emerged
from the dust ahead. He was alone, walking at a killing pace;
he wore high Italian boots, lederhosen, and an enormous
pack. As he tramped past he did not even look up. Lucas
watched his retreating back and realized then that this fel-

low was bent as much under the burden of youth — leder-hosen! — as of intellectual pretension, and almost forgave him. But back in town where the air was closer he disliked Selzac as much as ever.

Sam Wingluff's summons to the City Hall caused some familial static. "Joe's here," he said when Sally protested fear-fully. "He can take care of things this afternoon. They need me down there, Sal. It'll only be for an hour or so."

"Take your gun," she begged. "I'm not so much afraid for us as I am for you. That awful black eye — that fight this morning — it isn't *safe* down there —"

Self-consciously he got his pistol out from Sally's hatbox where it was hidden, the clip of bullets from under his under-wear in his bureau drawer. It bulged ridiculously in his jacket pocket. "Say —"

"Please, John. *Please.* I'd be so worried if you didn't have some protection —"

He could not imagine under what circumstances he would take the gun from his pocket and point it. When he kissed her she clung to him. "I'm just going downtown," he said.

He took Joe's car. For all he knew his own car was still in the street in front of the school, or had been torn apart and carried off piece by piece by those who by nature lay claim to all abandoned objects. In six blocks he knew it had been stupid to drive. Caught in the witless stream of traffic he took an hour to get downtown.

He crawled around the City Hall block. If it had not been Joe's car he would have abandoned it in the street as he had his own. Finally he drove it up over the curb, across the side-walk, and onto the grass under the City Hall maples — his grass; his maples; his vandalism, he thought grimly. But the lawns were ruins now anyway, turned to a campground and given another decade's use in these few days. Several dozen families were housekeeping here on the south lawn. Lucas stepped over babies asleep on quilts; an old man lay on his side on a blanket, a yellow maple leaf balanced lightly over his face; another old man sat erect on one of the benches, holding a shotgun. Guarding his bench the old man stared at Lucas ferociously as he approached. The gun barrel wavered slightly, following; the skin of Lucas's back prickled.

At the entry he was stopped by two kids in the cap, shirt, and armband of the Volunteers. They hooked their thumbs into their belts and planted their feet apart.

"Only authorized personnel allowed except to use the sanitary facilities," one of them recited tonelessly.

"Well, I'm authorized personnel. Hello, Arthur." The other boy was an acquaintance of Chris's. He had once taken apart Lucas's short-wave radio and in putting it back together had goofed in some way. The radio had never worked well since.

Arthur reddened. Gazing over Lucas's shoulder he muttered, also tonelessly, "Authorized personnel's gotta show their i.d."

"If you'd care to look directly at me, Arthur, you might be able to identify me as Mr. John Lucas. The man whose radio you busted," he said pleasantly.

Arthur and the other boy moved closer together. Lucas stiffened.

"Arthur. Now move aside here."

"Only city officials are authorized personnel," the other boy said doggedly.

"Except to use the sanitary facilities," Arthur repeated.

"Get out of my way."

The other boy slowly drew his billy from his belt.

"You do that, sonny," Lucas said evenly, "and you —"

"Mr. Lucas." Arthur's voice cracked although he still did not look directly at him. "It's permitted for you to use the sanitary facilities if you so request. Do you so request?"

"When I want to pee, Arthur, I'll do it on my own authority and nobody else's. And when and where I see fit." The boy looked so stern and anguished Lucas almost took pity on him. "I realize you're doing your job. I also realize you're no more suited to playing soldier than you are to repairing radios." He addressed himself now to the other boy. "You will stuff that club back in your belt, son, and move aside and let me through, or you will find out soon enough where my i.d. resides."

"Oh shit," Arthur burst out. "Let him through, for crissake! Can't you see he's gotta go to the *can?*"

"If he wasn't so goddam big, you wouldna — I oughta report you, Arthur, I oughta," the other kid said fiercely as Lucas walked past them.

Arthur's voice was high and defensive. "We gotta be able to make *some* decisions, don't we?"

The halls smelled of urine.

The office of the mayor smelled of smoke, confusion, and authoritative sweat. "It took you long enough," Sam Wingluff complained, mopping his neck.

"Look here, Sam, this is a public building. If you're the one responsible for those kids down there in front making it look like a goddam Latin American revolution —"

Sam regarded Lucas with steel completely foreign to his round amiable face. "Last night a gang of kids came in here and tore the records room apart, and broke the windows in the assessor's office. And another bunch brought two girls into this office and raped them." He pointed to the floor. There was blood on the rug. "Tonight I'm coming down here myself to stand a watch. Right at those doors down there, and I'm bringing a gun. Harry's coming tomorrow. We need all the grown men we can get for night duty. Kids have to have their sleep."

"When do you want me?" Lucas said.

"Anytime," Sam said. "Just bring that gun and come." He turned back to the table. "Look here, on this sheet, this cross section here — is it a duct or a ventilator, or maybe an electrical conduit? Tell us where it feeds out, will you?"

They bent over the sheets — the fire chief, the current Boys, Selzac, Harry, Sam — spread out on the big burl slab brought up from old Celeste Foster's sanctum. The gun in Lucas's jacket pocket swung heavily as he bent forward. Cursing silently, he took off the jacket and threw it on the couch. He turned back to the blueprints he had drawn years ago.

"That? It's an air-return shaft. It feeds out here."

"So. As I said." Selzac sent out a vindicated billow around his pipe stem.

"I can't see if it comes up . . ."

"All this complex here — here on this page, see, on the floor plan you can see where it's indicated — this is the central core, the utilities stuff. All wiring, heating, ventilation, plumbing, elevators, ducts, conduits are housed in this cluster here, through both stories —"

"But the *basement* —"

Lucas straightened. "Sam, you know there isn't any basement in this building."

"Ho." Selzac nodded and billowed darkly.

Lucas looked around. "What's the matter with you guys? You *know* all this. Sam. When this building was under construction you were a member of the Council. You watched every inch of this place go up. You've been mayor for three years and you've spent every working day in this building. So have most of the rest of you. Now you ask me where's the *basement?*"

"I wasn't asking you where it was, goddammit!" Sam rasped. "I was asking you why there isn't one!"

They all stared at Lucas accusingly. Selzac took his pipe out of his mouth and with its stem traced along a blueprint line.

"*Why?* For the love of — There isn't one because A, there was a beef from the soils-test engineers about the water table down here which as you all know is plenty high, and B, you boys hollered like stuck pigs about the expense of meeting the standards for reinforcement and sealing of a full foundation. You were there, Sam, and so were you, Harry — almost every one of you in this room now! In view of the expense you declared a full basement was unfeasible — that was your word, Harry, unfeasible. I remember because you said it in the same way your grandmother used to say it, '*un*feasible,' like that, when she couldn't think of any sound reason —"

"Let's keep personalities out of this, now," Sam said.

Lucas threw up his hands. "Hell, I'm not arguing. I didn't argue then! I'm not ape over basements. A utility core is neater and more economical in the long run, although not so much so in a two-story building, which is what I pointed out at the time. Don't look at *me*. The decision was yours, everybody was happy with it, and at the time I had my hands full trying to convince everybody that the finishes should be wood instead of concrete. Oh, *that* was a battle! What I mean we've got this big sign south of town that says *Welcome to the Lumbering Center of the World* —" He became aware that something in himself had frayed the knot of control. He stopped.

"Okay." Sam cleared his throat. "The subject under discussion now —"

"Is the nonexistent basement." Lucas shrugged. "Sorry, fellas. That was all resolved ten years ago."

They looked helplessly at Lucas's blueprints. Selzac hummed meaningfully to himself under his breath.

"This building is sound," Lucas offered. "The concrete pilings go down to solid bearing and it's tied together with steel."

"The thing is, John, now that you mention it, is the problem of wood." Sam hesitated delicately. "Wood just isn't much protection against fallout. That's an indisputable fact. You need thick concrete, preferably below ground."

"Sam. I designed a City Hall, not a shelter. You can't plan for all eternity."

Feet shuffled in the silence. "Well," Sam sighed, "we'll just have to do the best we can with what we've got. One thing, we know we've got to turn the rest of this building over to the refugees — with proper supervision of course — even if we can't reserve it for a shelter. All the public buildings are full now. The schools and the Vets Administration Building and the Recreation Center and the Elks' Hall —"

"This government pamphlet here says our best bet for a shelter is the basement of a two- or three-story building," one of the Boys said.

"Or at least the lowest floor," another said.

"What we could do, we could reserve the first floor here, put in emergency supplies and first-aid equipment. Then the lower floors of the other buildings — how many three-story buildings we got here in town?"

"The Professional Building?"

"That's full of doctors' and dentists' offices, they're using them."

"The hospital?" the fire chief said. "That has three —"

"Well, fine, Ed, except that I guess they're using all their space too, for patients, and they're pretty crowded as it is."

"Oh," the fire chief said.

"The churches?"

"We've been asked to keep those clear for services. So far no trouble there."

"The Roxy Theatre? Seems to me that place is the tallest in town."

"Superstructure," Lucas snorted. "Nothing but Hollywood Gothic, that crazy pylon. I don't see how it survived the quake."

"There aren't any more high buildings in town," Sam said.

Harry Foster, who had been staring out the window, turned. "We've got a big basement."

"You got an old house," one of the Boys said. "All those old houses, they got basements. Nobody puts in basements any more. How come about that, John? How come nobody puts in basements any more?" he said accusingly.

"Because everybody uses their garages to sweep the crud into now," Lucas snapped.

"Like John said, you can't plan for eternity," Sam the politician smoothed.

Harry said, "What I meant, the store basement."

"The store!" Sam slapped his forehead. "My God, the whole *block!*"

There was rejoicing. "And two stories —"

"Concrete!"

"Solid, pink concrete." Harry glanced at Lucas, from

whom he had taken a lot of digs on the store's architecture. ("If it had to look like something besides a department store why the Alhambra, Harry? And why pink? You could've copied Monticello and given it a more up-to-date air." "Grandma despised Jefferson," Harry said.)

"And that big basement!"

"It's mostly storerooms," Harry said miserably, "and the new Gourmet Center, of course. We'd have to clear out all that stuff."

Sam clapped on his hat. "We'll just waltz over there right now and take a look. You closed down afternoons like I ordered, Harry? Good. Good cooperation, Harry. We'll just inspect the premises, get things started. I tell you it's good to be able to *do* something! Now maybe that Civil Defense guy'll get off my back." He could probably see the headlines, MAYOR LEADS VIGOROUS ACTION.

Breasting the currents in the street they somehow picked up an escort of Volunteers. A flying wedge of billies locked into place before them; Sam Wingluff marched bravely on; the rest came behind, a fighting troupe of civic leaders. Lucas's gun banged against his hip. He hunched his arm over it stiffly. Harry groaned with every step.

Lucas looked for Chris but did not really hope to see him. To encounter him here would have been reunion, after an unthinkable time and distance.

"I insist," Harry said. "I'll be *offended* if you don't."

"Hell, Harry, I couldn't. Frankly I couldn't bring myself to eat toasted locusts," Sam said.

"Take 'em home then, take 'em home to Mrs. Wingluff or the kids. They're *nourishing*," Harry pleaded. You got little kids're hungry, Sam, you gotta fill their stomach with something. Locusts are high-protein."

"I haven't got any little kids. I haven't got any big kids either," Sam said. "Didn't you know that, Harry?"

"I didn't think," Harry said. "Sam, I swear I just didn't think . . . It isn't noticeable," he offered.

"It's one of the tragedies of our lives, Donna and I, we never had any kids. It's her fault," he said suddenly. "*She*'s the one's sterile."

"Try these locusts, Selzac," Harry pleaded. "I insist."

Selzac carefully put his champagne glass down on the floor — they were all hunkered against one of the counters — and received the tin from Harry. He turned it over in his hands, squinting in the dim light. "Hm," he muttered. "So."

"Heat 'em a little first, add a pinch of salt, you'll find they're delicious."

Selzac tucked the tin in his jacket pocket and picked up his champagne glass. He stared at it. "Empty," he mused. "Hm."

Lucas upended the bottle of Almaden Sparkling Burgundy over Selzac's glass. "Full," he said. "So."

"We both went to the doctor, we both had those goddam examinations, the doc he said to me privately afterward, there's no reason *I* couldn't have kids. My sperm count's right up there. Right up there," Sam repeated, popping macadamia nuts into his mouth and looking from one to another of them. "That's the thing to be sure of. That's what you look for, the number of sperm per cubic inch. You guys ever had a sperm count?"

"Cubic *inch*," Harry marveled. "My God, Sam, it must be millions." Harry liked his guests to be happy.

"Me full you empty," Lucas said to Selzac. "So? Hm?"

Selzac grinned suddenly. He had shockingly broken yellow teeth. With his wide flat face the snags made his grin look like a Hallowe'en pumpkin's.

"I tell you, you guys, you absolutely can't be sure unless you got a sperm count. Done medically. I mean it's the only absolute scientific proof."

"Sparkling Selzac," Lucas said, and poured him out a portion from another bottle, a good dry champagne this time. "Here's to the rule by slide, only fair rule." They touched glasses. Selzac grinned again.

There was a companionable silence. It was splendid down here in the Gourmet Center, sheltered and protected in the smell of cheeses and wine and dust and straw from packing boxes; quiet too, except for the grunts and sounds of cases being moved over in the storerooms by the Volunteers. The rest of the Council, at the prospect of physical labor, had disappeared. Sam had tactfully dismissed Ed the fire chief by instructing him to check on exit and egress regulations re public basements. He had tried to dismiss Selzac too, but by standing around looking dark and absorbed and humming to himself, Selzac had managed to remain. Lucas did not mind, now, that he had. The hideous grin was somehow disarming. It occured to him that this larval youth might possibly become at some later morphosis a mathematical, if not social, butterfly. Who knew? Full of champagne who could judge? "Who can plan," Lucas inquired earnestly, "for eternity?"

Sam reached over and gripped his knee. "S'okay, that wood on the City Hall. I'll tell you something. I *like* that wood. Even if it's not as safe as pink concrete — no offense, Harry — I *like* that wood. You know? It's —" he flailed the air to snag the word "— *woody*. You know?"

Lucas was touched. "Sam, you've got an appreciation. You've got esthetic values."

"Well yeah." He frowned. "Yeah. With wood now, it's, ah, softer, you know? Warmer. More in keeping. Hell, it may not be safer, but it's more *esthetic*, you know?"

"Sam, it's good to hear you say that."

"Hell, I mean, there're some values you just gotta keep. Otherwise what's life for?"

"Tell me something, Sam. You've had that mayor's office for three years now. When you go in there, into that office, into that room, do you ever feel as if you're —" How do you ask a man if he feels your creative presence? "Oh hell. I just wanted to know if you *like* the place."

"I sure do," Sam insisted stoutly. "Listen, it's a great office. No kidding. I mean, I recognize esthetic values, John, I think you know that. And I'll tell you something else. It's a terrific convenience having my own toilet. I've got this bladder difficulty —"

"Well, Sam, I didn't know you were going to be mayor when I designed that office, but I'm certainly glad you find the can convenient," Lucas said. "On the other hand I didn't know you might want to use the building as a fallout shelter, or I would have insisted on putting in a basement. And using concrete instead of wood exterior maybe. But then you can't plan for all eternity."

His head was beginning to ache. Champagne, no wonder. Sitting down here in the Gourmet Center drinking champagne in the middle of the afternoon — He thought about going home but there was the problem of Joe's car and then there was the household itself: even thinking of the intimacy of so many people was stifling. Would he ever again have a bathroom — any room, a cell, a closet — to himself?

"Eleven people," he said morosely. "Eleven people we've

got in one house. Talk about inconvenience to the bladder."

Sam said, "My wife's sister, she's a widow, she and her kids are down from Portland. She feels — my wife feels she oughta do something for them. Give them a party or something, introduce them. Can you beat that? *Do* something for them, when we — She's got a teen-age kid who eats like a pregnant horse. He's got the worst case of acne I ever saw. He's got a double-barreled advantage, that kid. One look at him at the table and everyone loses their appetite, which leaves more for him. He goes into the kitchen after he's cleaned up everything on the table and scrapes the pots!"

"You think that's something, you should see my kid Chris eat."

"I don't know, I had acne when I was a kid, not anything like that bad a case, but brother, I was on a strict diet. *I* wasn't allowed to stuff down just anything and everything —"

"Correction. Only ten people at our house," Lucas said bleakly.

"— And then when he gets through with the entire meal and the pots he pours himself the goddamndest biggest bowl of cereal you ever saw. We ran out of cereal yesterday though," Sam said with satisfaction.

"Raisin bran." Selzac spoke abruptly, his face alight. "*I* like raisin bran."

"Well say now. You might like to try some of this special Indian chutney." Harry hauled himself to his knees and groped around on the counter top. "It's chock full of raisins."

"I get constipated," Selzac confided, pocketing the chutney. "Raisin bran, it is splendid for that."

Sam eased down to the floor, crossed his legs, leaned back, folded his arms, and sighed. "Man, it's a relief. It's sheer blessed relief, getting out of that house for a while. All that women's talk. It's a relief, sitting here with you guys. You know?"

"She doesn't understand," Harry said somberly. "Phyllis just doesn't seem to understand that I'm needed someplace else besides home."

"Sally's kind of nervous," Lucas said. He struggled dizzily to his feet. "I better go home and check. They — they might need me."

"One more. One more for the road. Please," Harry said. "Please. We may not be able to get together like this again. Hell, you can't leave with a half-empty bottle sitting here," Harry blustered, covering.

XIX

SELZAC was talking about his father, who had built a great
bridge over the Raab and later blown it up in a gesture
of political protest. Harry had pressed upon him the last of the
cheeses, which Selzac, his pockets bulging, had set in a thrifty
pile next to him on the floor. Sam sagged against the counter,
asleep, his jowl nested in his collar. Lucas regarded him in a
wash of generalized sorrow: for the mayor in his exhaustion
of civic leadership; for widows, for orphans, for minor de-
pendents, for Senior Citizens; for housewives, abandoned
dogs, the President, hopeful children, domesticated fathers.
He wandered off to look for the employees' toilet. He found his
way up a staircase into a place as black as a Sierra night —
Foster's had no windows on the second floor — where he
bumbled about from rack to rack of ghostly silks, all polarity
lost; he felt that he was walking up ramps. Encountering a
furry thing he recoiled and his heart set up a rattle. He
plunged at last through a door into a small place whose odors
were of plumbing and air-spray. He leaned his head, thundering with the painful fumes of wine, against cool tile as he
relieved himself. He found another staircase which led to the
ground floor. He lurched along the dim aisles of yardage, no-
tions, and shoes until he came to the far fount of light, double

glass front doors. He fumbled with some kind of safety lock and finally in a hermetic whoosh was out on the late-afternoon street.

He did not remember that he had left Joe's car on the City Hall lawn until he had reached the downtown outskirts. He plodded on. What was impossible was, he now saw, impossible. Why should Joe's car survive and not his?

The lowering light bleached old houses, the semi-tenaments and vacant lots that stood between the downtown core (C-zone) and the sanitary distance to the residential area (R-1). This ramshackle strip (R-4) exuded a disembodied quality, as if it were being held in some forgotten file, waiting to be claimed for use by one or the other living factions of town. This street was an artery through which he had driven countless times, but never before walked.

ST. LUKE'S EPISCOPAL CHURCH
SUNDAY SERVICES:
CHURCH SCHOOL 9:30 A.M.
WORSHIP SERVICE 11 A.M.
INQUIRERS' CLASSES 8 P.M. WED.
REV. WILLIAM L. WHITLEY, PASTOR
DOORS OPEN EACH DAY 8-6 P.M.
COME IN AND PRAY

He blearily examined the bulletin board. Astonishing, unrecognizable, was this church approached by foot. From the car it had stature, steeple, stained windows, the old solid aura of reproach. Down here there was only shrubbery and seedy respectability. Just another building rooted in an ordinary sidewalk. Wear and tear. Needing paint. Grubby pennies clanking into the Sunday school plate. He craned his neck, and the foreshortened steeple rose shakily from the wooden flanks.

Its peak seemed to tilt somewhat. He returned his gaze to the bulletin board. COME IN AND PRAY. Ground-floor plea, spelled out. Down to business.

The small foyer was dark and clammy with the odors of a place filled only once a week. At one wall a rack of pamphlets stood against the dark wood. Paper advertising gleamed like reproachful eyes. He took one out and squinted at it hopefully but could not make out the lettering. He slid it in his pocket. The doors to the main chapel stood ajar. He walked through them. He stopped.

The ceiling zoomed upward so abruptly it whistled past his ears. The light — outside so solid and dull, barely utilitarian, — was bunched at the tall windows, transfixed a moment, and then flung out over everything — altar, pews, railings, lectern, font, choir, aisle, vestry, stall — over all the appurtenances of worship, light shattered in multicolored shards.

His numb head swelled. The height and the light were like a blow. The stillness hummed; the air had density and substance. An effect of levitation rustled through him.

Suspended in the lapping silence he moved down the center aisle. The sequence of pews dizzied him. He put his hand on the back of a bench. It was golden and polished, and so smooth the grain flowed away beneath his palm. He bent to follow it. How cleverly the contours of the seat-back curved. How adroitly sensual, with what intimate body-knowledge was this bench wrought. It led the joints as a drawing leads the eye. The polished seat eased the body forward; waiting was the padded rail; and once the knees succumbed all else had been seduced into the supplicatory position.

He put his hands on the back of the pew in front of him and rested his forehead. He closed his eyes. Upon his cheek he felt the fractions of light as it sluiced in low through the great windows; he could almost hear them splash against the palings of the organ. There was a quality of waiting in the tinctured air.

What was expected of him? Already he was upon his knees. He rested the enormous heaviness of his head against his hands and felt the tendons of his neck relax. How much strength it took to hold up the brain-case. And yet through the softened muscles he felt an increased pressure of expectancy. What else was he supposed to do?

Pray. He was expected to pray. "Oh Lord," he murmured experimentally.

The quality of waiting bore heavier. He could feel it in a ridge against his neck and across his shoulders. A fancy formed within him: that the shadowed curves of the ceiling were those of a huge ear, translucent, throbbing with attention, cupped to catch his very breath. He stirred uneasily. How to deflect this excruciating attention from himself?

"Oh Lord," he said aloud, "bless us."

The outward rim of the earflap inclined slightly. "Bless the poor and needy," he said rapidly, fending it off, "the weak. Everyone who needs Thy help. Bless the widows and the orphans and the Senior Citizens. Bless Sam Wingluff," he continued more urgently, "and husbands and fathers and the President and Prime Ministers and executives, all the people who have to lead. It's not easy to lead, O Lord."

Kneeling alone in this sealed place he all at once felt his fancy seized and carried off by a fierce conviction, as a hawk seizes a dove: he was attended. The Ear listened.

"Help us!" he cried. "Save us!"

His tongue was enormously thick. He felt he was about to faint. Released tears filled the cavities of his head and seeped into the orifices of his body. "Oh God," he gobbled, "You were supposed to have made us. You're supposed to be our Father. You're supposed to love us no matter what we do —"

The ceiling split. It opened and came together with a clap that shook down dust. Wildly the light scattered. He screamed.

"I'm so *sorry* . . ."

It had detached itself from the shadows behind the organ. It moved around the piled choir robes and stood near the rail. "I'm so sorry," Sarah Shaw said. "I — my foot slipped and hit the bars."

She came slowly down the steps. The aura of fading chords trembled about her. She came and stood by his pew. "I didn't mean to disturb you. I'm so very sorry."

He picked himself up from his knees. The gun in his jacket pocket banged against the bench. He steadied himself. When he could speak he said, "You — sitting there like a spider —"

She bowed her head.

"Damn you, Sarah. Up there at that organ — you could have let me know." He dragged out his handkerchief and violently blew his nose.

"But the organ was on. Didn't you hear the humming?"

That sense of weight, of listening: from a subliminal source. The throb of a resting organ. He pressed his handkerchief against his face.

"I honestly didn't hear you come in, John. I was going through my music, and when I looked up you were kneeling, and I —"

"You didn't want to speak while I was kneeling." He balled the handkerchief and jammed it into his pocket. "Seeing a person kneeling is like seeing him naked."

She was silent.

"I was praying," he said savagely. "I don't believe in it but I was praying anyway. Not the act of an honest man, Sarah. Nobody likes to be caught that way."

"I'm sorry." She lifted her face; he saw it for the first time here. It was so harrowed, so old, his fury drained.

"Forgive me, Sarah. I — I've been down at Harry's store drinking champagne and I guess I had too much."

"I'm afraid," she said. "I'm terribly afraid."

Although he did not want to touch her he took her hands in both of his. Her skin was cold; he had the feeling her hands might come off at the wrists and he would be left holding only these icy parts.

"I can't seem to be able to believe in it," she said in a remote tone. "The possibility of death. My own death, Marina's death, Howard's death, people I know . . . We all die someday but it's so hard to believe in it."

He felt a pang of fear. "But you pray. You must get some comfort. You come to church every Sunday, you must have some belief —"

She pulled her hands away. "How do I know if I believe in my prayers or not?" She said harshly, "If I can't understand about death how can I understand about prayer?"

From the days of his youth, past the fizz of youthful atheism, through the cooling years of the struggle for truth and the arrival at a cautious agnostic balance, there had still remained with John Lucas the acknowledgment that there were those who could believe. It had been for him like dwelling in the shadow of a mountain which he could never scale but could nonetheless imagine. He could imagine the possibility of the mists clearing and the sun striking the peak; and even if for him it seemed it must be a mirage there was still the possibility: it might be real. It was the weight of this enormous possibility, the testimony of seeing and believing eyes, which sustained his position of doubt. And now the balance was tee-tering. What if all these others, the holy Popes and the decent Sarahs of the world, were suddenly to cry, *I am not certain I see it, I am not really sure it is there . . . ?* The mountain would indeed be gone. The Eminence would be lost to a flat and final reality, that barren tundra open to the coldest winds, where naked humanity must huddle unprotected even by pos-sibility, their only shelter that of their own stature. No man was as high as a mountain.

This woman — this intelligent woman, this serene and strong person, this person of powerful gifts and invulnerable aspect, this church organist — stood before him disintegrated by doubt. She had begun to weep. Had he had any part in this corruption of belief? Terror filled him: that there might be nothing more. Nothing more than this anguished woman and himself, standing in an empty church; that they had had all their lives and now there was nothing; that they had made themselves no more than what they were; that they were all there could ever be.

The silence was an empty shape around them. They cast no shadow here.

In all of a life, in all of a single man's single life, there had to be something he could know! There had to be one un-clouded solid mountain, one single clear vision he could set his eyes on.

He raised his face to the high silent arches, the mysterious groins, the dim apexes; how could this silence be destroyed? How could veils be ripped off, Mystery pried open, the place revealed where the Secret dwelt? Why did it have to stay hid-den? Why in all these eons couldn't it show itself? Once — just once in a man's lifetime which encompasses the same slow years as a saint's — couldn't there arrive a sign? God was always demanding proof of man — even in this lowly nature proof of mercy, love, pity, concern. Honor thy father and thy mother. Do unto others. Offer unto Caesar. Brighten the Corner.

And Him? Oh there were corners here — dim and silent and terrifying corners, unlit caverns, yawning caves in whose blackness could only be sensed the drip of eons, unimaginable stalactites. Could He not even show himself in His own house?

He lunged down the aisle, mounted the altar steps. White linen, brass candelabra floated coolly againt the prisms of the window. The golden cross hung in the bisected light. The whiteness of lambs was blinding; the Babe's face was glazed with paralyzing innocence. The Wise Men worshipped knowingly, wearily, their ancient aspects pleated in strips of lead; in the highest curve the coronas of angels undulated with discreet love. WINDOW GIFT OF MRS. W. T. HALLENDAR, IN MEMORIAM. Light, colored bits, in fond memoriam of a lost Illumination.

Under the muffling linen, then? The Ark, the Residence? He laid hold of the cloth. The brass toppled, clanging like a gong. John Lucas gazed down at the naked table.

The echo of the gong rattled off; the smell of wax rose to his nostrils. The ruptured silence refurled fastidiously, as if withdrawing from an idiot's touch. The polished surface of the table had a faint network of old scratches.

The light had faded. The jeweled brilliance had sloped off and the dusk thickened unstirred. What man had the power to flush out this mighty Presence, to fight with it, bring it to the light of common day and look upon its face? An adversary: that is what a God would have to be.

The crumpled linen was heavy in his fists. He laid it back over the table, smoothing it awkwardly. He picked up the candelabra and set them back on the altar. Some of the tapers were broken. He groped in his pocket for the small knife he carried on his key ring; with its blade he pared down each candle until they were all the same length. He inserted them in the holders.

He stepped back, gave a stiff nod like a salute, and turned. Whatever else was due here, courtesy at least he could render.

XX

THE next morning Lucas called Sam Wingluff.

"You said you needed some help patrolling. Where can you use me?"

"John!" Sally said behind him. "You *promised* —"

"Don't ask me," Sam said. "*I'm* not in charge. They've got somebody else bossing the job now. Ask *them*." He hung up.

"You *promised* you'd stay with us —"

"I said I'd wait. I'm not waiting any longer." He dialed Sam's number again.

"When your own family needs —"

"Ask who?" he snapped to Sam.

"A-a-ah, I'm sorry. I thought you knew. They finally got here last night. Ripped off my chevrons and drummed me out. I can't say I remember our interview. Must have been impressive. Forgot to give 'em the keys to the city, I suppose," Sam said glumly.

"*Who?*"

"Who, hell, the Law. Don't you ever go to the movies? Martial J. Law & Co. Troops entering the besieged stockade. Snappy salute. Pass over the sword. *Relief reporting*, *sir*, and you can go to the showers now." Sam said bitterly, "I don't mind telling you I thought they handled it damned tactlessly.

Might as well tell a man he's no use any more. Unnecessary in his civic functions. Only the titular head. They elected me and now all they've got is a titular head. We've lost our powers of representation. Mark my words, people're gonna beef."

"Troops arrived? No, I didn't know."

"Troops?" Sally said fearfully. "Soldiers?"

"Real genuine uniforms all the way down to Arctic underwear. Some young squirt entirely covered with brass buttons is down there in my office right now sitting on a pile of signed and sealed documents the heft of a phone book which entitles him to turn the entire county into a military camp. Getting boot marks all over my nice bathroom, I suppose — pardon me, latrine. If you want to volunteer for anything call *him*. He'll probably run you through the FBI, short-arm inspection, and a session with the psychiatrist before he'll let you —"

The man who answered at Sam's office had a Southern accent. He asked for Lucas's age, serial number, criminal record and Reserve status, and told him to please remain near his telephone at stand-by.

"You can relax," Lucas told Sally bleakly. "They just want me to stand by. I don't think they're going to want amateurs."

That first fresh shock of terror which had welded them together could not be sustained forever. The bond crumbled and each of them was left alone. Even in the narrowing squeeze of household intimacy they were alone. They waited in the aimless, disordered way of children who have been sent outside, while in the house behind locked doors the parents desperately attempt to settle a quarrel which concerns their very existence.

Mark continued to build his tower, but John Lucas thought the child no longer remembered why. Surely Mark once believed, at the moment of its conception in his mind, that this tower was an urgent and necessary thing. Now he had lost the vision and only dull urgency remained. He prowled the house at night collecting: strings, beads, cups, envelopes, buttons, vases, shoes, pots, hangers, soap. He lugged them to his room and attached them any old way, without joy of creation, to the monstrous nest in which he was all but sealed. It was as if by surrounding himself with objects he sought to obliterate his own outline. Sally, raddled by worry and helplessness, alternately railed and wept over him. He lay and watched her silently and pleated the bedspread with his fingers. His whole body was shrouded in silence. Her words did not reach him but were lost somewhere in the furrows of his rumpled sheets, his nightclothes which he refused to allow her to change, hoarding in their fabric all the specks of protection he netted in his wanderings. He harbored silence inside him as if it were strength. Aroused one night by Sally's voice Lucas came upon her in the hall, squatting with Mark in her arms. "There isn't any Bigfoot," she was saying in a frantic whisper. "Oh Mark, you *know* there isn't any such thing as Bigfoot." In her grasp the child's limpness was a towering rejection. His head moved stubbornly back and forth, like a metronome. "But there isn't! Mark, can't you believe me? Can't you believe your own mother?" The head lolled rhythmically, side to side, eyes shut, face closed off. "Listen, Mark. Now listen. In the first place, if he's in the mountains, how'd he get *here?*" she said with cunning. "Right down here in the town? Why, they'd have seen him. They'd have captured him and killed him," she said, "so you see he *can't* be here. Bigfoot can't possibly get you because you're here in this town. You see? So you're safe. You're in a *safe place.*"

Mark continued to shake his head.

*   *   *

The other children were digging a trench in the backyard. Released from school, they joyously devised projects. Jennie and Cis, entwined in fiercest friendship, bossed the job; the younger neighborhood children — and some strange children Lucas did not recognize — brought shovels and spent the daylight hours digging up the lawn in back of the trees. The trench was now quite long and deep. It must have been hard work for such small children. They had to cut through a mesh of wiry tentacles (*Sequoia sempervirens* is surprisingly shallow-rooted, a surface feeder) and the ground was clayey. But they labored on it and only stopped for meals, quarrels, and bedtime. Perhaps they should not have been allowed to dig up the lawn that way, but it kept them happy and occupied. The house was crowded enough.

Inside, caution soaked the rooms like a gas. They trod cagily. Their encounters were servile with politeness. The radio, TV, all instruments of communication except their own real voices served them. A prime law of meticulous division had been enacted; it was only this tacit tenet which held their society together, like the bonding force between unequal bodies. All was apportioned with justice and exactitude: work, time, food, space, bathroom privileges. As they passed each other they hissed and bowed with Oriental courtesy. If they could have melted into the corridor walls they would. And it was always, it seemed to John Lucas, time for the baby's nap. That kid slept more than he could ever remember his own. Mike was in the throes of toilet training too; he was taken to the potty protesting, clutching his incipient manhood in an agony of indecision ("Do you? Do you have to go, Mike? *Potty*, Mike?"). Lucas found himself wondering uneasily if he, too, needed to go — a dozen times a day it seemed. In bathroom privileges Mike was a hundred times more equal than the rest. Lucas resented it, and was ashamed.

At the end of every meal Barbara silently took her plate, upon which she had hoarded a little mound of tidbits from her own portion, and to which Joe also silently had added, and went with it out to the garage. The dog Fritz, who was fitful and barking during the night and during the day dozed in morose apathy, would hear her coming and begin to ricochet off the door. Thump, thump he would crash against the door until it was opened; his jaws clomped on the food, his moment was instantly over. Barbara reappeared carrying the empty plate like a grim trophy of some barbaric — *she* would have them feel — rite. Sally had elected to ignore it but Lucas could see the skin at the edges of her scalp pull like a purse-string. Her waking face had begun to pucker from it.

They slept in strange and various places — in bedrolls, on couches, on chair cushions on the floor. Lucas and Sally had taken the living room. One night an unheard-of moon stole like a burglar in the tall windows and fingered their faces. Sally's was lovely then; the strings were loosened and her beauty fell over her face like a covering. Lucas watched her until the moon had once again been swallowed by the omnipresent fog. There were rustles in the chimney. Once he awoke toward dawn, and was certain that a note — a single clear soft black key — had been struck on the piano. The oscillations of the wire still hummed faintly in the studding of the walls and along the ceiling beams. He lay and stared into the shadows; but before the note had exhausted its tiny vibrative energies in his ear he was asleep again.

The outside world had become something to be ventured into with strategies, maps, and alternate routes. A hundred-dollar check tucked into the pocket of Hacker Hackett's rayon sports shirt held a place in an elite line which formed at off hours, after dark, at the back door of Hackett & Son. That ticket entitled the donor to purchase, at a single visit and with the further payment of a "luxury tax," a half-case of chicken gumbo soup, two frozen Chun King Chow Mein TV Dinners, six cans of chopped olives, a stick of margarine, two pounds of variously decaying fruits and vegetables, a quart of buttermilk, three boxes of Bisquick, an extension cord, and all the hand lotion and Drāno he could carry away. Other visits, other varieties.

There was looting in the cities and it was forbidden for unauthorized personnel to use the main arterial highways except at certain hours. Supplies to Sequoia got through very spottily. An entire van of Early American maple furniture managed to sneak past the line on Thursday. The Red Cross and Society of Friends sent out several truckloads of food, clothing, and medical supplies; all except one of these were intercepted fifty miles down the highway at the largest state park, where some five hundred families were camped in doubled quarters and there was a threat of a serious epidemic (diarrhea, vomiting) from a polluted water supply. The Mercy Truck that got through to Sequoia contained clothing, which nobody seemed desperately to need. The ladies of the combined Church Guilds were cutting up the clothing to make sleeping bags for those families camped in the designated areas of town.

Word went around that a few of the refugees were moving out of Sequoia for small inland towns in Oregon and California. Some of these towns made it known that they would throw up barriers of armed citizens to keep the refugees out. Sequoia had become famous overnight.

On Thursday afternoon an edition of the San Francisco

Chronicle mysteriously appeared on subscribers' doorsteps. They pounced on it like a note thrown in through the window of a cell. It was Tuesday's paper but nobody cared. News heard over TV was like a Chinese meal; it fed you but an hour later you were hungry. News in a familiar paper was lingering nourishment. They tore it apart and apportioned it with elaborate care. Lucas took the front page, Joe the green section, Sally the columns and editorials, and Barbara the classifieds and the funnies.

"I dibs for the funnies when you're through," Miss Lundgren said. "I can amuse myself sticking pins into Dondi. The little b-a-s-t-a-r-d."

"Why, I think Dondi's wonderful, just wonderful," Barbara said.

"Hm." Lundgren skewered her with a clinical eye.

"He's got a terrific philosophy, really. I mean, all those awful things happen to him but he's always so cheerful. I think it's wonderful for a person to be *cheerful* when things go wrong, I really do." She looked around the table.

"Barb," Joe said.

"He hasn't got any eyeballs," Lundgren said. "I can't stand kids without eyeballs. Now, Orphan Annie, I can stand *her*."

"They don't carry Orphan Annie in the *Chronicle*," Lucas said.

Joe said, "Orphan Annie hasn't got any eyeballs either."

Lundgren bent upon him a tolerant countenance. "Wrong. She hasn't got any *pupils*. It's the eyeball that counts. That kid's all eyeball," she said admiringly.

"Frankly I don't see what that's got to do with it," said Barbara. "Everybody thinks it's so smart to be cynical. Everybody —"

"Barb," Joe warned.

"I don't care," she said unsteadily, but she retired behind the funnies. *A near miss*, Lucas thought; *a close one*. He reached over and traded sections with Sally.

HERB CAEN

The Walking Caen: A city waits . . . and while the fog creeps in, the creeps creep out . . . Over the great Gate they creep, the deserters, the fearful, their car lights woven together in strands of panic, tightening about the lovely throat of the City . . . She stands tall, pale, silent, an aristocrat who has survived fire and thunder from below, composed and courageous while down in her streets the hoarse alarmists scrabble . . . Waiting . . . And down on the waterfront a Skid Rowgue takes a last pull on his chianti bottle, tosses it over the pier, and squints out at that deserted shadow in the Bay, the once-fortress island of Alcatraz . . . "Man," he says with cheerful contempt, "that's where I was once. That's where you are if you're scared. You're locked up, man," and with a hitch of his pants he rolls off to find some action . . . Free, man . . . And the frantic cars purl their choking necklace of lights across the bridges . . . and a City waits . . . and hopes . . . and has faith . . .

EDITORIAL

It is estimated that close to 18,000 persons have left the Bay Area since Sunday night. "It is precisely this sort of panic which the Civil Defense Program is suppose to avert," the mayor's Special Committee reports in an open letter to news media. "Why has it not done so? The obvious conclusion appears to be that the Program has been unrealistically planned." It seems to us, the editors, that this Special Committee, rather than complaining of the past, should be taking a close look at the future. Instead of casting blame, it should —

FREDDY CRITICIZED BY TEACHER

Berkeley, Calif: Alfred Weiss, science teacher who first broke the news of Freddy Gates's controversial claim to have spotted a Communist warhead missile he says is orbiting the earth, stated today at a press conference that Freddy should not have released his predictions to the public. "When Freddy said that the warhead had developed a wobble and that this might result in a disastrous failure of control over the missile, he was overstepping his field," Weiss said in a prepared statement. "Freddy is, after all, an amateur theoretical scientist and as such should not be involved in any judgments. That's applied science, and there is no place in pure science for such speculation." When asked if that meant Freddy was only guessing as to the nature of the orbiting body, Mr. Weiss, who appeared somewhat nervous, stated: "A venture into any other field such as the prediction as to whether or not the Communists would attempt to manipulate the warhead into a hovering orbit only obfuscates and hampers the theoretical scientist's approach. As his teacher I have tried very hard to guide Freddy to the scientific attitude. 'Facts,' I have said over and over again to him, 'facts only, Freddy. Everything else is clutter.' " . . . A spokesman for the AEC, when asked to comment on Weiss's statement, said only: "He's getting scared. All this reaction, all this panic have scared him. 'Pure science,' baloney. It's a fraud. If the U.S. public chooses to continue to believe these two fraudulent conspirators, which it seems to be doing, there is not very much anybody can say to alleviate the present widespread hysteria."

GLOSSOLALIA CONTINUES TO PLAGUE CHURCHES

The practice of glossolalia, or "speaking in tongues," has not been stamped out in the modern church but instead has gone underground, a high official of the Episcopal diocese said today. In many churches throughout the state there has been a resurgence —

Barbara, finished with the funnies, wandered off to watch TV. Sally winced as the sound rumbled from the living room. "My goodness," she murmured, "I keep forgetting how loud that thing is. Normally we just never have it on." This was meant to be a criticism of Barbara's intellectual poverty; Lucas saw that Joe understood this. "I think she's seeing if there's any news," Joe said tightly. They knew this was not so, that Barbara complained about interruptions in usual programming; but after a pause during which Sally smiled directly at Joe in a steady cold beam, and Joe stared at his paper, Lundgren slapped her hand on the table and got up heavily, saying that now Dondi'd gotten her bile flowing she guessed she'd better get back to work.

Lucas watched her go, enviously, to the quiet room where her only company was a sleeping child.

"Joe," Barbara called presently. "Joe!" They stared at each other; they hurried to the living room.

Barbara pointed to the screen on which a newscaster, flanked by two enormous globes, was reading from a script. The newscaster's voice was smooth but the script trembled slightly.

. . . repeat, claims that the so-called warhead satellite, whose existence has been the subject of so much controversy, may be visible late tonight if the cloud cover clears over northern California. Freddy Gates, the boy genius whose "revelations" concerning a secret Chinese death-weapon have sent a nation into near panic, tonight scored at least a partial victory when the official announcement was made an hour ago that there is indeed a new orbiting body, but that it is a recently launched communications satellite. In a statement just released to the press, Freddy said: "Yesterday they wouldn't admit there was something new orbiting. Now today — after many people actually saw something over western Canada last night — they come out with this new Telstar explanation. If it was just another Telstar why didn't they come right out and say so in the first place? Why did they cover up? They say I'm the one trying to fool the American public. If this cloud cover clears over California anybody with two eyes will be able to see that the satellite isn't even remotely like the appearance of bounce-relay globes. It doesn't even move the same. Because of its movements, not free-orbit at all, but erratic, I would say it is definitely being manipulated, probably in an attempt to get it into a hovering attitude." Shortly after Freddy issued this statement he was placed in protective custody by the FBI, which is said to be investigating evidence that the boy was seen only a week ago in the company of a well-known Communist agitator.

— And here is another bulletin. There is an unconfirmed report that a top-ranking Canadian scientist says that he observed the satellite in its pass over British Columbia last night, that it is definitely not a bounce-relay body as it has little reflective surface, and that there are distinct indications that Freddy Gates's theories are not beyond the limits of possibility. We repeat: this is an unconfirmed report.

— Here is an official bulletin from the National Civil Defense Headquarters in Washington. "The satellite which may be seen at approximately three-forty-three tonight over northern California is a recently launched experimental communications orb of radically new design. It is not a Chinese weapon. Citizens are urged to ignore rumors, utterly false and fed by enemy sources, among which Freddy Gates is under investigation as a suspect. To repeat: the satellite which may be seen tonight if the cloud cover clears over northern California is an experimental communications —

"What does it mean? Joe, what does it mean?"

"It means, Barb, that there'll be a satellite overhead tonight. And don't ask me what kind. Don't ask me any questions right now. Okay, Barb?"

"The children," Sally said wildly. "Where are the children?"

Down at the end of the lawn Cis, Jennie and Mike sat on the grass drinking Metrecal, their legs dangling down into their trench.

"How do you like our hole, Daddy?" Cissie asked.

"Hole," Mike echoed, pointing with his cup. He had trickles of Metrecal on his bare stomach, which hung out in the split between his T-shirt and jeans. He showed no sign of discomfort in the chill damp air.

"It's fine," Lucas said. "What's it for, a clubhouse?"

"Yeah. It's our Club Toom," Cissie said.

"Aren't you cold, Mike?"

"Cold," Mike said, grinning.

"I think it ought to be bigger though, don't you, Daddy?" Cis set her cup on the grass and slid down into the trench. "I don't think it's long enough."

"It looks long enough to me. How many kids are in this club of yours, anyhow? Looks like about eight or ten of you could easily stand up in there."

"Oh, we aren't supposed to stand up in here," Cis explained airily. "Come on, Jen, let's show him."

Jennie slid into the trench and they both lay down in the dirt at the bottom, Cis with her head at one end and Jennie at the other. They lay flat on their backs with their hands at their sides in stiff military position. They looked up at him anxiously. "See? Our feet touch too much."

"It's because I'm kind of tall," Jennie advised.

Lucas stared down at them.

"We're just going to have to make it longer." Cis sighed in a work-work-work way. She folded her arms over her chest and squinted up through the redwood branches at the sky, which was a grudging pewter with the coming sunset. "That's all there is to it, we'll have to dig some more."

With his heel Mike kicked some dust down upon his sister's face. She scrambled to her feet, put her fists on her hips, and stared at him with steely outrage. He immediately started to whimper. "*That* does it," Jennie hissed. "That's the end of *you*, Mike Anderson. You are no longer a member of this club." She pointed a finger, expelling him, indicating a limbo so remote that nobody, least of all a miserable two-year-old, could hope from whence to return. "No more Toom for you, Mike Anderson."

He put his thumb in his mouth and wept silently. Otiose tears of sleepiness and despair dropped from him. Down in the hole Cissie lay watching with judicious virtue. "Kicking dirt in," she clucked.

"Get up out of there," Lucas said harshly. "*Get out of there, Cissie!*"

He dropped down in and grabbed her arm. He yanked her up, boosted her by her rump and heaved her out. She landed on her stomach with a thump.

"Ow!" She began to bawl more from fury than from hurt. White-faced, Jennie scrambled out. Lucas began kicking in the sides of the trench. It was useless. The matted roots of the redwood held the clay fast; a few clods fell, the stench of mold rose in his face.

The children fled.

He fell to his knees and dug frantically with his bare hands at the hard sides of the Toom. How they had managed to burrow such a hole in such hard soil, what instincts had loaned them the strength, what deep urgency had informed their cunning, on these things he did not dare to speculate.

XXI

"WALK with me, Sally. Come on out and walk with me a
few blocks. We could stand some fresh air, get out of
the house."

The evening had worn on unbearably. They wandered from
room to room, yawning nervously, consulting timepieces.
Joe, his hands in his pockets clinking coins, passed on his
aimless rounds. He deferred to Lucas in doorways, standing
aside in unnatural postures of apology. Lucas knew this was
as irritating to Joe as it was to him but he understood it to be a
social tic, firmly and hopelessly rooted in the animal sense of
territory: Lucas's spoor was everywhere, long-deposited. This
was his house and not Joe's. He deplored this instinct but he
was as helpless against it as Joe, who finally retired to a corner
of the living room where he pretended to read but was actually
just fidgeting, waiting for it to be time when he could decently
lie down for the night for a sleep he did not need. Lucas was
irritated and saddened by this but he could do nothing about it
which wouldn't seem ridiculous.

"Come on, Sally. Walk with me."

"You're supposed to be standing by. You're not supposed to
be away from the telephone."

"To hell with the goddam telephone!" He had waited, he

had longed for the telephone to ring summoning him to some action, any action. Its silence mocked him. "We don't have to go far. Just a couple blocks. Just to get some fresh air — "

"I'm busy. I've got to get the children settled. They all need baths."

He lounged at the sickroom door.

Lundgren knew he had come, wordlessly, to consult her. "Kids," she snorted. "That Freddy Gates, nothing but a snotty little smart aleck. He's the reason everybody's so nervous, wondering if he's right or not, wondering who to believe. Well, you don't want to pay an unnecessary amount of heed to that little show-off. The world's being overrun with teen-agers everybody's scared to say no to, much less boo. He's just a symptom of the times, that's what Master Freddy is. We've got *adults* in charge, that's what we've got to remember."

"My arm hurts," Kathy moaned from the bed. "Lund-gren, my head aches."

Lundgren bent over the sick child. "I know, hon. It hurts now but it won't last. You want an ice cube to suck?"

"How long will it last?"

"The hurt or the ice cube?"

"Hurt."

"Let's see." Lundgren consulted her watch, an enormous utilitarian dial hanging from a brooch on her bosom. Lucas thought: *That watch runs faster than all the others in this house. It wouldn't dare lag . . .* She pursed her lips around the great teeth. "Hm. It's seven-eighteen now. I would guess that the hurt might be gone about, hm, seven-forty-two. The aspirin, you know, I gave it to you only five minutes ago. This little kiddo, she *lets* aspirin help."

"How long will that be?" the child whispered.

"Until seven-forty-two? Exactly twenty-four minutes."

The child wearily closed her eyes. "Okay . . . I guess I can wait until then."

"I'll wait with you." The nurse stroked the sheet, turned off the bedside light, and settled herself into the chair by the bed.

Lucas hesitated at the door. He longed to stay with them in this calm, dim kindergarten place, where the quality of waiting was filled with mercy, and the clock ticked assurance that pain would stop. The old nurse sitting in her chair seemed to gather to herself all the light from the evening. She was the gleaming center of gravity here, the great imperial figure of remembered youth, the matriarch presiding over the long mysterious wait of childhood. He turned, weak with a sense of homesickness not for a place but for a state lost forever.

The bathroom door was open! He leaped in, seizing the tower, from no physical necessity other than the same sense of conservation which prompted bears to gorge for a long cold winter. Sally was on her knees before the tub, wearily sloshing out the grime-ring — dirt from the children, from the Toom.

"Hey Sal? How about that walk now?"

"Wouldn't you think *she* could see to putting the children to bed? After all they're *her* children, half of them anyway. It isn't that I'm not fond of Jennie and Mike, they're really quite nice children although so noisy, sometimes I — But honestly, she doesn't lift a finger, John! She lets me do all the — "

Listening to his wife's bitter monolog he understood that this was her way of waiting. This was her way of fighting back fear and putting down the terrible helplessness. She had found something to cling to; and if it was resentment, who could blame her entirely? It was *something*. It drew her gaze from huge unspeakable questions and focused it on the small.

I have no such focus. I go around towing this freight of time, I am walking on my knees, there is an incubus aboard.

Can I tell her this? Could he in conscience interrupt her tirade, wrench her from her protection, force her to face with him his loneliness and uselessness and therefore open to her her own?

" — hate myself, but I resent everything she does, even little things. Yesterday she left one of Mike's dirty diapers in the toilet. I had to wash it out. I cried the whole time I was doing it — I was so *mad*, John, I don't think I've ever been so mad! Over a dirty diaper! You know what I did when I got through washing it out? I flushed it down the toilet."

I cannot feel her burden. Shocked, he stared down at her. Once the slightest bruise, the tiniest line of pain on that flesh had bruised and pained his own; once she had been a priestess in mysterious temples. Once she had been a woman of infinite craft, an artisan of the old school; in the early years of their love all was accomplished by her magic. There were no visible seams in the dazzle of her womanhood. True, over the years his eye had sharpened to the barely perceptible flick of the Black Queen as it nestled in his wife's soft palm; his ears occasionally caught the tiny click of the spring which guarded the puzzle box. Could she help it that the contours of her craft had gradually become visible to him? It was not in the nature of man to remain forever gulled, no matter how he might wish it, no matter how sweet the ritual.

Now as she crouched dejectedly before him, crumpled with bitterness, complaining, in need, he knew that he was powerless to rescue her. He could not feel her burden. All he had was clues: like trying to describe the color red, or the precise sound of an oboe, or a pain (his own). *He*, by God, had a burden. *He*, by God, could use some rescuing.

"You're not answering me! You're not even listening! You don't care! Oh, *you* have nothing to do, no work. You don't even help around the house. All you do is wander around — "

He sat down on the edge of the tub. She suddenly lay her face against the crotch of his neck but her body was stiff, watchful, untrusting. She too could not surrender her burden.

She too had once been innocent; she too knew and had suffered the loss of this innocence. To her, he had once been priest and magician. He had once been seamless in her eyes. The shoulder against which she now leaned so vigilantly had once, to her, been a mountain of smoothest marble transcending mere flesh, its warmth and strength clothed in the holy cloth of her most luminous imagination.

Together they suffered the decrepitude of love; the immutable law of mutability had pointed its finger at them. As he sighted fearfully up that long knobby old joint, as he sat on the hard edge of the tub with his wife's head heavy upon him, the only wonder remaining in him was that he had once believed — had perhaps only a moment ago believed — that the very essence of himself was impervious; to time, to change, to diminishment.

"Potty, Mike? Potty, honey?" A wailing, a pounding at the bathroom door: "Potty? Just a minute, *hold on, Mike* — Potty, darling?"

XXII

H E must have come a long way. He did not recognize this part of town. He had set out walking and he had walked blindly in any direction that opened to him, wherever the swarm thinned, toward any street where a stretch of sidewalk showed, any place where he could take one full free stride. He did not know how long he had been walking; once he looked at his watch: only eleven-thirty. He had thought it must be very late. At the entrance to an alley he had come upon two men; they were carrying rifles and they arose suddenly out of the dark. "Hey you," one of them barked. He broke and sprinted. It felt wonderful to run. He wove in and out of black places, around garbage cans, through sheds and garages, tipping over bicycles, setting dogs howling behind fences. He realized at last that nobody was chasing him, and gasping he leaned against a crumbling cold cement wall and mopped his face. He began again to walk. Whole neighborhoods passed.

The tall old house was built so close to the sidewalk that the corner streetlight flooded all but the farthest recesses of the porch. Halfway up the stoop a bald man and a young girl sat, basking in the yellowed light as if it had some warmth, a vacation sun. The man had his hand on the back of the girl's neck, massaging it as he talked, and in the other hand he nursed a large plastic pitcher. The girl watched as Lucas approached from the darkness. She had on a loose flowered shift which did not cover her knees and her hair was up in rollers. The bald man, his paw still on her neck, turned his head and took a huge draft from the pitcher. He offered the pitcher to the girl and she drank from it, her eyes on Lucas. She wiped her mouth thoughtfully and touched her hair with her fingertips.

"Hey," she called. "Hey. You." She crooked her finger.

Lucas stopped under the streetlight.

"Yes, you. C'mere."

His shadow moved hesitantly before him, zigzagged up the steps. He stood at the bottom looking up at her.

"Hi there." Still regarding Lucas fixedly she poked the bald man's ribs with her elbow. "Say hi to the man," she commanded.

"Well hi de hi and hi de ho." The bald man waved the pitcher. He had on some kind of uniform, gray gabardine shirt and pants, a dark blue tie loosened and dangling. His square face was deeply tanned — black it looked in this light — to just above the eyebrows where the pink skin fit like a skullcap. "Hey, thirsty traveler, you care to accompany us in a beer?"

The girl's sandaled feet rested on the stair above Lucas's shoulder. Her toenails were painted silver. The man handed down the pitcher and he drank — beer, tasting like plastic but cold and bitter and very good.

When was it he'd stopped drinking beer? They had had penny-ante parties with friends, he and Sally, long ago when they were first married — pot luck with peanuts and potato chips and quarts of Lucky Lager. After an evening of poker the taste of the beer was brown and metallic as the pennies in the pot. Those days they had strict limits on the game — no man and wife could possibly lose more than five bucks — but none on the beer. They'd worked hard all week for very little money. They deserved relaxation. Sally was nursing Chris then and the beer made milk; sometimes there would be two damp spots on her blouse where the bounty of her motherhood had overflowed; she would laugh and blush and they would have to go home so that she could nurse the baby. Lucas would watch as she lay on their bed with her breast as large and splendidly round as the baby's head; sometimes she would drowse, and in the warm quiet there were only the sounds of the baby's greedy smacks and the malty smells of milk, beer, and baby; the blue-veined skin of his wife's swollen breast was so luminous it seemed to be dusted with specks of silver.

He wiped his mouth and passed the pitcher back to the man.

"You could of got him a clean glass," the girl said.

"He don't look like the type guy who needs to drink his beer under sterile conditions," the bald man protested.

The girl prodded him tentatively with her silvered toe. "Hey. Listen. What's your name?"

"John."

"Hey John. Join the party. I'll even get you a clean glass, okay?"

"Party?"

"You damn right, party," the bald man said cheerfully. "Can you think of a better goddam time for a party? Can you — "

"Watch it," said the girl.

"Gee, I'm sorry, Sharon," the bald man said.

"I can't stand swearing around ladies," Sharon told Lucas, and delicately touched her hairdo.

The bald man looked serious and contrite. "No kidding,

you're *right*, Sharon. I admire you for insisting on respect. No
bull. A kid your age shouldn't hafta lissen to — "

"I mean either you're a lady or you're not," Sharon said.

"Jesus Christ you are sure *right*, kid." He looked at Lucas
sternly. "No bull, this little kiddo's got the right attitude,
check?"

"Check," Lucas said. "Well, I don't want to bust in on you
two — "

"Two! Are you kidding?" Sharon laughed without moving
any facial muscles. She was very young indeed and pretty.
"We got an entire soiree going on, everybody's out back in the
kitchen I guess is why you can't hear it." She got up and stood
on the porch with her pelvis tilted and one leg bent slightly at
the knee. The bald man gazed respectfully at the knee, which
was close to his head. "Well, I guess I'll go in and see if anybody's died in there without me. You're welcome to join us if
you *care* to," she tossed off over her shoulder as she ambled
inside.

Lucas went up the steps. The bald man struggled to his
feet and clutched Lucas's arm. He thrust his face close. "Lissen," he said, "that little Sharon's a ladylike-type kid."

"I can see that."

"Good. Ve-ry good. Because even though I just met her
that kid has made a deep impression on me. The oney thing
worries me is her drinking. You know? Kid her age, she
shouldn't be drinking beer outa pitchers."

"Aah will you quit your *worryin* about it, Eileen? I told you
we got plenty beer . . . Just hold them down, willya?"

Lucas held two cans on the kitchen counter while Milly
ripped off the softops. The foam spilled over his fists. He

swung around with them and they were plucked from his hands. Millie had two more ready; he held and she ripped. "Great improvement, these softops," she grunted.

"No, but I honest-to-God feel guilty about it," insisted the fat lady pressing into Lucas's back, "I just feel terrible about I haven't got my own bottle or something, Milly. Lissen, I could run over and get some wine we got, some Silver Satin that Vern likes? We got a whole unopened bottle — "

"*Get* it if it'd make you feel better, Eileen," Milly said good-naturedly. Her scrawny hands worked neatly, like machines. She and Lucas had got up a good rhythm: slam, grip, pull, swing, release, slam. "Hell, Ole and I don't want anybody suffering at any party of ours," and she winked at Lucas as she ripped off the tabs and the foam spilled over his fists. As fast as they opened cans somebody took them. In the exuberant kitchen crush Eileen the fat lady was a nice bolster at his back. The party had spilled over into the dining room again and out into the front hall. (Rigid custom, evidently, kept everybody out of the two symmetrical dark parlors.) Everybody could see that the dining room and kitchen were the heart and core of the living house. All love had been lavished here, in wallpaper gorgeously splashed with two-foot magenta orchids, in the giant TV set of bleached birch veneer, in the various blandishments of a Barca-Lounger vibrating chair, a plastic ottoman, a plush divan, a table with black-iron legs and linen-patterned Micarta top of orchid hue, and a glorious thriving potted philodendron which sprang from a corner, leaped up the wall, and reached its furthest glistening leaves unto the ten-foot ceiling.

"Not by accident," Milly hollered at Lucas as later they met in the throng near this thicket, "not by accident that thing thrives that way. I feed it twice a week, liquid fish stuff; by

God I swear I can stand here and watch that thing sprout leaves."

"Mo-ther," Sharon protested as she wafted by, "honestly."

"Sorry, honey, I forgot myself. She doesn't like swearing," Milly informed Lucas proudly. "Lissen, you got any house-plants, you give 'em fish stuff twice a week and sta-and back!"

An elderly man scrunched up with his nose an inch from the TV removed a finger from one ear and glared up at them. "Quit yappin, Milly," he ordered fiercely, "and get me another beer. I'm standin by here and I can't leave. *Somebody*'s gotta be standin by here," he snapped.

"Okay, Grandpa, okay. Everybody's standin by really, y'know, we're just doin it looser . . . Sharon! Get Grandpa another beer!" she bellowed. "Why, there's Charlene. Hiya, Charlene honey. This is my other daughter Charlene. Charlene, meet John."

"Hi, Charlene. I've got a boy about your age; he's eleven."

"She's oney five," Milly said, looking down absently as the child took hold of her beer can with both hands and drew it down to her own mouth, "but she's a big kid for her age . . . Charlene, that's enough beer!" she said sharply. "This kid, I never saw anybody so crazy for beer. She thrives on it, no kidding, like that plant thrives on fish stuff. Charlene, I said that's *enough*."

"Honestly," Sharon murmured, arriving with Grandpa's beer. She rolled her eyes to the ceiling. She had taken down her hair and it was now an enormous glistening globe that stood away from her head like a space helmet. She touched the helmet with her fingertips and smiled motionlessly at Lucas.

"There you are!" the bald man squalled, puffing through the crowd with the pitcher of beer held high in both hands. "Hey Sharon!"

Sharon sighed and sloped off, disappearing utterly. Lucas speculated there could have been a secret panel in that old house, somewhere behind the orchids.

"I wanna change into my pink dress," Charlene said to her mother. "Can I go change into my pink dress?"

"You already changed three times so no, you can't change into your pink dress. I already got a pile of ironing up to the ceiling — Well, hi there," Milly said to the bald man, who was bewilderedly looking around, holding the beer pitcher over his head. She reached out to shake his hand. He had to lower the pitcher and spilled some on Charlene. "Welcome, I'm Milly Oleson, I guess you would say your hostess? Any guy in uniform's welcome at this party, no kidding, glad to see you here. You all fixed? You got enough beer? Say, what kind uniform *is* that, anyway? I don't recognize it."

"Greyhound," the bald man said. His eyes roved anxiously around. "Say, I thought I saw that little Sharon — "

"Greyhound *bus* uniform, I shoulda *recognized* it." Milly smote her forehead. "Say, now, isn't that great? You and my husband Ole are in the same line of work. He drives a truck for Apex Distributing."

"Now I *gotta* change into my pink dress," Charlene cried. "He spilled it on me, see, he spilled some beer on — "

"I got the Silver Satin, Milly!" Lucas felt warm jiggly flesh at his back. Eileen waved the bottle triumphantly by his ear. "I slipped home and got it, and some Virginia Dare Tokay, it's all we got in the house but I thought you could use the extra."

"Well thanks, Eileen, put it in the kitchen then, but I keep telling you we got plenty of beer — Charlene, if you don't quit that — oh, okay. Put on your pink dress. What's the difference, who cares about the ironing. This isn't any time to worry about ironing. Put on your pink dress, Charlene, honey.

OLE!" she bawled, waving frantically. "OLE! THERE'S A GUY HERE YOU OUGHTA MEET!"

"Well," sniffed Eileen, "If you don't *care* for this wine I'll just as well take it back. Vern certainly — "

"Unbutton me."

Holding his beer in one hand Lucas unbuttoned the back of Charlene's dress with the other. "One hand," he told her. "Haven't lost the old cunning."

" — Ole, that's him over there, the blond guy medium heighth with the stomach — my husband Ole drives a truck for Apex Distributing, that's beer and wine? If there's anybody knows how to handle a big rig — You oughta go over there and introduce yourself to Ole, tell him you're a Greyhound driver, you guys got a lot in common. HEY OLE. SEE IF WE NEED ANOTHER COUPLE CASES FROM THE TRUCK! Oh shoot, Owen's got him all tied up. You want something done, do it yourself." Milly forged happily off.

"Christ, *Lucas!*"

Signaling with a beer can, Dalton Fox pushed his way over. It was as if they had met in Africa. "Some fat dame dragged me in from the street," Dalton bellowed. "Lord, this is great, isn't it? I haven't been to a blowout like this since I pledged. Hey, you *know* these people?"

"I do now. Great to see you, Dalton. You've sure got a nose for a party."

"If you want to know the truth, I'm on duty." Dalton's face clouded. "I'm supposed to be breaking up this bash. They called me — "

"They called you?"

"Hell, you know, that bunch of troopers or whatever that brass is running the show. I volunteered — "

"Yeah? I volunteered too, and I've been standing by ever

since, waiting by the goddam telephone, feeling like some teen-age girl with a face full of pinmples — You must sound more reliable over the phone than I do, Dalton. Or were you a war hero?"

"Take it easy," Dalton said. "Maybe my name's further up the list — F before L or something, hell, does it matter? You should feel lucky. This afternoon they had me out patrolling some goddam grocery store. Nothing but a bunch of screaming housewives. They should have something better for a man to do than scatter a bunch of crazy women. I mean, I *knew* some of those women . . . Anyway I'm supposed to be enforcing the curfew — what a laugh! — so at midnight somebody reports undue activity — " He broke off and said soberly, "I swear to you that's what they called it, *undue activity*. Aah to hell with it. Christ, this is wonderful. What a place. What a party. Look at that thing, willya. It looks like a living beast."

"Fish stuff," Lucas said. "They feed it twice a week."

"No kidding! Fish stuff. I'll have to tell Shirley, she has lousy luck with house plants . . . Hey, whattaya know, there's old Conrad. Hey, Conrad!"

A wizened little man in a red-and-white rayon shirt with Redwood Empire Machine Shop sewn on the front in script took a chewed cigar out of his mouth and hollered back, "She phoned me last night, she wants to come back!"

"Who?"

"Who'd ya think? My wife."

"Oh Jesus," Dalton muttered. He shouted, "You want her back, Conrad?"

"Hell no. I'm just beginnin to live! Wait — " He struggled over toward them.

"Last month I got Conrad a divorce from the bitchiest

woman in the county," Dalton said. "I never saw a man so grateful. He gave me season tickets to all the bowling league games . . . Hey Conrad, how'rya there, boy?" Dalton gripped the little man's shoulder.

"The thing is she's scared." Conrad scowled up at Dalton. "She was screamin and hollerin and carryin on something fierce over the phone. She says she don't want to die alone." He cleared his throat. "I told her everybody's gotta die alone when you die. You know? Lissen, Mr. Fox, I don't *have* to take her back, do I? She said she'd sue me if I didn't."

"Hell no, you don't have to take her back. She hasn't any legal claim on you any more. Except your alimony payments."

"That's what I figured," Conrad said. "Hell, I gave her six months' alimony in advance, it nearly busted me but it was worth it." He scowled ferociously, chewing his cigar. Then with thumb and forefinger he carefully removed the cigar. "I don't know. Twenty-two years of hell, I finally get so's I can wake up in the morning — I don't know. You know what my first waking thought is, Mr. Fox? I think, so help me, I'm free. She's not here. I don't have to lissen to her and I don't have to look at her. Christ. My first waking thought. You know? I have a cuppa coffee in peace, I go to work in peace, I work all day in peace thinkin I don't have to go back to her at five P.M. I fix me a TV dinner and I go bowlin, man I never did know such peace. I bowled two-thirteen last week, I dint tell you — or maybe you were there? You see our league game with Sequoia Plywood? We smeared 'em. Oh I was hot. Everthing — I just been *hot*, nothin could lick me this last month. You know? You guys ever felt that way? Not meanin any offense to your wives, of course."

"Yeah," Lucas said. "But not for a long time now."

"I kind of felt that way a minute ago myself," Dalton said.

"Well I'm sorry, I didn't mean to spoil the party for you guys, no shit," Conrad said with courtesy. "It's just that I wasn't sure if she hasn't got no legal grounds." He coughed apologetically to fill the pause. "I — I sure do wonder why she thinks she wouldn't be so scared, and all, back with me. I sure wouldn't be much *protection* for her, if it comes right down to it, would I?"

"I guess not," Dalton said.

"What I mean I sure as hell couldn't *save* her from nothin, could I?"

They were silent. Conrad shifted his feet, coughed again, then reached into his hip pocket and extracted a worn wallet. "I, ah, sure do hate to get free advice at a party," he said with delicacy, "so would five bucks — "

"Conrad, put your dough away. I didn't give you any advice."

"I don't want anybody to think I'm some kinda deadbeat," Conrad said stiffly.

"Listen, you gave me those tickets, didn't you? Over and above my fee? Well, that makes it square, doesn't it?"

"In that case I guess so." Conrad put his wallet back in his hip pocket and shook their hands. He turned, jammed his cigar back, and slowly threaded through the crowd toward the back hall.

"Damn that bitch to hell," Dalton said violently. "You know something? He'll take her back. If she keeps up with it. The tyranny of the weak!"

"Weak," Milly scoffed coming up and grabbing their arms, "a couple of you weak guys is just what I'm lookin for to help me get some more beer down off of the truck. Everybody's dyin of thirst."

They followed her out through the kitchen and the porch

stacked high with cardboard cartons of empties. The bang of the screen door behind him ruptured in Lucas some memory so sharp he felt at once against his calves the droop of knickers, felt the clamp of a leather airplane helmet — with goggles; there had been celluloid goggles attached to that helmet — over his ears and forehead. He paused on the step of Milly's back porch straining for the faint echo of his mother's voice warning him (she spoke in warnings then, his life was full of dangers to her) to be home at five. Thirty years vaporized in the *clusshk* of a screen door.

The back yard looked like a truck depot. It was lit in its entirety by a huge spotlight. Parts of machinery lay around, spilling out into an alley so narrow it seemed a car could barely get through; how the truck had been jockeyed in here he couldn't figure.

Dalton clambered up on the van and began shoving beer cases to the front. "Looka that, we haven't hardly made a dent in that beer yet," Milly marveled. Lucas wrapped his arms around a case and staggered to the back porch with it and came back for another. As he received it from Dalton they exchanged speculative glances.

Milly must have caught it. "Quit worryin. This stuff ain't stolen."

"Ah now — "

"You was wonderin if this was stolen beer," she said in an even tone. She squinted at them. Then she laughed and swatted Lucas's arm. "Well, I guess you don't know me and I don't know you so maybe you got a right to wonder." She leaned against the truck and lit a cigarette.

"See, Ole, he drives this truck and Tuesday when this liquor thing come up he was down to Garberville on delivery. The boss was with him that day, Earl Henkle? You know Earl

Henkle, he's got this big new home out by the golf course? You never saw such a snazzy place, I heard they got black light in the powder room, no kidding, he had somebody a lighting expert up from Hollywood, paid all his expenses up, airplane ticket and so forth, just to see things were done *right*. I heard he's got a waterfall in the living room too. Anyway Earl, he's one guy with money who doesn't just sit back on his ass, Earl keeps up. You know? Couple of times a week Earl rides with the trucks, goes all over the territory keepin in touch with the customers, keepin them happy, the personal touch, all the cocktail lounges and roadhouses, no place too small for Earl to sit down and buy the bartender a beer. It ain't by mistake Earl Henkle's the biggest beer and wine distributor in northern California. Anyway Earl was with Ole down to the Garberville area when this liquor thing breaks. A bartender told them, they was at the Green Mill. Well the two of 'em just took one look at each other and walk out of that bar and get on the truck and head home without a word. Ole thought Jesus, there goes everthing, my job, everthing, no tellin how long somethin like this will last. You know? Then Earl he says, 'I'll tell you what, Ole,' he says, 'I been thinkin. We can look at this thing two ways. Either we can bust out laffin because it's so stupid or we can bust out cryin because it's so bad. I never been one to cry much and I don't guess you are either, so what we'll do, we'll just have ourselves a good laugh.' So when they get back to Sequoia here and check in at the plant Earl tells all the drivers he personally is declarin an executive order of his own, which is a bonus and a holiday, the bonus bein what's on their trucks and the holiday bein of indefinite length, and what he hoped would turn out to be a good rest for everybody but not permanent. Which Ole thought under the circumstances was a kind of clever way of putting it. Anyway we waited a few days — I'll be frank to tell you we did a lot of hard thinkin about it, do you know how much good hard cash you could get for a truckload of beer? We thought a lot about how when everything was over we could maybe buy a trailer — we always wanted a trailer, gee they've got the niftiest trailers now, complete kitchens and bathrooms and bunks can sleep six or even eight, we always did want to take a tour of the national parks, the Grand Canyon and so on. We thought too about redecoratin the house, Sharon's been after us to modrenize the front, put glass brick around the porch and make a sunroom out of it and so forth — Well, anyway. We thought an awful lot about it, we must have spent that dough a hunnert times over. You know how it is. Well finally Ole said today, he says, 'One thing I always wanted to do. I always wanted to throw the biggest damn beer-bust this town's ever seen.' I thought about that for a minute and then I says, 'Well, we got the supplies.' "

Milly snubbed out her cigarette, swiped her hands against her slacks, and snapped her fingers at Dalton. "So let's put 'em to good use. Ole sure wouldn't like it if somebody died of thirst in there!"

"Milly, you tell a good enough story, there must be mostly Irish in you," Dalton said. "*I* don't mind drinking stolen beer."

She grinned up at him. "How'd you like a fatter 'n' redder nose than you got already?"

"You two can quit making love and hand down the beer," Lucas snorted.

"*Ro-oll out the bar-rel, we'll have a bar-rel a* — "

"*Aaahhhhgrr,*" warned a little kid on a tricycle, zooming past Lucas's calves.

"My, Charlene, you sure do look cutie-pie in that pink

dress," Eileen purred, lolling against Lucas cozily. "Look at that cute big old *bow* — "

"It's got a spot on it." Charlene lay on her back on the Barca-Lounger, her eyes foggy with beer and excitement. "I gotta go change into my yella, and I got some shoes with red straps — OW!" She suddenly began to jiggle violently. Somebody had switched the vibrator button. "Qu-i-i-i-i-t it," she complained as she lay rigidly bouncing, regarding the ceiling with astonishment. "Qui-i-i-"

"She's gonna get sick. Looka her face, it's turning green," Eileen marveled. She rubbed chummily against Lucas to share with him this wonder of nature. "Lookie there — oops."

Lucas waded out to the kitchen, where Sharon lounged against a counter, staring past the Greyhound man's eloquent dome as she attended the confidence of a scraggy young fellow whose pompadour was almost as lofty as her own; this young man was sheathed entirely in what appeared to be black patent leather. He stood out magnificently against the salmon-pink refrigerator.

" — took out every goddam spark plug in that entire buggy, cleaned every goddam one of them, took out the rings, cleaned them, took off the — "

"Sharon," Lucas said, "will you get a towel or something? Your sister's got sick in the Barca-Lounger."

He edged into the back hall and asked somebody where the bathroom was. They pointed, and he sidled down the hall through a group of women who giggled and put their arms around him and covered his face with fine wet beery smacks. They smelled like a nice warm henhouse. He kissed them back and pushed on. ". . . I put a layer of tuna, and then a layer of Cheez-It, and then a layer of macaroni — "

He opened a door to some dark room and found himself

between two gun barrels. He threw himself on the floor. Two young bucks gazed down on him. "Geez," one said. "How about that for quick reaction."

"He musta been in the war."

Lucas, heart hurling itself against his ribcage, got painfully to his feet.

"We're practicing quick draws," one boy said. He pocketed his gun, crooked his elbow, froze, and suddenly wrenched the gun from his pocket. "Gotcha," he said to the other kid.

"The hell you did. I had you covered before you — "

Lucas looked down at the guns in the kids' hands. They gleamed dully, oiled and heavy. Real ones.

"Get out of here," he said thickly. "Get out of here with those guns. Get out of the house."

They swung toward him, staring at him. There was a pause, during which Lucas's entrails began slowly to coagulate. "Oh?" said one of the boys. His face was blank. He licked his lips. "Says who?"

"You telling us what to do, mister? You giving us orders?" the other said in tones of wonder.

"I'm telling you to get out."

"I see." They nodded softly, almost affectionately. The guns were pointed at Lucas's belly. "You're telling *us*." One of them giggled suddenly, lurched, and caught himself. "He's telling *us!*"

Skewered on the aim of the gun barrels, Lucas fixed his eyes steadily on the boys' faces. His body throbbed with a pulse so heavy it seemed to lift him off his heels with every beat. A feeling of black rejoicing seeded in him, spread rapidly through his trunk and flowered out along his limbs. *Here it is*. The faces seemed to be huge, approaching. He raised his hands, his two fists.

"What's goin on in here? Chuck — Leo! What're you two kids — *Say, now!*"

Milly had them by the scruff, chastened, hustled out of there before Lucas had time to lower his arms.

Like the dog Fritz his moment was instantly over. Over; snatched away; and not even anything tucked in his belly to show for it.

Milly bumbled back, swearing. "Those goddam show-off kids! Comin in here with real guns. *Expect* a crazy stunt like that from Chuck but you wouldn't think that little Leo, well Eileen *said* she was havin trouble with him, all this goin on and all — Hey, you don't look too good."

"I was trying to find the bathroom."

Milly led him out to the hall and flapped her hand. "That's the door over there. Say, your Irish pal says you're an architect. Whatta you think about some advice here? You know that glass brick I mentioned? Around the porch? Well, whattaya think about tearing out these windows here over the front door and putting some glass brick in there too? Sharon says it'd tone up the whole place, modrenize it. Maybe blue. You can get it in that light blue."

As she spoke her leathery face spread out in multicolored wrinkles. The colors were coming from a fanlight over the door and thrown in by the porch light. He stared in awe at the beauty of the colored light as it flickered over Milly's wrinkles.

"Say, you *do* have to go, don't you?" She grabbed his arm and steered him toward the bathroom door, pushed him in and closed it after him. "We can talk about it when you're through," she called. "I'll rustle up Ole and you can explain it to him."

After he had splashed some water on his face and the noise of the toilet had finally died away, he stood leaning dizzily against the bathroom wall. It was cool and peaceful in here. Milly's towels carried out the orchid theme and had HIS and HERS and ITS stamped on them. It must be very late, he thought presently, to be so very quiet.

He went out in the hall again. There was the same quiet here.

How long had he been in there? Had the party ended? He felt a wave of panic. Had he passed out in there? Where was everybody? *He must get home!*

A single voice, metallic, sonorous, far, floated up the hall. He followed it back to the empty kitchen, where the beer cans and cigarette butts gleamed like mica, to the dining room door.

The party was over but they were still here, in this one room, bound and wrapped in tightest silence. The metal voice of the TV plowed on.

. . . landed in Washington only an hour ago. To repeat, it is now official that an ultimatum has been delivered to the Sino-Soviet bloc. Now for details: the President, haggard and grim as he appeared for the first time since last Monday, revealed that he has just returned from a secret meeting with the leaders of the Chinese Communist state, an unprecedented meeting attended by the heads of the world's other governments, which took place at an undisclosed hideaway believed to be in either Switzerland or Denmark. Making it clear he could not amplify at this time, the President read from a prepared statement:

"In an attempt to resolve the perilous situation which has arisen with the overthrow of the Chinese Government and the tragic assassination of its leaders, I have been for the last four days in conference with world leaders and with the Chinese Communist Army generals who are ruling in Peking. During this time it became clearly evident that their demands were intended to force, by intimidation and threats, a backdown by the free countries from our current world position. I do not need to remind you of the cost, in decades of painful negotiation, crisis, and effort, of reaching and sustaining that position. It is precisely upon that position of ideological boundary where our frontier lies; where exists the stronghold of hope for all peoples struggling for freedom and peace, and where are massed the ideals, treaties, and will which are the only guarantees for a conceivable future. . . . It is my opinion that the militarist faction, duped and seduced by impossible visions of absolute power, is staking all existing life in an unspeakable gamble. Let me say to them, and to you, and to all peoples: that gamble is doomed. The free world will never back down. We will never surrender, by one inch or one meter or one moment's pause, a single fraction of our position. We will not be threatened. We will not be intimidated. Nor will the rattling of an arsenal of horrors, new weapons, panic us. For — and let there be no doubt of this — we retain and will not hesitate to employ total retaliative power. . . .

"I return to you tonight from a confrontation in which the leaders of the world faced a small group of men who claim to speak for millions of civilized people. It is my profound belief that the militarists at this brief moment may control, but in no way represent, the great body of citizens of China and the Soviet provinces. It is my profound belief that the Communist peoples are fully as horrified at the traitorous seizure of their government and the murder of their rightful leaders as we of the free world. Every moment that this small faction of vicious men remains in control brings that great country, and the entire world, closer and closer to unthinkable disaster. . . .

"Therefore, I have called upon the people of China and the Soviet provinces to take immediate action; to arise in mass, with every ounce of power and courage at their command, and to purge themselves and the world of this most dangerous bloc in the history of mankind. This message is even now, as I speak, being brought to the Chinese people throughout the length and breadth of their land. Through channels and sources I cannot reveal they are learning of this call. They have assistance . . . Theirs, now, must be the courage to take action. Ours, the courage — for this brief moment — to wait. The wait cannot be long. Pray for them and for us all."

"He's just a man," someone said wonderingly. "Oh my God. He's just a man."

Someone else — a woman — began to cry.

Another sound arose. Unrecognizable at first, it became clearer as it threaded out of the stunned silence. "*Should auld acquain-tance be forgot, and ne-ver brought to mind,*" it rose slowly, eerily. It had the flat, dead-center tonality of the hymn-singer's voice. Lucas recognized it as Milly's. It strengthened, blossomed brassily. "*Should auld ac-quaintance be forgot, for Auld Lang Syne —*"

They straggled in. And then as Milly hit her stride and belted it forth lustily they came in on one surge; they roared it, swaying with it, shoulders and arms locked, one body:

> *For Auld Lang Syne, my dears,*
> *For Auld Lang Syne,*
> *We'll take a cup o' kindness yet*
> *For Auld Lang Syne.*

A<small>L</small>? Say, you may or may not remember me, but —"

"There's no Al here. Wrong number."

"Wait — wait! You *sound* like him. Al? You sure this — "

"This is the Lucas house. Check your number again."

"Lucas! Yes, yes — Al Lucas or Charlie or Bob or something — *don't hang up!* — listen — "

"*You* listen. You picked a lousy time to call strangers." He started to hang up but there was a frantic gobbling from the receiver. "Please," Lucas said, "please don't bother us now."

"In the holy name of God listen to me." the man said. "This is Len Moroney. We met at the Country Club. You took me home — "

"Oh . . . yeah." The man he had beaten up.

"From Seattle. You remember? Len Moroney? . . . Al? You still there? For God's sake don't hang up — "

"I remember you, Moroney. I'm sorry but I can't talk to you now. I'm with my family — "

He chuckled insanely. "Yes, family, lovely family. But what I was calling you about, Al — "

"How about your family, Moroney? They still up in Seattle all alone?"

Moroney chuckled again, as if this deliberate cruelty were a social thing. "Oh they're fine, just fine. But what I wanted to ask you — "

"I told you this is no time — "

"Please. In the name of God." All inflection had bled from the voice.

"What is it you want?"

"Help. Shelter."

The wire creaked with the nakedness of his need. Lucas was silent, appalled.

"The thing is — " Moroney laughed the frightful laugh of a captive who by clowning hopes to divert his captors from the hour of execution " — the thing is, Al, I'm out here, and they won't let me stay, and I said I knew you and they let me phone — They booted me out of my motel first — "

"You've been here in a motel all this time?"

"Well actually no, not entirely." He giggled hideously. "I was in the motel that one night, remember you took me down — say, it was great of you that night, really great, a perfect stranger going out of his way to — Well, I guess you're not that kind of guy, Al, who wants to listen to a gush of thanks and I know you're in a hurry, but I want you to know I certainly appreciate it. That's why I thought of you, Al, as a member of the Club — " He was evoking the name the way salesmen do, as if it had an arcane power, as if by merely speaking it he bound Lucas with a personal obligation.

"What Club? Who's *they*? Moroney, where are you?"

"That's what I'm trying to tell you," he said dangerously. "I — well say now, that didn't sound very polite, did it? What I mean, I'm trying to get my thinking straight here, make it as short and snappy as possible so as not to waste your valuable time, they said they'd give me five minutes — Let's see. I stayed in the motel that first night, then all these people started coming to town — God! Where did they all come from? — and there was this family came and offered the manager twice what I was paying for the room. I *know* that's what they did, because the manager came and told me I'd have to get out, there was this emergency policy that people could only stay one night. The family was waiting right outside the door, I *saw* them. I told him he had no right — it was a public service — I was there first — I would pay him double what the others offered — it was unconstitutional — " He broke off; his struggles were audible. "But he kicked me out, the goddam money-hungry bastard."

"Well, that's tough, Moroney, but — "

"Do you know where I've slept, Al? Anyplace I could — that night I got a prostitute — oh, I was smart, I found a good cheap one and I figured the price was right for her bed. I told her, 'Nothing,' I said, 'I don't want anything from you except a bed, a place to rest my weary head, shelter, that's all, sister.' She said no dice. If I thought I could spend the whole night just for the price of one clatter . . . A night in that fleahole for the price of five — *five*, my God, that tramp'd be lucky to rake in one a week, normal times. I made the mistake of telling her so, she kicked me out — uppity! Oh Christ, uppity! The whole goddam bunch of 'em, just because they can sell their bed instead of their — Listen, the world is made up of greedy people, Al, people crazy with greed. Let something like this happen, they make the most of it, they roll in it, they — "

"Moroney. What is it you want from me?"

" — and then one night the men's room of the Inn, it has a chair in there. All night long doubled up in that chair with my bones breaking in that stinking place, some pimply clerk comes in and informs me — that's the word he used, he said he had to *inform* me — nobody was allowed in there. I said what if I had to pee, then would I be allowed in there, what if I had a bad bladder or something — there's a bar at the Inn, every public bar has to have a restroom, it's law. The bars are closed, though," he said bleakly. "Did you know that the bars are all closed down? First I thought — I forgot to tell you, after I was kicked out of the motel and couldn't find any place, *before* I thought of the whore I thought of the bars, they usually have these padded leather corner seats you could curl up on. Well, they're all closed. They can't serve any more liquor, the emergency. Did you know that, Al?"

"Didn't it occur to you you could sleep outside? Curl up on a park bench or something?"

"*No.* No!" His voice shot up to a squeak. "No, I — " He brought it down with effort. Lucas had the feeling he was holding on to it with both hands, like a huge gas-filled balloon. "You kidding? You think there aren't people piled up double-deck on those benches anyway? There's one guy, an old guy, he's got a park bench staked out he hasn't moved off of for three days. I see him when I'm walking around, he's got a shotgun in his lap. He just sits there with that shotgun night and day. I don't know why, he can't *sleep* for crissake, he's so busy guarding that park bench he can't *eat* even, and what good's it doing him? What protection's he got? Out there under the sky, no roof over his head — He's crazy. Just like all the rest of them he's crazy."

"Moroney, a roof's no protection."

He groaned fearfully. "Oh yes yes, yes it is! Out under the sky it's terrible, you don't understand, it's . . . I'm not an outdoor type," he babbled. "I never went camping a day in my life. I — I don't *like* sleeping outside, Al. Some people are like that. Some people gotta have a roof over their heads. Outside

— dogs, people — who knows what could happen to a person?"

"You could try to get back to Seattle. It's no safer here now. You realize that, don't you, Moroney? In Seattle you've got just as good a chance now."

There was a pause. "No," he said in a voice so fatigued Lucas understood it had drained his final wisp of sane strength. "No. I've explained all that. Tell them, Al. Tell them to take me in. Please."

"Tell who?"

"This guy — this guy . . ." His voice trailed away; Lucas heard him say, ". . . I didn't quite catch the name there . . ."

There was a scrabbling in the background, a sudden howl; a crash in Lucas's ear as if the receiver had exploded, and then silence. The telephone wire hummed in a vast void.

"Moroney? *Moroney . . . ?*"

A distant sound of music arose. *Some En-chanted Evening . . .*

"Moroney — " There was a soft sound of breathing, close and intimate. The hair prickled on Lucas's neck. *"Who is this?"*

You will see a stranger . . .

The whisper sounded like nobody identifiable.

"Moroney, God damn it, speak up! If you — "

". . . Mr. Lucas? Good evening." A throat was cleared. "There now. Please forgive the interruption."

Suave, servile, unmistakable: the voice of Bledsoe. "Sorry he had to bother you, Mr. Lucas. But he insisted. Just insisted. And he *did* have the guest card, and the Diners' Club, or else we wouldn't have let him in at all."

"Bledsoe, what the hell is going on out there?"

"Oh everything's fine, fine, all in order."

"But Moroney — "

"He turned on us, Mr. Lucas. He turned around and was going for our guns — "

"*You shot him?*"

"Oh no no no no. Oh my goodness no. Ernie just tapped him with the butt. Very quick thinking. We wouldn't want to be responsible. On Club property. But everything's fine now, all in order. We'll just take him outside again. We only let him in — " Bledsoe's voice rose a trifle, indignantly " — because he said you'd verify the guest card, and we told him he could only have five minutes — And then he went on and on, and he did sound funny, and when he turned that way — Between you and me, Mr. Lucas, I don't think he's responsible. Pounding on windows that way, following us around for hours, from room to room, banging on the windows, yelling and wanting in — "

"Wait a minute. You're at the Club? You and Ernie — "

" — just us. Taking care of things. Keeping up our end — "

"And you've got guns?"

"We couldn't very well have kept out people without them, Mr. Lucas. You'd be surprised at the number of people who've showed up, way out here, not a one of them members, perfect strangers. Oh, we've had our hands full, Ernie and I. But so far so good. Tonight except for this Moroney it's been quite peaceable. I understand they've got soldiers back there in town now. Tonight Ernie and I felt we could relax a little. We turned on the Muzak . . ."

Bledsoe giggled suddenly. "You should see Ernie. He's dancing by himself."

Lucas had a sudden vision of Bledsoe and Ernie, two faithful retainers, two loyal dogs, roaming the Clubhouse and guarding the plate-glass windows with guns. Muzak playing softly from the ceiling; the bottles of the bar gleaming in neat rows, the glasses polished tidily; maybe they waltz a bit together in their waiting and loneliness; Bledsoe leads, naturally; at arm's length from each other, discreet, their bellies never touching, they twirl slowly and sedately between the empty tables, glide down the length of the buffet and the sneeze-rail . . . while outside in the dark Moroney pounds frantically on window after window.

"You're drunk, Bledsoe!"

There was a silence, behind which Lucas heard the harp arpeggios of "Any Old Time."

"How much of that liquor supply is still there?"

"Screw you, Mr. Lucas."

Lucas stifled an insane desire to laugh.

"The Board will have my resignation in the morning," Bledsoe said urbanely.

"Oh, stuff it. I don't care if you're gassed. Drink up all the liquor if you want. I wish I was there with you," Lucas said, "but I've got responsibilities here and I've got to get back to them. Listen, Bledsoe, when Moroney comes to, let him stay."

"I have worked very hard to get to my present position. I had an extremely tough childhood. This is the first time in my life I have ever tapped the larder, Mr. Lucas. I realize it's a serious offense. My career would be ruined — "

"Bledsoe, I said I didn't care if you drank up all the liquor in the Club or ate up all the — " Food; all that food out there in the Country Club supply room, the walk-in freezer: the cans of artichoke hearts, the garbanzos, the cheeses, the pink hams . . . He thought: *I must tell Sally this;* and then he thought, *but it doesn't matter any more*. The question of food had now become, in this last hour, irrelevant.

"Oh we've only taken what we need. Mere *sub*stenance. Nothing else. Never fear while Koogie's here."

"Koogie?"

"It's my childhood nickname," Bledsoe said wistfully. "But I suppose you wouldn't be interested in that." He seemed to pull himself together. "Well. Fine. We'll see you tomorrow then. Oh by the way, tell Mrs. Lucas everything's ready. Even though the decorating committee didn't come Wednesday . . . Confidentially, they haven't done one damn thing. *I've* done it all. But you tell her things are neat and tidy and all ready for the dance, Mr. Lucas. This afternoon Ernie and I went out by the water hole and picked some ferns for the tables. They look exquisite. Yes, *ex* — "

"*Dance?*"

"Surely you remember? Surely you're coming? Why, I took your reservation a good month ago! The Autumn Daze Dance," he said in shocked tones. "Tomorrow night. Big night. Why, Mrs. Lucas is the head of the committee! And I must say they haven't been too goddam dependable. But at least the kid got the Ice Statue done, it's in the freezer, and it looks — "

"Bledsoe," Lucas said heavily, "do you by any chance know what's going on?"

"Damn right. Haven't I been guarding this place for you? You think I haven't any sense of responsibility? I had a tough childhood. I didn't pull myself up by my own bootstraps for nothing. You know what did it, why I'm successful? It's because I'm *dependable*. No matter what happens, I make things go on as usual for people like you. Excuse me." His voice faded briefly. ". . . *Help him into the lounge, I guess, Ernie* . . .

"Dependability, that's what I'm selling. That's what my salary is paid for, and if all you nuts get together and decide you're going to have a Hay Fever Dance or a Fish and Chips Ball, then as far as Koogie Bledsoe is concerned and until I hear different then that's what you're going to have. If the world's still here tomorrow night then I'll be here as usual at the Country Club — alone if that's the way it turns out, wearing a red vest and waiting on tables if I have to — and by the way, I understand there's been some complaint about the red vests don't match the decor. I may not be responsible for things like sneeze-rails but I sure as hell don't mind saying I'm responsible for the red vests the staff wears. They give some class to the operation. If there's anybody on God's green earth who knows about that type of operation it's me, Bledsoe, and I will respectfully submit this remark to the next committee who tries to change the uniforms. And getting back to the other thing, you hired me to take care of a dance for Saturday night and that's exactly what I intend to do. Oh, I don't expect much credit for it. I don't expect anybody'll get down on their knees and kiss my feet for it. But I'll be here. I don't know where anybody *else*'ll be, Mr. Lucas, but Koogie Bledsoe'll be here tomorrow night at your goddam Country Club Ball."

XXIV

N o, Barbara. We're not going anywhere. Not now."

"But I left it unlocked! I'm sure I left it unlocked!" Barbara huddled on the edge of the couch, shivering violently, her hands clenched between her knees. "All those things — good things, *invaluable* things, Joe! All my good things, the furniture, the TV — "

"Barbara. People aren't going to walk into that apartment and carry out furniture. Not tonight. People aren't interested in furniture, Barbara."

"It may already be gone! All those lovely things — some things your own mother's, Joe!" She turned to him. "Your own mother's things — the Spode, and that little Wedgwood pitcher, that darling little lamp she got in Venice — *invaluable*, Joe, none of those things could ever be replaced, your own dead mother's things!"

"You got a couple of tranquilizers, Sally? Maybe if she had a couple of tranquilizers — "

"I don't know," Sally said indifferently. "I don't know if we have any tranquilizers." She was wandering around the room, holding her arms as if she were cold; every once in a while she would stop and listen. Lucas did not know what she was listening for.

Two-ten.

"How could I have been so stupid? *How* could I have gone off and left the front door unlocked? I remember, let's see, I remember going back to get the blanket for Kathy, I got it out of the linen closet, then I went up the hall and I got my purse from the table and I checked the stove again just to be sure, because of fire, then I put the key in my purse and I went out the door and — Oh I don't *remember!* I just don't remember *locking* it! With all those things, anybody could walk right in, all those lovely things . . ." Barbara's teeth were chattering so the stream of words seemed to be coming out of the sides of her clenched mouth. "And there's the *photographs*, oh Joe, those lovely photographs of our wedding, and the one of us cutting the cake together — "

"You want a drink, Joe?"

"I don't know. I don't know whether I want a drink or not. I — guess not."

"Okay." Perhaps some sense of propriety or dignity restrained them from the familiar comfort of a drink. Maybe they felt how easy it would be to burn up, in alcohol, all their available reserves. They stood in the kitchen jingling coins in their pockets.

"Maybe a drink would help Barb, though," Joe said.

"On top of those two sleeping pills, it might put her out."

"Maybe it'd be better if she was out."

TV sounds drifted in from the living room: a Negress singing "He's Got the Whole World in His Hands." Lucas thought of Barbara sitting huddled on the couch staring blankly at the TV while it played inspirational music, hymns, the National Anthem. *We have not been very good hosts,* he thought distractedly.

Sally wandered through. The dog had begun once again to hurl itself against the garage walls. Sally's face was empty. She had come at last to the end of all the things she could devise to do. She opened the cupboard and stood staring at the rows of cans.

Joe jingled coins. "What do you think?" he said presently.

"I don't know," Lucas said.

"You suppose that kid — there's an off chance he's right?"

"I don't know. The only thing, we can wait and see."

Joe consulted his wristwatch.

. . . *He's got the little bitty baby, In His Hands, He's got the little bitty baby* . . .

"What if that kid, that Freddy Gates, a kid named *Freddy*, turned out to be the law and the prophets?"

"Take it easy, Joe."

"I am! What'd you *think* I've been doing, for crissake?"

"Listen, you pop off at me — "

Abruptly they turned and lurched off.

Like a cat touring mouseholes he toured the children's doors again. Cis and Jennie were together in the same bed; they slept the ardent sleep of small children, entwined in twin-like embrace. The room was redolent with their cidery young breath. Mike, on an air-mattress in a corner of Chris's room, which he shared with his parents, slumbered in a roseate aura of damp rubber, in spite of a marvelously successful Potty at which Lucas himself had assisted not long ago. This room was stripped of the presence of his own son. It seemed to Lucas that Chris's going had cost him one third of his only hope for immortality; now that he had gone his sturdiest guarantee was lost.

In the dim nightlight of the sickroom Lundgren snoozed

upright in her chair, her head sunk on the broad bosom, her mouth ajar; as Lucas peered in, she opened her eyes, stiffly hauled herself to, and checked her watch. He withdrew wordlessly.

He hesitated before Mark's door. As he stood there he became aware of a moat at his feet across which he could leap only with more courage and imagination than he could summon. A yawning solitude separated him at this doorway from his son in there on the bed. The boy was awake. Lucas knew it; he was awake, lying silently in the darkness. From across the chasm which separated them he may have wished to call out to his father, wished to tell him something; perhaps his lips moved. But Lucas could not cross to him. These were the hours when real night is deepest; the hours of weakness were upon them all. He said aloud, "I'm here, Mark. I'm with you. Call me if you want me."

Sally screamed.

"*I'm here!*" Lucas roared. "*I'm here! I'm coming!*"

In the kitchen Sally stood by the cupboard screaming. "Chris!" she screamed. "Oh Chris Chris Chris! Oh thank you dear God." She did not run toward him. She stood by the cupboard and screamed his name, her eyes wide on the back door where her son stood.

He moved slowly toward his mother and put his arms around her and held her. Abruptly, almost ludicrously, she stopped screaming. She did not cry. She put her hands up to his face and passed them wonderingly over his skin.

Chris looked beyond her to his father. "I thought we'd all better be together," he said.

XXV

G OOD evening, sir. Are you prepared to meet your God?"
He had answered the doorbell with his gun in hand;
he had been prepared for violence.

Sinister indeed the stranger looked, but no common ma-
rauder: tall and gaunt in his black suit, all his trappings arrayed about him like a brush salesman's, he had prepared an
ambush on Lucas's porch.

"Sorry, I'm not interested." Lucas made a movement with
his shoulder to shut the door.

"Not interested in your own salvation?"

Lucas switched on the porch light. From the man's pale
unshadowed face and lashless eyes sprang a stream of coldest
beatitude. "The hour is at hand."

"Go home," Lucas said hoarsely. Behind the shelter of the
half-closed door he tried to bury the gun in his hip pocket, but
it snagged and the cloth ripped. "Go home," he said to the
man. "What are you doing on a stranger's porch?"

The man smiled tenderly. "We come to you in the name of
Christ Jesus. Through His mercy and forgiveness He has prepared for you a place in heaven."

"How do you know that?" Lucas said. "How can you possibly know a thing like that?"

The gaze of drenching piety continued to wash over him. There appeared in the man's hand a fan of pamphlets. He held them out to Lucas. "There is a place in heaven for all who repent. Whosoever seeth and believeth in Him shall not perish but shall have life everlasting. If you will read these, all your questions will be answered. Whosoever —"

"How do you know what my questions are?"

He smiled softly. "All sinful mortal man strives toward the light. Jesus is the light of the world. We are the beacons by which the light is thrown into the darkness. We carry His words to sinners that they may be bathed in that light and thence be saved."

"Do you have your own words? Could you answer me in your own words? By any chance did you ever in your life have some questions that weren't answered in those pamphlets?"

"My words are the Word of Christ Jesus."

Lucas had begun to sweat. "Tell me how you *know* this. Tell me how you found it out. Did it hit you like a lightning bolt? Did you lie awake at night wrestling with — angels maybe, suffering in the dark, fighting to see this truth? Or were you born believing in it? Don't quote to me — *tell me!*"

"God is within every man. The Word is within. Ignorance of the Word is sin. Whosoever does not believe on Him will perish and descend into the —"

"I've got children," Lucas said. "They're too young to ask questions. They believe what I tell them. If I told them I didn't know the truth about God, would they perish and go down to hell too?"

"Suffer the little children —"

"And then there're savages, and Buddhists, and intellectuals — all these people, millions of them, unlit by you Beacons — these all automatically are damned too? Is that your

Word?" He found he was trembling. "There are people who have *tried*," he said, "good people, people who are not wicked, these people have tried to understand not just your Truth or your Word but any Truth or any Word, people who've suffered trying to come to terms with some God — Are these people damned too?"

The man smiled even more tenderly, increasing the flow of wattage. The luminous aspect hung over his dark form so steadily it seemed to be a separate image, strung there from the porch light. He leaned over and with a deft flick of a bony wrist set the switch of the tape recorder at his feet. The metallic voice took over so smoothly it seemed to be his own. *Verily I say unto you that if ye trust on Christ Jesus ye shall not perish but have everlasting life. In the arms of the Blessed Saviour shall ye —*

"Turn that thing off. I asked *you*."

— from the flames of hell shall ye be delivered —

"*Turn it off!*" Lucas kicked out savagely.

The man bent and the voice stopped. He straightened and faced Lucas again. The incandescent visage hovered before him not one grain diminished. Patience hung like an iron mantle upon this man; under his austere suit his shoulders sloped off so narrowly they appeared to have been deformed by the constant weight of that patience. Could nothing — questions, brutality, ridicule, reason, blasphemy, desecration — *nothing* quell the flow of this pasteurized unction? Against such pitiless sanctity there was no appeal; nowhere could be sunk a barb of reason or attack but that this pale flesh would become holier. Martyred, he should have been a mass of scars from these encounters at men's doors; but nowhere was his tissue pervious.

He stood before Lucas in his black suit, this undertaker of

souls. On this of all nights he stood at Lucas's threshold, merchandising salvation! Encountering this faceful of macabre love unveiled by any decent reticence for a suffering household, it was to Lucas as if a naked woman had appeared on his porch with a fistful of pamphlets on sex. He had thought he was beyond shock; but there now came to him a moment when minor inroads appeared at one great spring to have become major outrage.

"You won't answer me. You can't answer me. You can't argue or discuss this with me. I know why! Why should you? *You*'re saved!" He was quivering uncontrollably. "You think I'm not, so you don't pity me. That's why you can stand here so coolly, backed up with your tapes and your pamphlets — your tickets to heaven, aren't they? That's why you can bring your own personal Christ Jesus and plunk him down on my doorstep like a prize kewpie, and smile when I ask you honest questions! *You think I don't have questions?*"

The man opened his mouth, but Lucas forged on. "Oh, I know what you're doing here! You're piling up points. With every fist shaken in your face another brownie-point! Every time you punch a doorbell you know that big IBM machine up there punches some more credits on your scorecard, brother, because that's the way you earn a nice plush lot in heaven, right? You work on commission, brother, for every sale you make and the more you suffer for it the bigger your bonus — because that Lord of yours, he sure does like suffering, doesn't he? Well, let me tell you something, brother —"

He was not listening. He had folded his hands in front of him, the fan of pamphlets spread modestly across his stomach. His face was raised to the light, sealed behind closed eyes, and the smile played tenderly on his moving lips as he swayed back and forth in exalted patience. With his head back he appeared to be awaiting a blow — the slash perhaps of the sacrificial knife; his Adam's apple bobbed on the crest of his collar, in the current of silent prayer.

The coldest fury he had ever known possessed Lucas.

"I see I've made you happy."

The change of tone aroused the man; he opened his eyes and saw Lucas's gun pointed at his face. He stared at Lucas across the barrel.

Lucas said softly, "How'd you like to be even happier, brother? How'd you like to see that heaven of yours, that nice property you've got lined up there, right away? No waiting? If it's that great," he continued in reasonable tones, "then you must be anxious to get there. Shake the dirt of this sinful world. Be among your own kind. Oh, I guess there's only a handful up there, just you Beacons, no worry of overcrowding —"

"*John!*"

"And here's my wife. Here's another one for you, if you'd like to try for extra points before you —"

"JOHN!"

Slowly he lowered the gun. He and the man stared at each other. "You understand now," Lucas said evenly to him. "You understand now?"

The man put the pamphlets into his pocket. He bent and closed the tape recorder, picked it up, and listing slightly walked away into the night. The mist dripped silently from the eaves beyond the porch light.

Sally leaned against the wall. "My God. My God." She closed her eyes.

"He was afraid."

She passed a hand limply over her breast. "You had a gun pointed at him. Of course he was afraid."

"If he really believed, why should he be afraid?"

". . . threatening . . ."

"I was not threatening him. I was enlightening him. What do you think he was pointing at *me*? Fear. Him and his pamphlets, his doom — The beacon of fear lighteth up all dark corners."

"Put it away. *Please*."

He reburied the gun in his jacket pocket hanging in the hall closet. He stood regarding the dark jumble of coats and tennis rackets. *His truth in his pocket, my truth in mine.* "I wasn't going to harm him," he said wearily. "I was doing the only thing I could think of to make him understand . . . what he was doing to me. He wouldn't answer me, Sally. He wouldn't *listen* to me. I was asking him honest questions. I wanted to get *through* to him somehow, and all I had was the gun."

"Then God help us all," she said faintly.

"Not *his* God."

She rolled her head from side to side against the wall. "How nice it would be to be able just to believe. Just to relax, forget about logic and intelligence and truth, and simply believe in something."

At 3:30 A.M. they turned out the lights in the house and went outside to the back deck. Barbara, stunned with sedatives, took her stance against Joe's shoulder and gazed heavenward as if waiting to be bathed in holy rays. Lucas and Sally stood apart from them and from each other. Chris, his arms folded, stayed by the door as if guarding it.

The sky over the lit town was a roseate mist, inflamed with a hectic flush. As they stood the flush faded; the muffled noise of traffic slowly, eerily stilled. A palpitation arose, like the slow beat of the distant surf beyond the arms of the bay. Out in the garage the dog Fritz, sensing the change, began to whimper steadily. Lucas thought he could hear the fog dripping from the redwoods.

Sally moaned under her breath. Her face was phosphorescent, a beaded pallor shone from her. Lucas thought he should move nearer to her but he was so cold he did not dare to touch her. They might have frozen together had they touched. The children were asleep. He sensed them strongly in the silent reaches of the house, unconscious, peaceful, composed entirely in sleep, forever innocent in their beds.

Six more minutes. The stillness had become a solid body clamped over him; he felt it close him off from the children, so that he could no longer hear their breathing, smell their warm sleeping breath. When they had been very young he used to awaken at night occasionally, and lie rigid, listening, fearful that this tenuous breath of his children might — from the very smallness of their lungs, the infinitesimal delicacy of their nostrils, pressed so heavily upon by the cold weight of the night air — have ceased.

The dog growled, and then set up a moaning whine. Sally made a whisper: "Shut up. Shut up." She repeated it with strangled ferocity, her face frozen up toward the sky. The dog continued to moan, as it is said animals do when there is a death in the house.

The sense of his sleeping children overwhelmed him; stiffly Lucas crept back into the house; as he passed Chris at the door the boy did not move. In the dark Lucas listened; the dog's whines seemed to come from below the floor, from a basement which did not exist. He groped his way along the bedroom hall, paused at Mark's door. "Mark? . . . Are you in here?"

A flare of pain exploded in his leg. It bore him sideways and he crashed against the wall. Something was upon him in a rush, swarming, beating, uttering small squeaks like a bat's, piping in a high monotone; its flaps and darts toward his face were like those of wings, frail, leathery, horribly dry. An odor familiar and unspeakable plugged his nose. He jerked his head away, gasping, and his temple hit the side of the door.

The quality of the silence had shifted. It may have been this which aroused him. A rumble — perhaps of his pulse — had resumed. The dog had been whining, he remembered. It had stopped. Yet there was still this sense in his eardrums and behind his closed lids, of a turning-up of lights and volume as at the resumption of a play after intermission.

A fearsome languor paralyzed him. He lay not daring to open his eyes. Some deep system of resistance, a leucocytic swoon held him. Beyond his senses there might still burn a remaining trace — a fiery hole, a singeing of the darkness — of some impossible event.

He thought vaguely of the dog. When had it quit whining? What the hell kind of watchdog was he, anyway? Barked all night and all day and then when somebody — a thief? madman? — sneaked in, became silent . . .

Abroad; something was abroad! He came to with a gasp.

His head billowing wildly, he pulled himself up. He listened. Nothing. He plunged down the hall, his arms sheltering his face. In the kitchen he stopped and listened again. There — a scrabbling out there, by the back door, the breezeway, the garage maybe. He wrenched the door open and fumbled for the breezeway switch; he got a palmful of splinters before he located it. The breezeway and the garage step flooded with light. Beyond the step, in there, back where the wood was piled, a shadow jumped. Something dropped with a clatter on the cement floor.

Sally, half-crouched against the woodbox, swooped and snatched the gleaming thing and held it tightly against her chest. She turned and confronted him.

All but unrecognizable, wild, her face was stretched so tightly it seemed the skin must split across the cheekbones. An incoherent hiss escaped like steam between her teeth.

The dog Fritz lay on the cement floor of the garage, on its side against the closed overhead door, a jerking, filthy bundle of fur. It moaned; a slow froth oozed from its jaws; its legs moved stiffly in a rowing, clawing motion. As Lucas watched, the bundle gave a great heave, tottered to a tipsy stance on its feet, pivoted slowly around in a circle twice, and collapsed again. With a long bubbling gasp it subsided and was still.

Sally glared at him as if the force of it would physically fend off his approach.

He reached out and touched one of the arms she was holding to her chest. She shrank from him.

"What's that, Sally?" he said stupidly. "What's that you're hiding?"

He had to force it from her. She struggled briefly and then let it drop. It made a ringing rattle as it rolled away. He picked it up. It was an empty can of Drāno. He turned it over in his hands wonderingly. He shook the can; a few hard grains rattled.

"I don't know what everybody expects." Sally's voice was flat, her lips barely moved. "Somebody has to watch out for these things. You have to draw the line somewhere."

BEWARE, he read, POISON. He dropped the can. It rattled away like a castanet.

"Somebody has to do what's necessary." Her bloodless voice continued. "Somebody has to take the responsibility. There's the children to feed."

"Sally, Sally."

She crouched in the dusty light. "I know what you're think-ing — oh, I know! You're thinking I've done a terrible thing. Do you know how much food that dog ate? Do you know what's been going on? Do you know she's been feeding him secretly — *extra?*"

"With everything else we have to face —"

"Do you know I found an empty can of ravioli in the gar-bage? We haven't had ravioli for three days! *Right on top of the garbage*. I found it just a while ago — just before —"

"Food isn't important now," he said. "Why didn't you save your strength?" He sat down on the step. He put his hands over his face.

"Oh isn't it? Isn't it?" She said cunningly, "Well, you're just not *thinking*, that's all. *I* began to think, all of a sudden, while we were out there, waiting, and the dog was making all that noise — I was listening to him make all that noise and I sud-denly thought *very clearly*, if that wasn't a bomb up there we'd still be here. And *they*'d still be here, and the *dog*'d still be here, and the children — the children'd still need food, and what would we do if the children started to get hungry and there wasn't any? And that empty can of ravioli. And Mark's so sick. So sick, and if he was hungry too, and we didn't have any food for him . . . I thought, *somebody* has to take care of these things, *somebody* has to . . . I was thinking very clearly . . . and I knew . . . I —"

Presently she crept over to him. She put her forehead down against his knees. "I don't remember now what I knew. Just the children."

He took her head between his hands and brought his own cheek down against it. They crouched there together for a while.

"I have to tell them. I have to tell them, don't I?"

"I don't know . . . Yes, I guess you have to tell them."

He helped her up, and walked with her back into the house.

"I have to find Mark," he said. "He can't be left alone any more."

"Come with me first. Please, I can't . . ."

Barbara and Joe still stood out in the night, their faces turned to the sky with the rapt, listening attitude of sleep-walkers. Somewhere a single whistle, deep and stern, had arisen out of the dark.

Joe turned toward them. "What do you think?" His voice seemed to rustle, suspended. "It's after four o'clock. What do you think?"

"I don't know," Lucas said. "Did you see anything?"

"No. Not with this fog . . . But it's after four o'clock . . ."

"Barbara, I killed your dog."

"When was it supposed . . . three-forty-three?"

"What do you think?" Joe asked again.

The whistle, rising, was ominous and majestic, like the throb of engines deep in a ship's core. "I don't know," Lucas said.

"I put some Drāno in a can of ravioli and he ate it in one gulp."

"Over fifteen minutes."

"There may have been a miscalculation."

"Christ," Joe said with sudden violence, "a miscalculation! Now *that*'d be something. Getting us out here to wait to be blown apart and there's been a miscalcu —"

"Just like he ate the ravioli you sneaked out to him."

"If he could miscalculate the time he could've miscalculated the whole thing," Lucas said. "There's that possibility."

"Oh God," Joe croaked.

A siren, a honking, had joined the whistle. Sally's voice rose. "I'm really very sorry Barbara but somebody has to think of the children. Growing children have to have enough food."

"Oh God, do you suppose — Barbara quit pulling at me! *How much are we supposed to take of this?* Barbara will you for once get the hell *off* me —"

". . . K-killed Fritz. She killed . . . I want to go home, Joe. Joe please take me home —"

There was a din in Lucas's ears as of animals shrieking; it had risen to an unbearable pitch. "Be quiet," he muttered; and then louder, "Be quiet!" He began hammering his fists against his ears. "Oh God, *what is that noise?*"

Light flared in the living room. The square form of Lundgren stood at the French doors. In her whiteness she had an aura about her as of some old ghost. Her very face had a gray luminosity; her hands were folded at her stomach; each knuckle was composed in the gaunt symmetrical order of stony heads on a frieze.

"That noise," she said in flat tones clearly audible above it, "is whistles and bells and horns and sirens. The news came on the radio. They overthrew those generals and took back the government." Her voice cracked. "The crisis is over."

She paused, and looked into their faces, each of them in turn. "The children are awake," she said severely. She squared her stiff old body, turned, and marched back to her duties.

XXVI

B Y noon the town was emptied. The exodus had begun the night before; all throughout the remaining hours lights wove in a slow, orderly, almost solemn procession along the arteries leading out. The dawn rose on the shabbiness of public places nearly abandoned; through the mist gradually emerged the dew-soaked litter of the courthouse grounds — paper, charred campfires, a child's sock, a forsaken cat mumbling balefully among the bean cans — and the old man who refused to surrender his bench. He huddled dazedly in the early chill, nursing his gun, until it became apparent that he would need explaining to. "It's over," a kindly woman called to him. "You can go home now"; but he raised his gun in his stiff trembling old hands and pointed it at her, and eventually a posse of two police, the fire chief, the Presbyterian minister, and the school psychologist came to help him. The minister and the psychologist approached him cautiously from the front while the policemen and the fire chief sneaked up behind. The old man, squinting desperately into the strengthening light, wavered his gun between the two as they eased closer, step by step, talking. "We are your friends," the minister said. "We only want to help you." "A nice hot cup of coffee'd go good right now, wouldn't it, Pop?" the psychologist

said heartily. "A real good hot breakfast. Come on, I'll stake
you to some ham and eggs, a stack of flapjacks, a good hot cup
of coffee, then we can talk. Can't settle things on an empty
stomach, eh Pop?" Saying not a word the old man tucked the
gun between his stubbled chin and his shoulder and squinted
down the gun barrel. "I don't think we ought to get any closer
to him," the minister muttered. "He's kind of nervous. They've
almost got to where they can grab him now." But the psychologist continued to advance, all the while gazing with understanding down the gun barrel and saying, "Kinda tired of
that bench, I'll bet, Pop. Now after a good hot breakfast and a
friendly chat, no strain, no hurry, we can decide —" The old
man pulled the trigger and blasted the psychologist dead.
TRAGIC AFTERMATH IN CITY PARK, Daggett ran in his special afternoon BACK TO NORMAL! edition of the paper.

Because Kathy could not yet be moved the Andersons had
arranged for Lundgren to stay on with her for a few more
days. Joe would come back for her. Barbara, pale and listless,
sat on the couch and watched him gather their belongings and
carry them out to the car. Occasionally she wept, thinking of
all the beautiful things she had left untended, unwatched, behind the door she had forgotten to lock. "That little jade Bud-
dha from Gumps," she wept, "the ashtray Kathy made in kindergarten. The plants, without any water. The plants will be
dead."

Joe had recovered his car, relatively undamaged, from the
city park. There was no trace of Lucas's; it had disappeared
utterly. Joe finished packing the car and got the children
dressed. "Potty, Mike?" he said. "You want to go potty before
we leave?"

"And his little silver christening cup and spoon he got from his godmother — they'd be sure to find that, it was out on the kitchen counter . . ."

Cis and Jennie clung together and were separated only with promises of future visits. Lucas could not imagine the circumstances under which those promises might be kept. He and Joe shook hands in a manly silence which failed utterly to conceal their relief. They both knew that never again would they seek each other out; they had been imprisoned together; they knew too much of each other. Mike jigged around anxiously clutching himself but still refusing to be taken a final time to the potty — *my potty now*, Lucas thought; his spirits did not lift. The dog — Joe and Lucas had buried it in the children's trench (Toom after all), and tamped the dirt back, and now there was only a raw scar beneath the redwood tree — was not mentioned.

After they had left, Sally went into the bathroom and emerged much later with fresh makeup over raddled eyes and a swollen nose. She did not look at Lucas and he did not comment. To weep alone, to enter a battle alone — there was not always a choice. Help was not always available.

Lucas went to Mark's room with a sense of dread. He prepared ground at the door: Mark understood that it was all over? That things were back to normal? That he didn't have to worry any more? The boy lay in bed as in a burrow, watching, motionless, as his father worked his way in. Lucas removed a monogrammed oyster fork (where had he found *that*? It had been packed away, never used, with wedding silver) from its wrapping of ski sock which in turn had been stuffed into a toilet-paper tube impaled by a clothes-hanger. Mark understood that he was safe now, didn't he? Presently he could get up, maybe tomorrow go outside and play. He would feel a lot better if he got up and dressed . . . Lucas had gained the bed. Gingerly he sat down on it. Mark pulled the covers over his head. As he did Lucas had a fleeting glimpse of his face. His dread crystallized.

"Mark." The body was rigid under the covers. "Mark, what are you afraid of?" But he knew. The child had built not a nest but a trap. It was not a shelter Lucas had dismantled but a barricade, intricate, hopeless, a maze intended to baffle a Yeti. But the animal who had penetrated it was intelligent. Lucas, sickening, perceived how helpless a child was against what must seem to him this massive, terrible intelligence.

Gently he drew back the covers. Mark slid further down, until at the bottom of the bed there was no shelter left.

"Look at me, Mark. You know who I am. You know I'm your father." In one heave Lucas stripped the sheet completely off. The boy was curled tightly as a drowned worm. Lucas took the head between his hands.

"You know it was me you hit last night, don't you? Look at me, Mark!"

The laying-on of hands ripped some protective swaddling. The boy gasped, drew in his breath, held it; in the face between Lucas's palms the eyes slowly filled with recognition.

Crouched over him on the bed Lucas poured desperate remedies into this dumb aspect as if at any moment it might close again: "See, you know it, you see me now, you know I'm your father and I love you and I won't let anything hurt you. You see now I'm not Bigfoot, there isn't any Bigfoot, it's all over. You undertand that, Mark? There isn't any —"

"You killed him?"

"I didn't *have* to kill him, there *isn't* any —"

The boy's gaze was clear, unveiled, and glittering with rejection. His son saw him as through a solid pane of glass —

posturing, mouthing, a lying puppet dancing the Dance of Parenthood, that ritual dance of gods inevitably deposed.

"You promised," the boy said.

"Mark — how can I promise something that's not real? You've got to get back to real things now! You have to understand —"

The boy had shut his eyes. There was a tremor under the bluish lids.

Where had he gone? Anguished, Lucas said, "All right, Mark. I promise. I'll kill Bigfoot for you."

The boy remained folded, apart, disbelieving.

Lucas left the room trundling grief like a wheelbarrowload of rocks.

All afternoon, wandering past Chris's door on makeshift duties he half performed and then forgot, Lucas's rockload became heavier. Had this son, too, sealed himself off from him? Last night when the news had broken Chris had gone silently to his room, got his sleeping bag, taken it to the far end of the garden beneath the trees, and spent the remaining hours of the night there. After the Andersons had left he had gone back to his room and closeted himself.

There was no answer to Lucas's knock. He opened the door.

Chris was sitting on his bed, his arms hung loosely over his knees.

"Glad to see you back, Chris."

The boy's head sank into his hands.

Lucas hesitated, moved to the bed. "It hasn't been a — very good week, has it?" He grimaced painfully. "The understatement of the century."

Slung in the center of his silence Chris did not move.

"Chris, you aren't still out of joint about my not . . . It wasn't cowardice, you know."

His shoulders moved. He mumbled something.

"What? I didn't hear you."

"I said it's no use." He raised his head. Lucas saw with a shock the change in face. Where before had been only blurred intimations of the coming man, youthful cartilage, was now a sharp edge of hardened bone. Under the boy's flesh the man's skull resided. Could this be a scientific fact — that such a thing might happen in only a few days?

"It's no use," he repeated dully. "Nobody can do anything. Nobody can change anything."

"I don't know what you mean. I don't understand you."

"I mean nothing's really changed. Everything's the same." He flung up his hands and let them drop again heavily. "Oh, I don't mean the situation. I just mean — everything else. Everybody. We're all such a goddam buncha — of — *creeps*."

Believing he glimpsed the enormity which his son faced, Lucas sat down on the bed in a wash of relief. "You're not unique," he said. "Whatever's happened to you you're not unique." Now they could unburden themselves together, share as one man to another the anguish of helplessness; together they might plot its remedy, together heal and be healed, shore up their immortal ramparts and their human manhood. "We all feel the same way. It's a terrible thing not to be able to *do* anything. Listen," he said eagerly, "listen. My God, Chris, I tell you, this is a thing we're going to have to —"

"*Do* anything?" Chris laughed bitterly. "Well congratulations. I just want to congratulate you, Dad. You didn't *do* anything."

There was a pause. "Creeps," he repeated. "All creeps."

"Chris, I don't know what *you*'ve been doing. Is that it?"

His head had gone back in his hands. He was silent.

Lucas felt a prick of fear. "You think you're so all-fired bathed in wickedness, maybe you better tell me what you *have* been doing."

The boy hesitated. Lucas saw a flicker of childlike, Puritan anguish. "Okay. Remember you asked."

"Go ahead."

"I knocked a woman out. You *asked*," he cried fiercely. "I didn't mean to, it wasn't my intention, but she kept screaming at me, and hitting me —" He touched his groin. "We were supposed to get them out of these people's garage, and she wouldn't go or get out of my way, I gave her a shove, I *thought* it was a shove . . . And then this other place, I — don't remember how that happened either, there was this kid, a junior high kid I guess, he grabbed my gun —"

Lucas must have made an involuntary noise; Chris stopped and stared at him the way a teacher stares at the class dunce, waiting for his silence to get through. "Like I said, this kid was all excited, clowning around in that stupid gang of his, he grabbed my gun and I tried to get it back from him and it went off. It tore a big hole in his foot."

"Go on."

"There was a lot of — we had a lot of fights. Some of them were kind of lousy. I *tried*," he said carefully, "to do what we were supposed to do without hurting anybody. But people just kept . . . I got hurt myself, not too badly but banged up, and I banged up a lot of people myself. I couldn't help it. They just wouldn't — cooperate."

Co-operate! What was that joke about the scalped man? . . . It only hurts when I laugh.

"That wasn't the worst."

"Chris —"

But he was relentless, with the savage implacability of the confessor. "What was probably the worst, and I can't figure it, I think I'm *supposed* to think it's the worst." His face was very white. "I'll bet *you* think it's the worst."

Lucas was silent.

"I raped Marina Shaw." He opened his hands and looked down at them, and then closed them into fists. He began beating his fists softly against his knees.

"It was before — it was when it all started. When we first heard. Remember Sunday, I came back and you asked me if I'd been with McKnight, you thought I'd — well, I was with Marina." The fists beat on the knees in a steady rhythm. "I started to walk home when we heard. I thought I'd better, you know, get back home. I started out and I saw Marina over by the Fourteenth Street playground, and she was crying, she was real frightened, she was going home too. She — she was crying terribly hard, Dad. I told her I'd walk home with her and we started through the playground and she was crying so hard she — Jesus. We sat down on the bench behind the Rec building, you know, where they keep the equipment and the ping-pong stuff. We sat down there for a minute and I — I tried to talk to her, I gave her my handkerchief, I don't know, I tried to make her stop. She kept saying now her father would never get his book written. I mean, Christ, that's all she could make any sense! She was really hysterical, I tried to make her stop, I — Oh God, Dad, I don't know! I honest to God don't know how it happened! I just — was trying to make her feel better, and I guess I kissed her, and she hung onto me like some kinda life raft, she was so — Well, I didn't exactly feel like kissing somebody out in the open like that, I — We went inside and it happened. It just happened."

White, he was entirely white. His face was a white mass, his knuckles pounding his thighs were a white ridge. He rocked back and forth like a man with a stomachache. "It just happened . . . Dad . . ." The call came over the white expanse, far, faint, frightened. "Can't you say something?"

His son, the solid and pigmented Chris, sat before him. A tremendous fatigue settled over Lucas. This long haul — beginnings, assessment, judgment; the towing of the huge freight of parenthood, the caravan of half-truths in the endless linkage of refrigerated dicta, baled official messages, parlor-car wisdom — overwhelmed him with revulsion. He ran his palm over his face.

"I just wanted to comfort her! Can you understand that?"

"Yes."

"I lost my head. I mean, it started, and I — didn't seem to realize it until after, what I'd —" He broke off. "You aren't listening to me!" he cried furiously. "You think I'm just making excuses!"

"No. No." How could he say to his son: to comfort with the flesh is bad. How could he say: there are times when the flesh is the only comfort.

"I sure was crazy, thinking you'd understand! How would *you* know? How could you be expected to —" He may have come up blank against something in his father's face, lifted now to his regard; for he stopped, his arguments shattered. His mouth quavered. "I'm not asking you to excuse me."

"Chris," Lucas said, "you're my son. I love you. How can I judge my own son?" He touched the boy's shoulder.

Chris inclined his head stiffly toward his father, his hair just grazed his cheek. They sat that way for a moment. It seemed to Lucas that a membrane separating them had at last become permeable, that giant molecules of unbelievable intricacy might at last slip through between them. He tried to think of some final word, a plea perhaps, for future charity. "It's not easy," he said at last.

XXVII

BLEDSOE received them. With that mixture of pomp and iron obsequy which is the mark of good servants and high-bred Labrador retrievers he personally relieved them of their coats. He saw to it that the Club liquor supply — not yet legally distributable as the governor, flown to Washington "to personally shake the hand of our victorious President," had neglected to rescind his Executive Order — nevertheless was abundantly available. He moved among their orgiastic clots, wafting approbation like Air Wick; if they were here to rejoice, imbibe, and feast upon their acquittal, then Bledsoe was there to attend properly to the rites.

Lucas attempted to hook his eye, to reassure him that he would overlook his bizarre revelations of the night before, but Bledsoe's gaze was not to be trapped. Lucas considered addressing him as Koogie, but humanitarianism won. He turned to his duties of celebration.

Duties they were. He could not summon a sense of carnival. He could not full-heartedly carouse. He seemed unable to surface; like a depth-dwelling fish his organs had become acclimatized to pressure; he sensed that to haul himself up to the rarified occasion might be dangerous; they might no longer be resilient.

Dutifully he drank. Dutifully he danced. The night like all nights was enclosed in mist but the decks smoked with light and the curtains stirred to the music of Sheldrake's Flying Six orchestra. The waters of the pool on the terrace below rocked gently in their green underlit depths and floating gardenias cast shadows like tropical fish. Dutifully in these Byzantine blandishments Lucas shuffled about, dancing with partner after partner, with Sally, with Betty Foster, with Phyllis Mc-Kinney, with Shirley Fox, with Betty Wingluff, with Tinker Belle, with young Mrs. Hannibal, with Mrs. Patricia Hue. Orchestra leader Leon Sheldrake, who played trumpet, had some defect in his windpipe which caused the side of his neck to swell out like a misplaced goiter with each blast of his horn. In the fast pieces this sac expanded to excruciating fullness, was sucked back to near collapse. The effect was stupefying. Lucas hovered near the dais with his partner, gazing at this mysterious defect, hypnotized by it, his melancholy increasing.

"I love you," Mrs. Patricia Hue said. "I have loved you ever since I first clapped eyes on you."

"When was that?"

"At the Roses' Christmas cocktail party, December twenty-third, 1957."

He transferred his gaze from Leon Sheldrake. The superstructure of Mrs. Hue's hairdo bobbed against his thorax. It was always difficult for Lucas to dance with her, she was so short. In order to talk to him she had to throw her head back like a chicken taking water. To hear her he had to bend over awkwardly, mindful not to wrench her right arm out of its socket. Although he knew she tried very hard not to, she always got lipstick near the middle button of his jacket, making it appear he had been kissed on the belly.

"I decided it was about time to level with you," Patricia Hue said. "I suppose you think I'm drunk."

"No. No, of course not," he said politely. He jockeyed her carefully around in the crush. Leon and the orchestra carved away at the music with a deadly fairness in the apportionment of notes; each was given its due share of the beat and nothing more. The gullet pumped in and out like a small bellows fanning the steady blaze.

"I figured I needed to keep my wits about me tonight," Patricia Hue continued. "Besides, dancing with you I don't need to drink. I feel strong and steady and safe. Al now, he needs to drink to feel that way. Gin to him has become holy water this last week. Beware the man hooked on anything holy. Makes them mean." Her face floated beneath him like a nearsighted waterlily.

He said uneasily, "Listen, you don't want to talk that way. Even kidding, which I know you are."

"I am not kidding. I don't mess around with serious matters like love or death." She wiggled her head around on her neck and winced. "I get so stiff looking up all the time like this," she said irritably. "Can't we sit down somewhere — you sit down and I'll stand up and talk to you? There's a lot I have to say to you now that it looks as if we might live a little longer."

"Quit that," Lucas said sharply. "Can it, will you?"

"That last got to you? Talking about love and death, it's best to use euphemisms. Here we were dead for sure — pardon me, *passed away* — and now we're not. Kind of embarrassing, no? Makes you wonder what to do with your hands. But I'm warning you, you'd better listen because it's a kind of no-holds-barred moment for me. I hope you can understand this. I just realized something last night, when we were standing out in our back yard, Al and the cat and I, waiting for that damned satellite. I stood there looking up at the sky, the way I'm looking up at you now, and I couldn't see a thing through that fog. My neck got stiffer and stiffer, the way it does when I stand and look up at something — which is most of the time. You know what happened? I got mad. *Mad!* Here I was standing there the way I had all my life — waiting, getting a crick in my neck, watching for signs from above. The Word handed down from that Great Big Face up there. Patient little old Patricia Hardy Hue with her nose pressed against the glass. All my life like that! You know what I began thinking? *How dare they make me stand like that!"*

"I know," Lucas said suddenly. "I know exactly what you mean."

"Don't be silly, you couldn't know what I mean. You look *down* on people. Anyway, what I thought, standing there getting madder and madder, I thought, It's my life. I don't mind taking what comes — everybody has to do that — but I'm damned if I'm going to just stand around with my neck hanging out like some kind of sacrificial lamb. I mean I realized this was a big thing and a worldwide thing but when you got right down to it, it was *personal.* You know?"

"Yes," Lucas said.

"I thought of all the things I'd waited for in my life. All the things I'd wanted that never came. I thought of you — you might as well listen to me because I'm going to *make* you listen, no use in your hanging up there like some distant planet. You're too polite to put your fingers in your ears and I've got a good grip around your waist. You're too kind to pull away from me — gentle is what you are, actually. Did you know that you are really a very gentle man? I'm sorry to take advantage of it but I told you I'm dead serious . . . Where was I?"

"Waiting for the satellite," Lucas said coldly, "out in your back yard with your legal husband."

"Oh legal, yes, I get your drift. The protection of decency — I can't blame you, because you're *decent*, too. Gentle and decent . . . It was *decent* of you to want to plant those trees, John. Oh I remember how they kidded you, and how you simply took it, and went on fighting for it. My heart bled for you. I cried once when you stood up at a Council meeting and they laughed before you'd even opened your mouth . . . Oh Lord I'm rambling."

She rolled her neck painfully. "There we were, waiting, my legal husband and I — dear old Al, drunk and whimpering and scared half out of his pants," she said contemptuously, "that's how *he* waited, that's where *his* week went. But that's not my point either. That's *his* problem. Everybody's got to settle it with himself. *My* point is that I was so mad, thinking of all the things I'd wanted so badly and just waited for. You. I remember once I sat across the dinner table from you — it was about, um, three years ago, at the McKinneys' — and I remember watching you, and thinking as hard as I could: *Listen, John Lucas.* Listen. I'm sending you a message. Now hear this. This is Patricia Hardy Hue calling. Calling from across the table. I love you, John Lucas. Do you hear me? Come in, John Lucas. Over."

He was sweating. "Patricia, I —"

"Shut up," she said fiercely. "I'm not finished. For years I've sat across tables from you and sent you signals. For years I've yakked with you at parties — about things you were interested in, your kids — I'll bet I know more about whatsisname, Mark's dental problems than anybody outside the orthodontist. Architecture. Trees. Preserving old houses — those men and their funny little city government, they just didn't *know!*

— Art. Books. I spent weeks once struggling through a book you just happened to mention. It was not only boring, it was difficult. But I read every word, thinking, *he* has read these words. For years, in the brief moments allotted to me by the prevailing winds and your social duties, I have listened to you and through it all I have sent you these signals. 'How's Mark's bite now? I saw the house you did for the Searles.' Everything I said to you was a call."

"I'm sorry. I didn't know."

"You certainly didn't! Either I'm a lousy sending station or you're completely lacking in antennae. I don't know. I tried hard enough. Maybe it finally got too automatic. Like saying the Lord's Prayer when I was a little girl. I used to try and think about the *meaning* of it while I was saying it, but the words had been used so much. You know? By the time I got through I knew I'd just been mouthing them again, there wasn't any power in them. OurFatherwhichartinheaven. The trouble may have started with the fact that I used to think that *art* was an active verb, as if to 'art' something. I got hung up from the very start, thinking about the Father up there in heaven, so mysteriously arting. It started me out confused."

Leon Sheldrake's gill went in and out, mercilessly, dangerously.

"I was only a child," Patricia Hue said. "It just hadn't been explained to me. I was a good little kid. I was trying. I really tried to speak with God courteously and earnestly, just Him and me."

"And you never could get Him alone."

Her face was white and strained; she had been looking up at him for so long. "There ought to be one moment of grace in everybody's life," she said.

Her eyes filled with tears. She ducked her head, swiping

her face blindly against his shirtfront. "I stood there in that crummy back yard Al never mows waiting for the end of the world and listening to Al moaning and sniveling, and the cat rubbed against my leg and scared me half out of my skin — and right there in the middle of all that, and being so mad, I decided what I could do. I decided that if this was the moment I was going to die, it'd have to be my best moment. I realized I was just as scared as Al was — I was moaning and crying *inside*, I was that scared. You know the fear. We all of us have to know the fear, sooner or later. Maybe if I'd been drinking as much as Al I'd have been down on my knees too. But seeing myself that way — I don't know. Maybe it's a matter of appearances. I wasn't going to appear that way in front of *anybody*, not Al or the cat, not myself. And then I thought about how it was inside me, I could see *that* — and I don't know, maybe it was appearances again, I couldn't stand the picture of little Patricia Hardy Hue, whose insides only God and I could see, bowing out that way. So scared! The only way I could change it was to stop being afraid. Just to face it. It was the only thing I could do," she said. "It was the only moment of private grace I had any more chance for."

The music had stopped. They released each other. "Well. As it turns out I still have it ahead of me," Patricia Hue said. "But meantime I thought I'd let you know how I felt. It's one way of fighting back at the way things have always been. I'm not going to send any more signals out that're never received. It wears me down, and I need all the strength I've got. That's all I wanted to say to you."

Couples had wandered back to their tables; through the windows Lucas saw Sally in her white dress, alone, leaning against the railing over the pool terrace. "Once I wanted to parachute into a girl's back yard," he said. He looked at Patricia Hue helplessly. What else could he have offered this woman?

She did not appear to have heard. "All I wanted was to tell you," she said. She turned and walked away across the empty floor.

"Personal pushbutton power for each and every individual." Kohner's voice shrilled above the babble at the bar. "It's worth consideration, I tell you!"

Dalton winked at Lucas. "Doc here has an idea we should run the world from our living rooms. He's got this parimutuel machine."

"I thought it was an Addresso-Graph," Sam snickered.

Lucas signaled Ernie for a drink.

"Frankly it sounds kind of wildeyed," said Harry Foster. "Who wants a machine running his life?"

"Goddam impersonal, if you ask me," McKinney said.

"Impersonal? *Impersonal?*" Kohner cried. "You aren't listening! Hell, what's more personal than direct action?"

"I wanna take direct action, I'll tell you how I do it. I use this —" McKinney tapped his forehead, "and this —" he held up his fist. "No machine's gonna replace *this* man."

"In certain functions anyway," Dalton said.

"The mind boggles," Dave Neale said dryly.

"Heh. Heh-heh," giggled Al Hue.

"I'm not talking about sex," Kohner spat, "I'm talking about government and you know it. A way to get power back into our own hands —"

As he sputtered on, waving his arms, Lucas had a vision of a vast console imbedded in the wall of Kohner's living room. Lights flash, dials spin, gauges tick; Kohner sits before this, deep in consideration; presently he raises his hand, extends his forefinger, a flash of lightning spurts between this forefinger and the big button, the central navel — *zoom*, he has acted! His electronic *esse*, the forefinger of Jehovah, has registered its digital power. It has become the force which drives the world.

Poor little Kohner.

"Hold it a minute," McKinney was saying. "Hold it just one minute here. This is a *world* government gimmick?"

"Hell *yes*, world government — but no gimmick! You think we're the only people with a right to our own statement?" Kohner agitatedly batted his glasses up and down his nose.

"You'd let a bunch of Commies have an equal —"

"After what *they*'ve just —"

"What are you, one of those Love Everybody nuts?"

"Ah lay off, Roy. Why argue? C'mon, have a drink —"

"There wouldn't be any Communists." Kohner's voice was low now, quavering with the effort to control his temper. "Nor any socialists or fascists or anarchists or democrats or republicans. All social systems would be resolved under one —"

"An end to the two-party system?" Harry said incredulously.

"That's what he is. I've got you pegged, Kohner. You're another one of those Love Everybody nuts."

"Love?" Kohner blazed. "Me? Do I look like somebody who *loves*, McKinney?" He suddenly thrust his face toward McKinney and spat. "Does that look like love, McKinney?"

There was a pause. The spittle had missed McKinney and was lumped in a forlorn little wad on Kohner's own lapel.

Dalton muttered, "Ah come on. This is no time for arguments."

"Come on, Max," Dave Neale said. "You're surrounded by Pharisees. Let me buy you a drink."

"Yeah," Harry said. "Buy'm a drink. Tonight we're supposed to be celebrating. Tonight's a *happy* night."

Kohner laughed suddenly, his bitter high cackle. "Why? Why should this be such a happy night, chum?"

"My God listen to that, willya," McKinney said. "He doesn't think we should be happy. Maybe he thinks the Commies should be happy. Hey." He punched Neale's arm. "You happy, Doc?"

"Max?" Dave Neale said, ignoring McKinney. "What're you drinking?"

"Don't — handle me, Dave," Kohner said. "Just don't try to *manage* me."

"Hey," McKinney said, punching somebody else's arm. "You happy?" He punched a few more arms. "Everybody's happy but you, Kohner. How come? You think your machine'd make us happier?"

"It might allay the Sitting Duck Syndrome," Kohner snarled. "Which is what you guys are suffering from and you don't even know it."

"Who's suffering except you, Doc?"

"Kohner's Personal Power Machine, all you have to do is push a button —"

"Lay off him, McKinney."

"I don't need your protection, Lucas."

"Christ, Kohner, who's protecting? I just don't like to see a man outweighed, is all."

"Up you, Lucas," Kohner said thickly.

"You happy?" McKinney punched the arm of a man sitting on the end barstool. "Hey. You there." He punched again.

With great slowness and effort the man turned.

Lucas's impression had been that Moroney was a fat man. Here was a wraith. He had dwindled fantastically; his clothes

hung on him in deep folds; his head was shrunken like a talis-
man of a cannibal tribe, the face pleated skin, as if the bones
had been removed from under it. Between these appalling furrows the eyes dully regarded McKinney. The comatose glance
slid over him and returned to the untouched drink in front of
him on the bar.

"Not happy?" McKinney cried. "Aw. Come on. Turn
around and be happy. Be sociable. We're celebrating."

Across Moroney's shoulders passed a twitch like that of a
drowsing horse.

"What's with this guy?" McKinney complained. "Who is
he? He's not a member. Hey. Hey, fella."

"Roy," Dalton said, "come on. If he doesn't want to —"

"How do you know he doesn't want to? Christ, can't he
speak for himself? What kind of fink would sit there and not
celebrate?"

"You show him," Kohner called. "Lead the way! American-
ism! Renaissance of spirit! Brave new world! Courage the by-
word —"

"Hey," McKinney said, close to Moroney's ear, "listen, fella.
You turn around, tell me who you are, introduce yourself, I'll
stand you a drink. How's that for a deal?"

Moroney was stone.

"We want to make you feel welcome here at the Sequoia
Golf and Country Club," McKinney said expansively.

"Maybe he's just gassed or something," Dalton said.

"Gassed! Crissake, he's at a party, isn't he? I offer him a
drink, I welcome him —"

"Certainly not a particularly *gracious* guy," Sam muttered.

McKinney put a forearm on the bar and stared into Moroney's face. He withdrew, pondering. "I've seen this guy before," he said darkly.

"Lay off, McKinney," Lucas said out of some deep unease.

"Why should I lay off? I simply want to know who this guy is, is all. I know I've seen him before. I don't like being snubbed by a guy I know I've seen —"

"His name is Moroney, he's in the lumber business, he's from Seattle, he's been here all week. Now will you lay off?" Lucas snapped.

"Seattle, huh?" McKinney leaned over. "You got a family in Seattle, Moroney?"

Moroney stirred. He muttered something.

"A family. Wife and kids," McKinney marveled. "Isn't that nice? You know that everybody's gone back now, don't you, Moroney? Everybody's gone back home, left dear old Sequoia to us natives. Bled us dry, ate all our food, ruined our town, and now they've all gone back home again. Now that it's *safe*. You knew that, Moroney?"

Lucas caught a glimpse of the liverish whites of Moroney's eyes. ". . . didn't *eat*," he mumbled, and mumbled some more as McKinney bent his head solicitously, listening.

"No kidding! Just don't like to travel? Well now."

"Say, that's really a shame," Harry said. "Wife and kids up there in Seattle all alone."

"And he's a traveling salesman?"

"How about that, a traveling salesman doesn't like to travel!" McKinney roared delightedly. "Doesn't want to travel on home! Your wife that bad, Moroney?"

"No," Moroney said with sudden clarity. "She's very lovely."

"*I'll take you home again, Kathleen, to where your heart will feel no pain*," Al Hue sang.

"— Or maybe you figure Seattle isn't safe yet," McKinney said heavily. "Maybe you're scared to go back, Moroney? Is that it?"

"*Acro-o-oss the ocean wild and wide —*"

". . . Not . . . safe," Moroney said with difficulty. He put his elbows down on the bar and lowered his head and wrapped it in his forearms as if expecting a blow.

There was a pause.

"Ah, forget it," Dalton muttered. "Come on, leave him alone. Let's go have dinner."

They moved off.

"And there's their sitting duck." Kohner, gazing at Moroney's back, clamped his hands tightly. Slowly he opened and closed them again. He sat clenching and unclenching his tiny fists.

"Now there," Harry Foster declared in hushed tones, "is what I call a *centerpiece!*"

The Ice Statue, a maiden twice life-size, reclined full-length on a dampening bed of ferns in the middle of the buffet. Safe behind her sneeze-rail she lounged, one impossibly round hip rising majestically above the greenery like a denuded dome above timberline. Ranging down the alluvial slopes, irrigated by the glacial thaw of her hair, under the dizzying hillocks of her breast, in the grottoes of waist, thigh, ankle, the offerings were banked: bleu cheese, crab aspic, artichoke hearts, garbanzo salad, macaroni and pimiento salad, shrimp soufflé, pickled beets, sour cream, turkey, spiced peaches, pigs' knuckles. The sauces were at her instep. That art student, chipping away with numbed fingers (or toes?) — what dreams must have drenched his cot! The Ice Statue, were she alive and warm, could have nourished at that bosom an entire generation of art students. The young man had evidently been weaned too early.

"I guess we decided against scarecrows," remarked Lucas.

"Hammond thought it'd be a fun gizmo to do something representational," said Tinker Bell, reaching in below the armpit for an anchovy. "He said he was ready to recapture the *basics*."

A morose sympathy for young Hammond expanded in Lucas.

"Center*piece*," Harry repeated, digging with his elbow at Lucas's ribs."

"*Pièce de résistance*. Peace on earth."

"All that food! It must have been in the freezer the whole time," Sally whispered.

Behind him Lucas heard Sarah Shaw's sudden laugh. It rasped like a cat's tongue up his nape. "It's got nipples. The boy put nipples on it."

"We're all adults here," Howard said.

Sarah laughed again, a little wildly. Lucas listened with every pore on his back wide open to catch the inflections of Sarah's laugh: *did she know?* "Oh that poor kid," Sarah said. "All that loving work, and the nipples are melting."

"All this time. And it never occurred to anyone," Sally murmured, staring at the buffet table.

"Eat, Sally," Lucas said. "Eat. Here, have some soufflé. Have some artichoke hearts. Some anchovies —" He took her plate from her and heaped it high, and higher, until the food began tumbling from the piles. "Some olives, some bleu cheese, some garbanzoes —"

Howard did not dance with women, he ingested them. He took a stance like a praying mantis and with his elbows, shoulders and wrists he swathed his victim. Under Howard's prongs Lucas's wife had the appearance of being trapped half in and half out of a monster's mouth. Her bottom shimmered frantically. Lucas watched, knowing that she did not need to be rescued; she did not want to be rescued.

Not so Lucas himself. Who would think that he was praying, dully and without hope, for rescue? He sat by Sarah at the table and waited for the axe, the terminal blow to what once had been treasure and comfort.

Sarah sat, matter-of-fact and stolid, her hands folded primly on the table like a schoolmarm.

Lucas shifted from one buttock to another. "Look, Sarah, I . . . Do you —"

"Yes, I know about Chris and Marina. I guess you've been wanting to know that."

Dread like dust settled over him. "Yes."

"I don't want to have to defend Marina to you, John. I just can't do it."

"Defend . . . *Marina?*"

Sarah blinked stonily at the dancers writhing past the table. "She's my child. How can I judge my own child? Besides, she was honest, if that's points. She came right out and said it. 'I seduced Chris Lucas,' she said. Sixteen years old and she used that old-fashioned word. It sounded so peculiar, coming out of her mouth that way. 'See-dooce,' she pronounced it like that." Sarah thrust out her lips in a gentle pout. "Cute sayings of kids."

"Chris said a cute thing too. He said he'd raped Marina."

"Oh no," Sarah said mildly, "no, no. It wasn't that way at all. Marina's a very honest child. She *said* it was her fault, so I believe her. She said she was kind of upset, and Chris was so scared. They were evidently both so scared. She put her arms around him, and then she —" Sarah cleared her throat briskly. "At least that's Marina's version, generally."

"I cannot believe," Lucas said in formal tones, "that a boy Chris's age could be —"

"A rapee? It does sound unlikely. Do you suppose," Sarah said after a pause, "that neither of them *knows?*" She ducked her head. Her voice teetered precariously. "Oh my. They don't even know which one's to *blame?*"

Across the dance floor, dim and churning, Lucas caught a glimpse of Leon, laboring away at his trumpet as if in a death-struggle with a brass gargoyle; his gills strained in and out and it was unbelievable that he could last another note; his esophagus would surely burst and come flying out; Leon Sheldrake would become the sacrificial lamb on the altar of their celebration.

Even more formally, Lucas said, "I think Chris — understands his responsibilities though, Sarah. I'll see to it he — does what's right. In the event . . ."

"In the event she's pregnant? *What's right* — you mean marry her? You shock me, John," Sarah said in strangled tones. "Just for one moment, a single moment, they should be lashed together like contestants in a sack race? Nobody has the right to tie up anybody else like that, not his body or his mind or his soul, for an entire lifetime."

"And you shock me, Sarah! You think they're not tied together by the consequences of their actions?"

"Their action took place at a time when it looked as if there might be no consequences." She rested her elbow on the table and rubbed her eyes. "Oh John, let's not moralize for them. I've got enough to figure out for myself." She gave a small dry laugh. "A loss of faith is certainly an old-fashioned problem, isn't it? So outmoded. Victorian. What can I tell my child? How can I guide her? All is anarchy. No single Word. *Death,*" she said suddenly, and poked him in the chest with a forefinger. She repeated in gonglike tones, "Death, our own personal ex-pi-ration! The one faith we never believed in. Why is it always such a surprise? We see evidence of it all around us. History reeks of it. But that inscrutable old buzzard Death, we don't believe in him any more. He's old-fashioned and irrelevant, like the Devil. In these bright and sanitary times, John, in this — deodorized progressive kindergarten with piped-in Muzak to drown the grunts and screams, who gets to look a buzzard square in the eye?"

Hers was the face of unbearable loss, anguished, bitter. "What happens when a black thing suddenly appears rattling its wings, that hideous old red eye looking straight at us? We call it an apparition! We relegate it to Disneyland, or a zoo — on Sundays we take the kids and a picnic lunch and go stare at it there in its cage. When the youngest kid asks what would happen if it got loose we say, 'But darling, it can't get loose, see the bars?' And when we hear him scratching around in there and a dreadful stink oozes out, we smother it with mental health and occupational therapy. Tsk tsk we say, can we *help* being human, we all have bad dreams, and then we jam some more Mature Attitudes down the kiddies' throats."

Lucas lit a cigarette; his hand was not steady. With cold deliberation, calculated brutality, he said, "Maybe. That may all be true. Things look that way when you've quit."

"Quit?"

"You're a quitter, Sarah. You saw something you didn't want to believe so you lay down and quit. You saw death so you died."

She stared at him with her lost and bitter face. "Why, how coachy you sound. I feel like an entire football team between halves."

He stabbed his cigarette into the ashtray and stood up. "Let me know," he said politely, "how Marina is. Will you promise to do that, Sarah?"

"Certainly, coach," she said. He left her sitting at the table alone. He cut in on Sally and Howard Shaw.

"Go back to your own wife, Howard," he said. "Go back and take care of her. She hasn't got anybody to communicate with."

"Who has?" Howard Shaw said bitterly. "All this time, didn't you once listen to me?"

In the dining room the deserted Ice Maiden aged. Her beauty ebbed in relentless trickles. Her melting cornices buckled, exquisite hollows thickened, clear lines smudged, breasts sagged. The clumsiness and formlessness of age was upon her. The trickles would soon become a freshet, the stream a river, and into the amorphous ocean she would vanish, carrying with her traces of her garnished glory. In the puddle beneath the buffet table green fern-fronds floated like traces of algae. There was nothing Lucas could do for her, either.

"Help him!"

He struggled from the depths of the slippery plastic chair. The voice was tight as a wire. It sliced through Lucas's doze, through the background of other voices whose dreary arguments had set him nodding in the dimness of the men's lounge. Fingers dug into his collarbone.

"Help him, Lucas!" Kohner crouched over the chair, his face contorted with urgency. Lucas shook off his clutch and sat up.

The room hummed with a peculiar pitch. A group was clustered tightly around a couch at the other end of the room.

The argument had lowered in volume but had taken on a peculiar intensity. Vibrating like a swarm of wasps they hovered in attentive, almost enraptured postures. From their center emerged a different sound, high, insistent, monotonous.

"No, no no. Not safe. Never safe again. It'll come."

"*What will come, Moroney? What?*"

"You know. You know!"

"*Tell us, Moroney. Tell us what's coming.*"

"It's still there. Up there, terrible. You know, you know."

"*What's up there, Moroney? Tell us.*"

"You know . . . Flying around up there . . ."

"*Airplanes, Moroney? Is that what you're scared of? That why you're scared to go home? Scared to go outside? Is that it, Moroney?*"

They were evoking his name as earlier Moroney had evoked Lucas's; as if it had a magic power to bind. They were drunk. But that did not account for the eerie malevolence in the sound which emanated from them like an odor. Lucas could smell it, a feral, witless force. He had smelled it before.

These were not men; he identified no single voice. This was, he recognized all at once, the true phenomenon of mass; the condition in which the weight of parts no longer defined the whole; the microcosm that had leaped the quantum gap to macrocosm and was no longer restrained by the same rules. Once set in motion its parts were fused; it would run its course as a single force; it fed on itself; it needed no other impetus than its own primary state; it outstripped its parts.

Faced with its mindlessness Lucas grew cold. The dynamic pulse throbbed in the room, threatening to suck heat and reason from them all. Kohner's hand on his shoulder was frantic.

"Get him away from here! Help him, Lucas!"

"*. . . Aa-ah. The satellite, is it? Freddy Gates's folly. Is* *that what you mean, Moroney? Is that what you want us to consider? Is that your warning? You wish us to consider an imaginary gizmo dreamed up by a crazy kid? A Commie agent who thought he could scare us? Is that what you seriously wish us to believe, Moroney?"*

"You believed him."

There was a pause; and then the hum rose abruptly to a new sinister level. The cluster broke for a moment. Lucas saw Moroney sitting on the couch. In the dim light his ravaged features seemed to have sunk entirely back into his skullbones. The clear light of sudden sanity shone from the death's-head. "You can't trap me," it said. "You believed that kid. Just because he's locked up now doesn't mean he was lying. It doesn't mean that satellite couldn't be still up there. Flying around, and around, and . . ." Madness had closed in again; but still the stubborn sound continued, ". . . around and around . . ."

"For God's sake, Lucas," Kohner hissed, "I'm telling you, get that fool away from them!"

"How? How, Kohner?"

"I don't care how!"

He lurched to his feet. The sudden action made his head swim. He hesitated. The group ringing the couch was hooting wildly. Now that he was on his feet they seemed far away, small, absurd. They looked like a bunch of schoolboys playing bully at recess.

"Maybe if you could just walk in, turn their attention, ease him out —" Kohner gnawed distractedly at his nails. Crouched by the chair he seemed so ridiculously terrified Lucas felt a spurt of disgust.

"They're just drunk. Can't you see it's just a crazy drunken brawl? What do you want, me to go thrashing around in there like the White Knight, rescuing some fair maiden —"

"They're scared." Kohner's glasses flickered. "People're dangerous when they're scared."

"Come off it, Kohner. Moroney's the guy who's scared. He's unbalanced, he's a natural coward —"

"We're all natural cowards! Why do you think those guys are after Moroney?"

"Because they're loaded, and they're looking for somebody to rag, and Moroney's it for tonight. What'd you think they're going to do, lynch him? Listen, I know these guys and so do you. Christ, I eat lunch with them, I play golf with them! They may be gassed but they're not barbarians."

He was all at once tireder than he had ever been in his life. A tinge of nausea curled in his mouth. "If you want to rescue somebody who doesn't need it go ahead, Kohner, but count me out. I've *had* it for tonight. As a matter of fact I've had it for the week. All week long I've been waiting for a call to help, to do something, to be useful, anything. I've been sitting around like some poor dumb beast in a feed pen, waiting — What kind of world have we *got*, that that's all an able-bodied man can do? And now you come up and ask me to rescue a screwball from a Country Club party. From my own friends! To hell with you, Kohner. You and your goddam drama," he said bitterly, and got out of there.

Leon Sheldrake had folded his gullet and his music stand, listlessly flapped his boys through the terminal tootles of "Goodnight Sweetheart." Lucas found Sally drooping at the Shaws' deserted table and together they shambled through the last dance.

Till we meet tomorrow . . . It was long past overdue, to-morrow was. When they awoke then it would be to the resumption of sane time, to the ticking of order, to the long slow tempo of reason. Tomorrow: its breaking would once again be a commonplace thing.

Sally went off to get her wrap and Lucas wandered to the men's room. He scooped palmfuls of water over his drugged face. The door sucked open and Kohner bumbled through.

He did not recognize him at first; Kohner seemed to have become entirely bald. He stood blinking in the dead white glare of tile, both hands thrust out before him like a somnambulist's. Lucas saw it was not hair which he had lost but his glasses. Without the great magnifying lenses his features had a shocking nudity. He moved his face about as if it were a sensory organ. It came to rest on Lucas.

Kohner did not attempt to squint. He took a wide blank fix and shuffled toward him, palms outstretched. He touched Lucas's chest.

"You, uh, lose your glasses?"

Kohner regarded him with the empty stare of a baby. He was, Lucas saw with surprise, quite young. Even the blind eyes looked unused; they were without expression, speculation, fervor, or any trace of light. What had seemed to be a vital gleam had, then, burned only in a set of optical lenses.

Lucas said vaguely, "I'm sorry, Kohner." He did not really know what for — the weakness of the little man's eyes, the loss of his glasses; perhaps for the youth and nudity of his face, or the vanished vital thrust. He mopped his own face with a paper towel.

"Why should you be sorry? You didn't lose anything." Kohner's voice was slack. "Nothing ventured nothing lost."

"Ventured — Are you still talking about that Moroney business?" The eyes rested on Lucas weightlessly. "Kohner, they were riding him. Just riding him." A suspicion formed.

"You didn't mess into that yourself, did you? Is that how your glasses — You didn't get into a *fight* with them, did you?"

"I didn't fight. I don't — fight. My glasses weren't broken," he said thickly, "they took them off me. They took them off my nose and put them in their pocket. They just took off my glasses and turned me around and patted me and told me to run along."

As if he had been seized with cramps he wrapped his arms around his belly and leaned over one of the basins. His face was beaded with a ghastly pallor but he was not sick; he only leaned over the basin, doubled up.

They had patted him. Lucas slowly balled the paper towel in his hands. "They're just a bunch of stupid drunks, Kohner."

"I never fight. I'm always too . . . scared."

"So, well, maybe you're a lover not a fighter."

The little man raised a face streaming, murderous. "Don't you pity me! And get it straight about this lover crap!"

Lucas hurled the towel into the trash can. "Okay then, what kind of man *are* you, Kohner? All this about saving Moroney —"

"I may not be able to love but I have to care." Clutching his belly he twisted away from the bowl. "My God. I'm not insane! A sane man has to *care*."

A terrible grin moved his mouth, with nothing in it of triumph or of pleading. "They've got a rope. Lucas, they're out there with him and they've got a rope."

"Bon voyage!"
"Give our regards to the wife and kiddies!"
"Enjoy your trip, Moroney!"
"Breathe that nice fresh air, Moroney!"

Off he zoomed into the night, his screams caroming back over the snarl of the KaddieKart, while on the grass they capered. The waters of the pool lit their jigging faces. "Fare-thee-well! *Aloha!*" Howling against his lashings Moroney struggled; the Kart rocked, the tiller swung, back in an arc it tilted headlong, bumped over the gravel approach; back into their reach he swept. They belted the tiller gleefully and off he careened again, screaming into the blackness.

Lucas launched his weight at the center of the mob. Helpless in their mirth they gave way; he felt the heft and balance of himself as their bodies melted before his impact. Then he was out in the dark, running.

Moroney and the Kart bore suddenly down upon him. He lunged and snagged what felt like rope; it burned through his fingers. Again he grabbed blindly and the tiller swung, cracking him across the chest. For an instant he was borne along in Moroney's lap. Mindless screeches clawed in his ears and foul breath, the odor of terror, assailed him. Then the Kart tipped, swerved, and Lucas was thrown off. He lay stunned in the grass for a moment. He picked himself up and lunged after the diminishing roar, cursing. His body felt heavy now. The smell of Moroney clung in his nose.

He was almost within reach of the Kart as it approached the grassy lip of the terrace, shot between the scattered mob, and plummeted with a leap into the lit green waters of the pool.

Lucas was pinioned under the weight of pain. The air he labored to draw was so sharp each breath seemed to crack another rib. Pain held him utterly; he was cradled in it. Beyond it sounds percolated to him as through the glass of an aquarium.

He stirred; his head was lifted, drawn against familiar flesh. He gasped and rolled to his elbow. Through the chlorine mist he saw a dark form next to him writhing in slow, formalized swimming motions. He started up; pain gouged his chest again.

"Easy, John, oh easy, easy, darling . . ."

He croaked his wife's name and tried to ask her a question.

"He's all right. He's okay. You got him out, oh darling, lie back and rest, easy . . ."

I got him out.

Down in the boil the face was a sunburst center of erupting eyes and cheeks, an undersea Sol radiating green explosions. Lucas tore at the bonds. The silent shriek shattered in his face. He surfaced sucking in a gardenia; he spat and retched and dove again. A solid jar directly over him bore him straight down. He grazed the cement at the bottom and fought back up, and was entangled; as he struggled Kohner's convulsed blind face appeared like a bouquet in his hands. They hurled each other away and together burst again into the air. Together they dove again, and again, and endlessly again, into the center of that churning undersea shipwreck, the gaseous boil. Lucas did not remember past this except waking to the pain.

Over by the pool they were clustered, their faces green as fishes' in the watery light; like fishes in aquarium silence they hung, agape.

Lucas fell back into Sally's lap; she nursed his head. He lay on the grass, beside him Moroney, burbling, hawking, writhing, alive.

I got him out.

Under Lucas's back the grass was like wet fur. As he lay utterly drained a warmth from the earth began to seep into him. Slowly it penetrated, spread, filled him with vital heat. A vision of genesis and sequence seized him. Hand over hand he had worked his way out over unthinkable brinks, teetered on the edge of revelation, stared fearfully down into chasms; but within him history uncoiled its living tensions, from somewhere the vital will flowed freshly back. Beneath him the mighty planet still ticked; above him and eons of his kind, the darkness still hung beautiful in its serene geometry. Like a slow measure of sound, ripe, grave, eloquent, a major-keyed processional, the sense of celebration came at last to him. His pain ebbed, a pulse resumed.

XXVIII

T H E hour gonged with the thinness of dawn. He stood in the kitchen holding his sleepless son; together they kept watch, he and this child who could not surrender the terrible vigilance. They were waiting for Bigfoot. He had promised his son the nightmare's death.

Out in the garden, under the redwoods, the Yeti waited. He brooded and lurked; occasionally he snarled softly and rubbed his body against the tree. The sound of fur on bark was dry, hollow, scratchy. He reached up and grabbed the lowest branch and shook it in sudden, witless fury. The branch was twenty feet from the ground. The tree clattered; rusty fronds showered down upon the Toom where the dog lay buried.

The boy whimpered.

"Don't be afraid, Mark. I'm with you."

The beast was covered with the night's blood. Kohner was dead. As Lucas lay on the ground slowly filling with awe and strength, Kohner lay under the water, his life draining in silent bubbles, trapped beneath the machine from which Lucas in his mightiest and last effort had wrenched Moroney. The little man's final exhausted struggles had gone unseen. The ring of paralyzed fish-faces were blank, perhaps blinded by an interior vision. Kohner had been very small.

The long night was almost over. The morning which would light them all, the implacable dawn freighted with its daily load, crouched just below the horizon. Once again the dark coagulated in grains of feeble light. Still Bigfoot waited. The prey he smelled was guarded by the father's arms.

Who could take action against a nightmare? Stunned by revelation, who could make promises to a child? What unspeakable effort, what marshaling of scattered forces, what powers of love and craft could summon a sane man's will to this commitment?

Keep watch with us, somebody — Kohner, Chris — somebody wait with us! Help me face the coming day. Equip me with adrenalin, reinforce my sovereign will; for I am unarmed, I have only my two naked hands, and this is an official Wilderness Area.